THE GREAT EXHIBITION

An *Honest Heart*

A NOVEL

Kaye Dacus

B&H
PUBLISHING GROUP
Nashville, Tennessee

978-1-4336-7721-2

Published by B&H Publishing Group
Nashville, Tennessee

Dewey Decimal Classification: F
Subject Heading: HONESTY—FICTION \ LOVE STORIES \
INDUSTRIAL REVOLUTION—FICTION

Scripture reference is taken from The King James Version.

1 2 3 4 5 6 7 8 • 16 15 14 13

CHAPTER ONE

Oxford, England
March 1851

*T*he Siamese silk slid sensuously through Cadence Bainbridge's hands, catching on the rough spot on her thumb where she'd pricked it yesterday. Two of her apprentices worked silently on hemming gowns hanging from dress forms in opposite corners of the workroom, in front of the large windows where the light was the best.

Ten-year-old Nan, the youngest and newest girl to come to learn the seamstress trade from Caddy, hummed a monotone as she secured buttons down the back of a green muslin bodice. The sound crawled up Caddy's spine to tingle under her collar at the back of her neck and tighten her shoulders until she thought she might scream.

Caddy cut into the expensive imported fabric with more trepidation than she usually experienced in cutting a new gown. She'd drawn the pattern from the fashion plate her customer brought to show her, and it was a more complex design than

1

anything Caddy had attempted in the eight years since striking out on her own after her apprenticeship ended. The knife-pleats alone would take days to form for a skirt as full as this would be when finished.

Footfalls on the creaking stairs broke the monotonous drone of Nan's humming. Caddy set the silk aside and rose, tucking her shears into the extra-deep pocket she'd sewn into her skirt.

"Mother, if you needed something, you should have sent Mary to fetch me."

The frail older woman stepped down gingerly from the last riser and patted Caddy's cheek. "Do not worry about me so. Mary is having a much-needed afternoon off."

"What do you need? I shall get it for you." Caddy put her arm under her mother's elbow to provide support.

But Mother pulled away. "'Tis a lovely spring day, and I plan to avail myself of it by walking to the greengrocer to visit with Mrs. Howell for a little while."

The greengrocer was less than fifty yards up North Parade Avenue from the seamstress shop. But Mother had not walked so far on her own in over two years.

Caddy turned to her young apprentice. "Nan, please walk with Mrs. Bainbridge. If she tires, find a place for her to sit. You can finish your work after you walk her back home."

Nan stood and laid the bodice on the seat of her chair. "Yes, miss." The way the child's tongue caught between her front teeth made it come out as *Yeth, mith*.

Caddy raised her brows.

Nan blushed as red as her hair. "Yesssssss, missssssss," she over-enunciated.

Caddy nodded, and Mother extended her hand to the ten-year-old. They ambled from the workroom and into the store-front. Caddy's shop clerk stepped out of the way to let them through, then entered the workroom. "The hackney is come to take you to Chawley Abbey."

"Thank you." Caddy closed her sewing kit and tucked it under her arm, motioning to the two remaining apprentices. "Letty, you will go with me. Alice, you stay here and help Phyllis if she needs it in the front. And mind Nan when she returns as well."

"Yes, miss." Both young women set into motion—Alice returning to her hemming job and Letty replacing items in her sewing kit.

Caddy checked her appearance in the long, unframed mirror mounted on the back of the stairwell door. She combed loose wisps of straight brown hair back into the soft wings covering her ears to the twisted braids at her nape. Smoothing the tatted lace collar at the high neck of her blue-and-green plaid gown, she took a deep breath and prepared herself for the unpleasantness to come.

"Come, Letty."

The fifteen-year-old reached out for Caddy's sewing kit, and she tucked both under one arm. Caddy pulled a bundle of garments wrapped in white linen from the bar where several dresses hung in a row, waiting to be finished or altered, and carried it out like a prince rescuing his maiden fair—both arms supporting the weight of the gowns and keeping her arms high enough that not even the bundling fabric touched the floor.

A blast of chill, damp air stopped Caddy in the front doorway. She'd need to return for her cloak.

"Afternoon, Miss Bainbridge." The driver touched the front brim of his tall hat. "Back to Chawley Abbey today, are we?"

"Yes, Thomas, thank you." Caddy carefully stepped up into the coach and draped the bundle of gowns across the backward-facing seat before climbing down again. "I will be right back." She hurried into the store—and stopped short at the sight of

Alice standing beside the button cabinet, holding her cloak. If it weren't for her girls, sometimes Caddy wasn't certain she'd stay in business.

She flung the cloak around her shoulders, and it billowed behind her as she rushed back out the door to the carriage.

Letty chattered incessantly the entire hour's journey—about the young men she fancied who worked at the shops and public houses in North Parade, or lived above them; about the new hat she was trimming from the scrap bag; about her plans to open a shop of her own in London someday. Banbury Road and the increasingly fine homes marched past the coach's narrow windows. Caddy's gaze drew across the grand edifices of the ancient colleges and churches as the carriage took them south into Oxford proper, then through town toward the road leading to Chawley Abbey on the western outskirts of the city.

The drizzle and cold wind didn't seem to deter any of the noise or bustle of the city center, and several times, Thomas drew the cab to a stop, yelling at someone or something blocking their passage. Caddy drew the curtain shut and leaned back in her seat, trying to block out the tiresome scene.

Letty leaned forward and would have opened the window in her door had Caddy not reminded her of the purpose of their journey with a hand on her arm and a nod toward the bundle of dresses on the opposite seat.

When they turned into a quieter lane, Letty leaned back with a sigh. "I cannot wait to visit London in May. I tingle with pleasure every time I imagine the displays of fabrics and clothing from around the world. Won't it be delightful, Miss Bainbridge? Not only to see all of the treasures the world has to offer, but to be able to spend the day in Hyde Park in London?"

Caddy held in a shudder. She'd lived in London for a time and had been grateful to return to Oxford. "Prince Albert's Great

Exhibition should be quite educational, yes, Letty." Caddy was going mainly because she promised her girls she would take them. But she did want to study the fashions of the ladies in London, and also learn more about fabrics that could be imported. The best part of the Great Exhibition was the increase in Caddy's business—many local women had come to her over the past few months to have new dresses designed for their upcoming jaunts to London for the Exhibition.

She reminded herself to thank God for Miss Buchanan and Lady Carmichael. The daughter of a baronet and wife of a baron were by no means the highest-ranking ladies in Oxford society, but they recommended Caddy's services to their friends and acquaintances—almost to the point that Caddy had more orders than she could fulfill with only three apprentices. Perhaps she should take on one more.

Letty's flow of raptures about London and the Exhibition, as she imagined it would be, stopped only when the carriage did in front of Chawley Abbey. Though not massive, the gray-stone manor, with its crenellated roofline and tall, square central tower was imposing. Several small windows in the shapes of crosses and the high, mullioned stained glass windows bespoke its original purpose as a monastery.

A footman met them at the carriage and took the bundle of gowns while Thomas Longrieve, the cab driver Caddy used most often, offered his hand to Caddy and Letty for assistance getting out.

In the entry hall, Letty paused, as usual, to take in the soaring open tower above. Caddy hid her annoyance. She'd learned long ago not to openly show her awe of the homes she entered, lest her customers feel she was too provincial to do the job for which she was hired. And she'd tried to pass that along to her apprentices, but with varying degrees of success. "Come, Letty. No dawdling."

With obvious reluctance, the girl dragged her gaze down from the lofty ceiling and followed Caddy and the footman upstairs toward Lady Carmichael's dressing room. In contrast to the entryway, the rest of the abbey seemed dark and cramped—the rooms small and paneled, painted, or papered in deep, heavy hues.

A wooden staircase wound around the walls of the home's second, smaller tower. Caddy's right knee protested each step up. Mother had been right—she should have had the doctor look at it after she wrenched it in her spill on the icy street a few months ago.

Rounding the landing halfway between the second and third floors, irregular movement caught Caddy's attention, and she looked up just in time to see the footman stop and flatten himself against the banister, head bowed. The way he leaned back made Caddy's heart pound—he could so easily overset and fall to his death on the stone floor below.

"Jenkins—" But she stopped her question. Looking up past the footman, she realized why he'd stopped.

A few steps up stood a man—she could tell he was male by the shape of his shadow. He stepped down and into the sunlight streaming in through the tall, etched window in the opposite wall.

Caddy immediately bent her aching knee into a curtsy. "Mr. Carmichael. I hope we are not disturbing you." Though why he should be coming down the servants' stairs instead of the massive staircase in the front of the house, she couldn't guess.

The Honorable Mr. Oliver Carmichael, Lady Carmichael's eldest son and the future baron, raised one brow. "I do not believe

I've had the pleasure." He came down another step—putting him even with the footman and only two steps above Caddy.

"Cadence Bainbridge, seamstress. My apprentice, Leticia Ayers." She looked over her shoulder at Letty, who executed a perfect curtsy.

"*Miss* Bainbridge, I hope." The tone in Mr. Carmichael's voice sent a shiver down Caddy's spine. She'd been doing this work too long and encountered too many husbands, sons, and fathers of her customers not to recognize his meaning.

She forced a tight smile. "If you will excuse us, Mr. Carmichael, Lady Carmichael is expecting me." She nodded at Jenkins, who seemed grateful for the escape. Caddy couldn't blame the servant.

For a moment, Mr. Carmichael seemed to consider not moving out of the way, but at last he relented and pressed his back against the wall so Caddy and Letty could pass.

Reaching the top of the next half-flight, Caddy glanced to her left. He stood there, looking up . . . at her. He grinned, then sauntered down and out of sight below them.

In the dressing room—larger by half than Caddy's bedroom—she unwrapped the gowns and hung them on four vacant hooks lining the walls, ignoring the lingering crawling sensation on her skin from Mr. Carmichael's expression and tone. She adjusted the trimmings on sleeves and bodices, and Letty followed behind, fluffing out the full skirts.

A clearing throat drew their attention to the door. Dressed in an understated blue gown, Lady Carmichael's lady's maid hovered in the doorway. "If you are quite finished primping, Miss Bainbridge?"

Caddy bit her tongue. *Let the unpleasantness begin.* "Yes. We're ready."

Letty melted into a dim corner of the dressing room, while Caddy stepped back so that the gowns would be the first thing Lady Carmichael saw.

The lady's maid disappeared. Caddy took a deep breath—then held it.

The baroness swept into the dressing room, her emerald-green taffeta afternoon dress whispering across the expensive Oriental carpet. Caddy assumed Lady Carmichael had chosen to wear the gown, her most recent London purchase, on purpose, to put Caddy in her place—as simply a good-enough local dressmaker, but one unable to compete with the couturiers in London.

Not a blonde hair ever out of place. Her lips and cheeks rouged. Her mouth pulled into a constant bow of petulance. The world lived to serve Lady Carmichael—and Caddy was part of that world.

The baroness's expression did not change as she examined each gown, her forefinger pressed to her puckered lips, forehead crinkling in concentration. The lady's maid, who'd returned with her mistress, eyed the gowns with equal disdain.

She gave each of the four gowns the same level of scrutiny, then turned toward Caddy. "The blue first."

"Yes, my lady." Caddy nodded at the maid and motioned Letty forward. Between the three of them, they had Lady Carmichael out of the green taffeta and into the blue silk-satin dress with the eight ruffled flounces around the full skirt in short measure.

Before allowing Caddy to start pinning for alterations, Lady Carmichael turned to look at herself in the full-length cheval mirror. "No. Too many ruffles. I'm a baroness, not an unfledged debutante."

Caddy chose not to remind the baroness of the fashion plate she'd given Caddy showing a similar design, then asking for additional flounces to be added. "Perhaps if we removed every other one?"

"I still will not like it. The color is hideous." She turned from the mirror as if it pained her to look at herself in the gown.

The color had been "simply divine" when Lady Carmichael picked out the most expensive satin in the shop. Caddy helped Letty and the maid remove the dress from the baroness.

As Caddy expected, Lady Carmichael found fault with each of the remaining three dresses, but she reluctantly agreed that the green-and-ivory-striped ball gown brought out her green eyes, and the pointed Basque bodice flattered her already narrow waist, especially once Caddy pinned it tighter than she wanted to. She would leave a bit of an allowance, just so the baroness could breathe, and so the seams wouldn't split when she moved her arms—or any other part of her upper body.

The maid assisted Lady Carmichael back into her London dress while Caddy and Letty carefully bundled the ball gowns in the linen again.

"I expect the gown to be ready by Friday." With a terse nod, the baroness stalked from the room.

Two days to finish a dress that wasn't needed for almost two more months. Why would Caddy have expected anything else?

Letty opened her mouth to speak, but Caddy shook her head. Thankfully, unlike Alice—who seemed to have no ability to curb her curiosity from erupting into questions loudly asked and overheard by inopportune people—Letty held her silence until they sat in the carriage as it rolled down the drive, back toward Oxford.

"Did Lady Carmichael not choose all of those designs and fabrics herself?" Letty absently fingered a cluster of ribbon rosettes sewn onto the sash at her waist.

"Don't do that—you'll ruin your work."

The apprentice looked confused, so Caddy touched the back of Letty's hand. The girl clasped her restless hands together.

"Yes, Lady Carmichael chose the fabrics, colors, and styles. But as a customer, it is her prerogative to change her mind once she sees them fully realized. What looks wonderful in a fashion plate is almost never as flattering in reality."

"But what will happen to the three gowns she didn't want?"

Caddy glanced at the girl in surprise. "Leticia Jones, you have worked with me for over five years now. What *always* happens to the garments customers decide they don't want?"

"They are put in the shop as ready-made to be sold to someone who cannot afford something custom, or someone who does not have the time to have a gown made. But these fabrics—they are so very expensive. Who of our customers other than Lady Carmichael can afford these?"

"Perhaps the American niece of Sir Anthony Buchanan is in need of another ball gown."

"Do you think she would be charitable enough to take the yellow one with all the red silk roses on it?"

Caddy had to laugh. She agreed—that particular gown would be hard to sell to anyone. "I think Miss Edith Buchanan would love to see Miss Dearing in something so . . . overwrought. Perhaps I should take it tomorrow when I go to Wakesdown to see Miss Buchanan."

Caddy regaled her apprentice with stories and descriptions of some of the worst garments she had ever been commissioned to make, and both were laughing when Thomas stopped the cab in front of the store.

"I couldn't hear what you two were talking about." Thomas handed Caddy down from the cab. "But it does my heart good to hear you laughing so, Miss Bainbridge."

"It did my heart good to be laughing, Thomas." She handed him a folded bank note, enough to cover his fee with a little left over for good measure to show her appreciation for his consistent and continual service to her. "I had almost forgotten what it felt like. But Mother seems to be feeling much stronger, and I am blessed with work, so why shouldn't I be light of heart?"

Letty handed Caddy the bundle before climbing out of the coach. They both thanked Thomas again, then ducked into the warm shop. Phyllis, a former apprentice who'd shown no aptitude for sewing but had quickly proven she had a head for numbers, stood at the ribbon rack with two young misses. Beyond her, Alice pulled out a bolt of burgundy wool for a middle-aged woman who would most likely be taking the fabric home to sew her own dress. Which was exactly why Caddy had expanded into a shopkeeper in addition to being a dressmaker. Women who could not afford to pay someone else to do their sewing still required fabrics and notions. So Caddy kept a wide assortment, from muslins strong and inexpensive enough for a farmer's wife or a factory worker to the Siamese silk waiting in the workroom to be made into a fine evening dress for the Bishop of Oxford's wife. It was her first commission for a courtier—as Bishop Wilberforce also served as Prince Albert's chaplain, and they spent more time in London than Oxford—and she prayed she would not mess it up.

The front door rattled, and the bell hanging from it chimed. Caddy turned to help the customer.

And she lost the ability to breathe.

The largest man she'd ever seen trundled into the shop, a bundle in his arms not unlike the one she'd just handed Letty. Thick, muscular arms. Arms bare from the elbows down, covered only in white muslin above. His hair was a cross between golden and brown, and his chiseled features reminded her of the statues of the angels in the Christ Church Cathedral.

Heat flooded her face when she realized she'd been staring. "How can I help you, Mr.—?"

The bundle in his arms moaned.

Caddy's stomach knotted. She rushed forward and pulled back a hood to reveal—"Mother!"

CHAPTER TWO

$\mathcal{N}$eal followed the brown-haired woman up the steep steps to the living quarters above the shop. The enclosed stairs were narrow enough that he had to turn sideways so that he did not risk further injury to the one in his arms. Although, after carrying the barely conscious woman down the street from the Howells' store, he wasn't certain it was injury that had felled her. She weighed next to nothing, and her gaunt face and grayish-yellow pallor indicated a protracted illness.

The younger woman, obviously the proprietress of the shop below, opened a door that led to another narrow staircase. Starting to feel winded, Neal followed, again turning sideways. In the cramped hallway above, the woman opened one of the doors and stepped back, motioning Neal inside.

A wooden bedstead almost filled the small bedroom, a night-stand wedged between it and the wall on the far side, an armoire blocking the door from fully opening. Neal edged cautiously between the wardrobe and bed and laid his moaning bundle down in the plush quilts.

"Here."

He turned and accepted a thick woolen blanket. A scent of lavender and lemon wafted up when he unfolded it to lay over the woman on the bed. He pressed his hand to her forehead. Cool and dry. No fever. He lifted her hand and pressed his fingertips to the inside of her wrist. Hmmm. Faint and slow heartbeat. No wonder she'd collapsed upon standing.

"Sir, thank you for bringing my mother home, but—"

"How long has she been ill?" Neal leaned over and pulled the older woman's eyelids up, then looked at the insides of her lips and at her gums. Pale. Too pale. Probably a weak heart.

"Pardon me, but who are you?"

Straightening, Neal turned toward the door. For the first time, he really looked at the woman standing there. Not tall, but not petite, with a healthy build. Well dressed, but not ostentatious. Modest but fashionable hairstyle. Her wide blue eyes bespoke her concern and fear for her mother. Neal's heart ached for her— the mother's prognosis wasn't good.

"I do apologize." He edged toward her and extended his right hand. "Dr. Neal Stradbroke."

Her hand paused halfway to his. "Doctor? Was she so bad they had to call for a doctor?"

"No. I happened to be in the Howells' shop when your mother collapsed, and I offered to bring her home, Miss . . . ?"

The woman shook his hand with a firm grasp. "Bainbridge. Miss Cadence Bainbridge." She nodded toward the woman on the bed. "My mother, Mrs. Bainbridge."

Neal pulled his tingling hand away from Miss Bainbridge's and returned to her mother's side. "How long has she suffered from a weakened heart?"

"She has never been strong, but she has been in decline for four years . . . since my father died." Miss Bainbridge slipped into the room and wedged herself between the footboard and the wall. "Is she . . . will she recover?"

"I would need to do a complete examination before I could make a diagnosis." Neal smoothed the silvery-blonde hair back from Mrs. Bainbridge's papery forehead. "But if your mother has been ill for so long, I imagine she is already under a physician's care."

"Yes. But . . ."

When Miss Bainbridge did not continue, Neal looked at her over his shoulder. "But?"

"As you can see, she is not getting better. I am certain her current doctor is highly capable, but . . ." She shrugged.

"But you wonder if having another doctor examine her might lead to a different diagnosis, a different treatment?"

She nodded.

He crossed his arms. "I would consent to examining her and rendering a diagnosis only if your mother decides it is what she wants—and so long as her current doctor is informed. And I will need her nurse present. I must be able to ask questions of the person who knows her symptoms best."

"I could—"

He held up his hand. "'Tis better if family members are not present during such an examination. Patients often try to hide their true condition if they think it will worry their loved ones." A number of emotions crossed Miss Bainbridge's face—the kind of face he imagined could grace one of the queen's famous china dolls.

"Her nurse has Wednesday afternoons off. When might you be able to come back and do the examination? If Mother agrees, of course."

"I am in North Parade every day. Or, rather, I will be from now on. I've taken lodgings above the apothecary opposite Howell's

Greengrocer." He looked down at himself, and embarrassment heated his skin at the realization he'd stood here in a lady's presence without his coat—his sleeves rolled up, his waistcoat rumpled, his collar unbuttoned, and no tie. His own dear grandmamma, God rest her soul, would have dragged him out by the ear and tanned him for such atrocious manners. No matter that she'd been more than a foot shorter and a good seven to eight stones lighter. He would have let her do it, because he deserved it for betraying his upbringing in such a manner.

"Good. Once Mother awakens, I will speak to her. If she agrees I shall send you a request for a formal examination." Miss Bainbridge pursed her lips into a perfectly kissable bow.

Perfectly kissable? What was wrong with him? He inclined his head toward her and edged toward the door. "If you will excuse me, Miss Bainbridge, my crates await unpacking." No hat to tip, he inclined his head again, then fled the small bedroom.

No entanglements. No involvements. No getting close to anyone. At least not until October. Not until it ended. Not until he had no further risk of anyone learning the truth about him.

"I agree."

Caddy turned at her mother's weak voice. She scooted around the bed to the spot vacated by Dr. Stradbroke moments before. "Mother? How are you feeling?"

"I am feeling like I need another doctor to examine me and see if he can determine a different diagnosis and treatment for my malady." Mother pushed herself up into a sitting position, and Caddy helped her arrange the pillows behind her to prop her up.

"What happened at the Howells'?"

"I believe the walk was too much for me. I was so tired by the time I arrived, I was grateful to sit down in the office, for I could not have climbed the stairs on my own. Nellie Howell was kind enough to come down and visit with me there. We had a nice long talk; it has been far too long since I saw her last."

"She called on you a week ago."

"Yes—and a week is too long between visits for true friends." A little color came back into Mother's cheeks, Caddy was happy to see.

"You are correct, of course." Caddy tucked her smile into a frown of concentration so Mother would not think she laughed at her.

"When I stood to leave, I . . . I am uncertain what happened. The next thing I knew, that very handsome, very tall young man was holding me in his arms and carrying me home."

"You fainted, Mother. I knew you should not have walked so far. You've likely set yourself back with this ill-conceived exertion. I never should have let you go."

Mother grabbed Caddy's hand with more strength than Caddy knew she possessed. "Who is the mother and who the child here?" Her voice crackled with fire. "Do not forget that it was I who raised you, dear girl. I who taught you to walk, to talk, to run, to sew."

Caddy rubbed her mother's arm in what she hoped was a conciliatory manner. "Yes, Mother. I am sorry." She swallowed back the other words of reproach piling up in the back of her throat. "So you heard Dr. Stradbroke's offer to examine you and see if he can find a different diagnosis?"

"Yes. And I completely agree. Dr. Fieldstone is a very capable man, I am certain. However, he is . . . well, old. And set in his ways. Perhaps my cure lies with a younger man, a man schooled in new medical techniques and research." She squeezed Caddy's hand before pulling away and smoothing her hair back. "And he is very handsome, is he not?"

How had the blankets become so entangled when her mother hadn't moved? Caddy set to straightening them. "I hadn't noticed whether he is handsome or not."

"Mmmm."

"I shall be downstairs working." Caddy moved the bell on the washstand closer to the edge so Mother could easily reach it. "If you need anything, ring for me. Do not attempt to get it for yourself. Unlike Dr. Stradbroke, I do not possess the strength to carry you back up the stairs."

"So you did notice his muscles—"

"Mother!" Caddy would have whirled and stomped from the room, much as she had done in her early years whenever her mother teased her about meeting a handsome man. But the wardrobe behind her and the bed in front of her pressed her skirts so that she had to push her feet against the floor to be able to move at all. "That is enough. Rest now. And—"

"And ring if I need anything. I know, I know."

Shaking her head in resignation, Caddy returned to the shop. The girls clamored to learn more about the handsome stranger who'd carried Mrs. Bainbridge home. Caddy staved off the most curious of the questions and picked up the bundle of gowns to take back into the workroom.

The jingling chimes on the door stopped her. She turned to greet the customer—and her breath caught in her throat.

Oliver paused just inside the door. As he suspected, the shop was nothing close to those on Oxford's High Street. And comparing it to anything in London was laughable. But though he'd otherwise never deign to set foot in a women's dress shop, much less allow himself to be seen in North Parade, he'd decided he needed a closer look at M'lady's charity case.

The plain-looking woman who'd come to Chawley Abbey earlier today shifted the bundle of gowns in her arms to those of one of the young shop assistants. Miss Bainbridge smoothed her hands down the full skirt of her dress, a concoction that might get her noticed in this part of town, but that would get her laughed out of his mother's drawing room.

"Mr. Carmichael, how may I assist you?" Miss Bainbridge's wide blue eyes betrayed her surprise and trepidation at his presence.

"I have come on an errand from my lady mother. She has decided she will take the blue dress in addition to the green. She would like both delivered on Friday." He sincerely doubted the rustic would be able to meet his mother's demand—and perhaps that was M'lady's plan, to avoid being seen in anything this backward shop would produce by giving unrealistic deadlines.

Miss Bainbridge reached up to tuck a stray lock of hair back into her plain hairstyle, and her hand trembled. Oliver kept his smile to himself—mostly.

"Please let Lady Carmichael know that I will be happy to have both gowns finished by Friday." She clasped her hands together at her waist. After a long pause, she cleared her throat. "Is there anything else I can do for you, Mr. Carmichael?"

Oliver rubbed the tips of his thumb and middle finger of his left hand together. For the first time ever, a woman seemed eager to be rid of him. Every woman he'd ever met—with the exception of Edith Buchanan's spinster American cousin. But who could countenance Americans anyway?

If one of his mother's or sisters' maids were to get hold of Miss Bainbridge, she might pass for one of their own. Certainly, with the correct hairstyle and a proper evening gown, she could fool anyone into believing she was one of the gentry, if not low aristocracy, rather than in trade.

"Miss Bainbridge, though I am certain you carry . . . many fine wares here, I do not believe there is anything I might find that would suit my personal needs." He ducked his chin and glanced at her in a way that made most ladies' fans start fluttering at twice the speed.

Red climbed into Miss Bainbridge's cheeks and she looked down. "No, of course not." She curtsied and looked up again. "Good day, then, Mr. Carmichael."

Oliver forced his jaw not to fall open. He'd been dismissed. He, the Honorable Mr. Oliver Carmichael, future Baron Carmichael of Chawley Abbey. Dismissed by . . . by . . . a tradeswoman!

He bowed, keeping a smile on his face. "Good day, Miss Bainbridge. Until next time." Settling his hat on his head so that it would not crush the curls his valet spent so long perfecting each morning, Oliver departed the shop, mentally shaking the dust of the place off his boots in the few steps between the door and his horse.

The long ride from North Parade to the heart of Oxford did nothing to dissipate his annoyance—in fact, each hoofbeat acted as a hammer, nailing the memory of the ignominious interview deeper into his mind.

He handed Caesar's reins over to a groom and entered the club. The sweet, acrid scent of smoke greeted him a brief instant before the majordomo did the same, taking Oliver's cloak. Behind him, a footman handed Oliver a snifter of brandy.

Oliver wandered through the ground-floor rooms and, as expected, saw no one of merit. He climbed to the first floor. The footman at the top of the stairs inclined his head upon recognizing Oliver. The club's dedication to keeping the gentry separated

from the men who truly deserved to be here was the only reason he and his father had kept their membership once the club
opened to membership from wealthy but non-titled men.

"Carmichael—there you are. You should have been here
above an hour past." Doncroft waved him over to the table. "Join
us. Radclyffe has no heart for cards today, which means I have
not been able to take the entirety of his allowance yet. Perhaps I
can take half of yours, and that will make up for it."

Oliver turned one of the two empty chairs at the small round
table to the side and sat. He slid down into a posture of repose
and stretched his legs in front of him, crossing them at the ankle.
"I have no heart for cards myself."

"I know why Radclyffe is disconsolate. His father informed
him today he has started negotiating terms with Dr. Suggitt of
Christ College for a possible marriage for Rad with the man's
horse-faced youngest daughter. If you have nothing to compare
to that tragedy, then ante up." Doncroft began shuffling the cards.

Oliver launched into his tale of woe about how Caddy
Bainbridge snubbed him and practically ordered him from her
shop.

"She should have realized the honor of my presence there.
M'lady wanted to send a servant with the message, but as I was
already coming into Oxford, I volunteered to carry it for her.
How could that . . . that . . . peasant treat me thus?"

Doncroft and Radclyffe had the audacity to laugh. "Alas, poor
Carmichael. Snubbed by a seamstress."

"Is she pretty?" Radclyffe asked.

"Prettier than Suggitt's daughter."

"You are nigh on closing the deal with Miss Buchanan, are you
not?" Doncroft started dealing cards.

Oliver nodded.

"Then why worry about some no-name tradeswoman from North Parade and whether or not she falls at your feet? You have your choice of women now—though Miss Buchanan's fifty thousand pounds would be tempting even if she were not a beautiful specimen of womanhood."

"I could *make* Cadence Bainbridge fall at my feet, as you put it." Oliver pressed his palms to the arms of the chair and pushed himself upright.

Doncroft seemed to forget the cards. "You could try. Make her realize what an insult she paid you by wooing her, then walking away."

Radclyffe leaned forward. "And I say you cannot. Women like her are not easily charmed. Filled with ice and iron, they are, those confirmed spinsters."

Oliver weighed the opinions of his two friends. "I'll place money on it. Fifty pounds says I can make Cadence Bainbridge fall in love with me before . . ." When? How quickly could he work his magic on her? "By the day the Great Exhibition opens— May 1."

"Make it one hundred, and you have yourself a wager." Doncroft extended his right hand across the table.

Oliver considered a moment, then took his friend's hand. "One hundred pounds says I can make Miss Cadence Bainbridge fall desperately and completely in love with me."

CHAPTER THREE

*E*nvy roiled in Edith Buchanan's stomach. How could it possibly be right that the viscount would choose her old, plain cousin over her?

She returned the flirtatious attention of the earl's son to her right, dragging her attention away from Lord Thynne and Katharine on the far side of the sitting room. It was bad enough that the embarrassment of penniless cousins had been forced upon her. But Katharine and Christopher Dearing's rustic manners and nasal American accents were like a slap in the face each time they came into the same room as her.

Now Lord Thynne favored Katharine. Edith wanted to scratch the too-serious expression from her cousin's face. Father had invited him here for the express purpose of having him fall prey to Edith's charms and propose to Edith. Not the American nobody.

And Christopher Dearing! Loud and obnoxious with his observations and commentary on the differences between British and American lifestyles. His excitement over the Great Exhibition made him sound like one of the servants. His constant questions about the railway system in England made her ears ache.

She could just scream from the boredom and annoyance. However, she did not want to lower herself to being as uncivilized as they.

Oliver Carmichael returned with a fresh cup of coffee for Edith. She beamed up at him. While he was heir to only a barony, nowhere near as large an estate or prestigious a title as a viscount, marrying a future baron was a step up for the daughter of a baronet.

His two friends who usually followed him like trained hunting dogs had found their own amusement this evening—flirting with several of the other young ladies. With the house party in its third week, Edith had grown tired of these after-dinner sessions of talk and flirting before the evening's entertainment began. And the "entertainment" usually consisted of each of the young ladies showing off her talent—or lack thereof—at the piano or spinet or harp, each trying to outdo the other in the quest to secure a proposal from one of the men of the party by playing or singing or both.

Edith never lowered herself to such an exhibition—she did not need to. Men came to her naturally, drawn by her beauty and elegance.

Her gaze drifted over to the far side of the room again. Lord Thynne leaned close to Katharine and whispered something in her ear.

Edith's dinner soured in her stomach. "Charades," she called, cutting off Mr. Carmichael's anecdote of his visit with his mother this afternoon. "And I choose . . ." She looked around the room at the dozen and a half guests. Whom would she honor with going first? "I choose Mr. Oliver Carmichael to lead off the game."

Carmichael pushed his languid form from the armchair, bowed, and kissed the back of Edith's hand. "It would be my honor, Miss Buchanan."

Edith ducked her chin and gazed up at him through her lashes, pursing her lips into a coquettish expression. As expected, Mr. Carmichael's gaze dropped to her mouth and lingered there a moment before he stepped away to help the other men rearrange the chairs and settees into rows.

To her great annoyance, Lord Thynne and her cousin did not join everyone else, but stayed in their corner, conversing as if joining the game were beneath them. With a sigh, she sank onto a spindle-legged settee in the center of the audience. Spreading the ruby satin silk of her skirt to cover most of the seat, she clapped her hands and enjoined Oliver to begin.

Just to prove to the viscount and her cousin that she did not care if they snubbed her, she laughed longer, shouted her guesses louder, and clapped more enthusiastically with each round of the game. And she invited Oliver Carmichael to sit with her, necessitating a pause as she rearranged her skirts to give him room.

"When will you be going to London, Mr. Carmichael?" Edith leaned closer to her companion, hoping Lord Thynne could see that she had already cast her romantic interest elsewhere.

"M'lady has determined that we shall arrive the last week of April. She believes she will be disturbed by the crowds coming into London for the Exhibition if we arrive any earlier. We have secured seats in one of the observation boxes for the opening ceremony. I would be honored if you would join us."

To give herself time to answer without betraying the excited leap of her heart at the offer, Edith shouted a wild guess at the young woman currently acting out something that resembled nothing at all. "I am flattered at the invitation, Mr. Carmichael. I shall speak with Papa about it."

Even though her father, a baronet, was part of the aristocracy, his title did not make him a peer of the realm—like Lord Thynne—so he had been unable to secure seats in the grandstands that would flank either side of the stage from which Queen Victoria would proclaim the Great Exhibition officially open. Of course, joining the Carmichaels in their box would be tantamount to proclaiming an engagement.

But she had more than a month between now and then to settle the matter—to see if she could win back Lord Thynne from her cousin. Or to at least keep Katharine from becoming Lady Thynne and a viscountess while Edith settled for becoming a mere baroness. And that would not happen soon, for Baron Carmichael was healthy and robust and did not seem likely to be giving up the title to his son within the next twenty years. She would *not* be calling that American upstart *my lady* for years before being addressed thusly herself.

A slow smile spread across her face as Mr. Carmichael rose to take another turn at the game. Fortunately, Edith had the foresight to notice Katharine's interest in the man Papa had hired to redesign the gardens and set one of the maids to follow Katharine and report on her doings. And one of those doings had been a clandestine meeting with that man in the garden folly two weeks ago. But as that had been before Lord Thynne had officially begun courting Katharine, Edith had not yet shared that knowledge.

She would wait. Eventually, the American would do something that Edith could use to engineer her downfall. It was just a matter of time.

Neal stacked four stoneware plates on the shelf. Not being particularly adept at carpentry, he hoped the thing would hold. Three tin cups and two bowls joined the plates, followed by four teacups and saucers, the only luxury items he had brought with him from Grandmamma's house. The rest he had left in place for the young couple now letting the farm.

A banging on the door interrupted setting up his kitchen. He rolled his sleeves down and buttoned the cuffs before opening the door.

"Are you the doc?" A young man—who looked barely old enough to shave—twisted a felt cap in grubby hands.

"I am."

"My ma's trying to birth a baby, but it won't come. The midwife said to fetch the doc. Can you come?"

"Of course. Let me get my bag and I will be right along with you."

Carrying a candle into the small room he'd designated an office, Neal checked his medical bag to ensure he had all the equipment he might need for a difficult birth. He shrugged into his long coat, not worrying with a frock or waistcoat, then followed the boy out into the night.

He'd yet to hang a shingle or to let his neighbors know who he was—other than the Howells and the Bainbridges. But, like the small town where he'd lived with his grandmother since age twelve, North Parade and the adjacent community of Jericho must not be a place where many secrets could be kept.

He sighed. He'd hoped moving to Oxford would help shield him from anyone finding out about his background. Hopefully, the committeemen would be unable to find him here, leaving all communication on his side.

Following the lad down North Parade Avenue, Neal looked up to his right. The lowest floor of the redbrick storefront was dark, but windows in the three floors above revealed life went on over the seamstress's shop. His right hand tingled from the memory of shaking hands with Miss Bainbridge. He stretched his fingers and then curled them into a tight fist to rid himself of the sensation.

He knew nothing about her save the facts that she was a seamstress and she was passably pretty. And her mother suffered a weak heart—something that often ran in families.

No. He sped his step to catch up with the lad hurrying ahead of him down the darkened street. The last time he'd risked his affection on a passably pretty young woman, when part of the truth of his origins became known she'd sent her brothers to warn him away from ever coming within sight of her again. It hadn't taken long for his patients to stop calling on him and for his income to dwindle to nothing.

Thus his removal to the North Parade section of Oxford. He could not risk his heart—or his reputation—like that again.

The young man finally stopped in front of a row house of a different sort altogether from those on North Parade—low and stone, with a steeply pitched, gabled roof. Neal had to duck to keep from hitting his head on the lintel upon entering.

At the sights, sounds, and smells that greeted him, all thoughts but for the woman in front of him and her condition fled his mind.

The breech birth was difficult and dangerous at moments, but Neal welcomed the screaming, wrinkled little girl near dawn. He stayed long enough to ensure the health and welfare of both mother and daughter before taking his leave. Two steps out the door, he realized he had no idea how to get back to his dwelling. The father of the new baby roused his son where he slept on the floor outside his mother's room to show Neal home.

"Before you leave, Doc." The father reentered the house.

Neal waited what seemed a long time, stifling his yawns and wanting to be at home in bed.

The man came back out with a writhing burlap sack. "We got no coins, but I hope this will suffice for your efforts."

Neal took the bag, making sure he held the top tightly closed. "Thank you. I am certain this will be more than sufficient." He hoped it was something useful, and not something he'd have to rid himself of secretly.

The boy took him as far as the end of North Parade. Neal shifted the sack into the hand with his medical bag and fished in his pocket. He flipped a copper pence to the lad, whose eyes widened with delight when he snatched it out of the air. "That's between you and me." Neal winked at him. "No one else need know about it."

"Thanks, Doc. If you ever need someone to carry or fetch for ya, Johnny Longrieve's the lad for you." The boy clenched the coin between his canines—to check its authenticity, Neal supposed—then took off at a run back down the alley.

Neal shook his head and trudged up the street toward home.

Home. An apartment of two floors consisting of five rooms above the apothecary's shop. But the furnishings were decent and the rent low enough to be suitable for someone of his station.

How could he call it home when no one waited there for him? Home was the farm in the country where Grandmamma tended her garden and provided midwifing services to anyone within the range of the old draft horse she rode.

He circled around to the back of the contiguous row of buildings and climbed the steps to the door of his abode. Before another day passed, he needed to secure a horse. The stable behind the shop was large enough for three, and the apothecary only had the one he rode in from his home each day, leaving plenty of room for Neal to keep a horse.

The bag dangling from his hand squawked. Ah, yes. His payment.

Setting his kit on the table in the middle of the room that served for kitchen and dining, Neal crouched down close to the floor and untied the string from around the top of the bag. Two small chickens protested their confinement—one white, the other a mottled gray-brown. Hens and, he hoped, layers. He'd enjoy having his own source for eggs.

He looked around the room. "What am I going to do with the two of you?" He'd need to build a small coop. But until then . . . he couldn't keep them in the burlap sack. Carefully, he turned the bag on its side, then started tugging at the stitched end to encourage the hens to climb out.

When they realized what he meant for them to do, they jumped out amongst much flapping and squawking and flying feathers.

Using three of the four chairs from the table, a couple of old blankets, and some twine, he created an enclosure for the birds. As he laid parcel paper and newspaper in several layers over the floor in the small area, the two chickens ventured into the room that Neal planned to use as a sitting room.

They gave him quite a chase, even in the small rooms, but he eventually caught them and lifted them over the wall of woven wool into their makeshift coop. A bowl of water and a pan of bread mashed with the carrots and parsnips he'd overcooked and not eaten with his dinner followed, calming the new residents.

"What shall I call you?" Neal leaned over, resting his arms across the high back of one of the chairs. The white one looked up from the water bowl, head cocked as if waiting his judgment. "You'll be . . . Matilda. And you"—he motioned toward the gray-brown one that ignored him—"you'll be Sheila."

Matilda and Sheila explored the confines of their new, albeit temporary, home, then both flapped their way up onto the seats of two of the chairs to roost.

If only he could feel at home as easily as they seemed to be able to do. Yawning, he stumbled up to the top floor and dropped into bed. Despite the early morning sunlight streaming through the bare windows, he fell asleep almost instantly.

More banging at his door brought him upright in the bed, shaking off sleep as if he'd had plenty—though the angle of the dusty golden beams across his floor indicated he'd been home less than an hour.

He tossed a glance at the chickens—undisturbed by the banging, their heads forward and slightly down in sleep—then opened the door.

In the hallway, fist raised to bang again, stood a petite woman of indeterminate middle age.

"Please, are you the doctor?" The woman wrapped her hands anxiously in her apron, and her white frilly cap lay askew on haphazardly pinned braids.

"Let me get my bag."

❧

Pushing herself up to sit on the edge of her bed, Caddy rolled her head from side to side. When Lady Carmichael paid her for the two ball gowns on Friday, she needed to invest in a higher quality down with which to make a new pillow. She tossed her long brown braid over her shoulder and tightened the belt of her dressing gown before padding downstairs. The smell of brewing coffee meant Mother must be awake already and had sent her nurse, Mary, down to make it for her.

Her slippers, made from scrap-bag pieces, created no sound, and she made certain to step on the squeaky third stair to announce her presence so she wouldn't startle Mother if she were in the kitchen with her nurse.

The kitchen was empty. Frowning, but happy to have a few moments of peace before the day started, Caddy poured her coffee. It was one expense that she indulged in, because she preferred coffee to tea in the mornings, as did Mother. She clamped two thick slices of hearty rye in the toaster and set it on its rack on the hearth where the bread got the benefit of the heat of the open fire but wasn't scorched from touching the flames.

While her bread warmed and her coffee cooled, Caddy made her way down one more flight of stairs to the ground level and let herself through the shop to get the newssheet she paid the newsie to deliver to her front door each day.

Before she could grasp the knob, it rattled, then the door swung open. Caddy gasped and stumbled several steps back.

Mary rushed in—with Dr. Stradbroke on her heels.

"Mary? What's wrong? Is it—?" Caddy pressed her hands to her mouth.

Sympathetic concern filled the doctor's eyes. "Mary said she could not awaken your mother this morning, so she came to fetch me."

Breath stuck in her throat, Caddy whirled and dashed for the stairs, unconcerned for propriety or hospitality. Once before, they had been unable to rouse Mother . . . and Caddy did not want to think about the fear-filled days that followed. At least Father had still been with them then. Now—

Winded from running up two flights of narrow, steep stairs, Caddy pushed her mother's door open and came to an immediate stop.

Mother lay in the center of the bed, flat on her back, her silvery-blonde hair spread out on her pillow like an overly large halo. Her arms lay folded on the white lace counterpane over her chest. All she lacked was a nosegay of flowers for the scene to be perfect.

Caddy rubbed her throbbing temples, her hand covering her eyes. She wasn't certain if it was to keep from seeing the expression on Dr. Stradbroke's face or to keep him from seeing her embarrassment over her mother's obvious play-acting. She knew Mother wanted her to marry, but faking illness to throw Caddy in the doctor's path was taking it a bit far.

Dr. Stradbroke paused in the door and took in the scene. The only indication he gave that he noticed anything amiss was a slight lift of his brows—which Caddy saw between her fingers, curious as to his reaction.

Lowering her hand, Caddy crossed her arms and pressed her fist to her mouth to keep from calling out to her mother to stop her pretense.

The doctor set his bag on the bed near Mother's feet, opened it, and withdrew his stethoscope. He pressed the wide end to her chest and tilted his head to listen through the narrow end.

"Hmmm." He put the horn-shaped implement back in his bag. He pressed his fingertips to the inside of her wrist and withdrew his pocket watch.

Caddy could hear it ticking from her position at the foot of the bed.

He laid Mother's arm down gently at her side. He moved forward and leaned over her head, lifting each eyelid and examining her eyes for . . . Caddy couldn't begin to imagine what he could tell from her eyes except, possibly, that she was just feigning her swoon.

After using almost every instrument in his bag—and probably not with the use for which they were meant—Dr. Stradbroke deliberately and methodically put everything away. He straightened the coverlet, brushed a stray strand of hair from Mother's forehead, and then turned to face Caddy.

"I fear, Miss Bainbridge, that your mother's condition is grave." The doctor crossed his arms, his brown worsted frock coat unable to disguise the thickness of arms better suited to a farmhand or laborer than a doctor.

Caddy's heart jumped. Could it be possible her mother wasn't faking her illness? "Grave?"

"Yes. I believe the only treatment that will bring her around is an ice bath. Do you have a tub in which she can be fully immersed?" Dr. Stradbroke turned his head away from Mother and smiled with a shake of his head, his blue eyes dancing.

Caddy almost laughed with relief. Mother wasn't ill, and he'd seen through her ruse and decided to play along. However, Caddy thought *she* might need the ice bath in another moment, if Stradbroke kept looking at her like that—bringing her into his humor with the simplest of expressions. "I have one I use for dying fabrics. Would that work?"

"Yes. I shall see to acquiring the blocks of ice—"

A low moan from the bed interrupted him. A smile stole across his face—but he straightened it into a visage of concern before he turned to look at Mother. "Mrs. Bainbridge?"

"Wh-what . . . happened?"

"You were in a swoon, ma'am, and we were unable to rouse you." He leaned over and pressed the back of his large hand to her cheek, then rested his palm on her forehead. "How are you feeling now?"

"I do not know what ministrations you provided, Doctor, but I seem to be regaining strength by the moment."

The doctor's broad brow furrowed. "Are you certain, Mrs. Bainbridge? I find that a shock to the body—such as full immersion in an ice bath—can be quite efficacious to restoring one after a swoon."

Caddy grabbed the railing at the foot of the bed and squeezed, letting the carved wood bite into her palms to keep from laughing at the doctor's solicitousness toward the malingering woman in the bed.

Mother struggled to push herself into a sitting position, and Dr. Stradbroke helped her arrange the pillows to prop her up. "Yes, you see, I am already much better, thank you."

Sidling along the bed to the end, Dr. Stradbroke snapped the latch of his kit closed and picked it up. "If you are certain, I'd best be going about my rounds, then."

"Yes, yes. I am certain. Cadence, you will walk the doctor to the door, please." Mother waved an imperious hand.

Caddy whirled and started down the stairs, hoping the doctor was behind her, but unable to look at him, knowing how red her face must be from the way it burned. She stopped at the foot of the stairs in the kitchen and turned back toward him.

"Doctor, I cannot begin to apologize for my mother's deplorable behavior this morning."

He lifted one hand, smiling at her again. "Think nothing of it. I am only sorry I interrupted your morning in such a way."

Caddy glanced down—and resisted the urge to cross her arms over her chest. The dressing gown covered her corset and petticoats well enough. But it was a dressing gown and nothing fit to be seen in by anyone other than her mother, Mary, or the girls. Especially not a man. "How . . . how much do we owe you for your services?"

He shook his head. "I did nothing other than provide comfort to a woman who is, truly, very ill. I find that when people begin to face their own mortality, they become . . . eccentric. If I can bring them a measure of peace or happiness by feigning ministrations, then it is my pleasure to do so."

"But there must be something. I cannot allow you to leave without some type of recompense." Caddy tightened the already tight sash over her dressing gown.

Neal seemed to consider for a moment. "I—no. I cannot ask it of you."

She stepped forward, eager for some way to repay his kindness toward Mother. "What? Anything, please."

"My grandmother used to do my mending and darning. But since her passing . . . suffice it to say that stitching wounds together does not prepare one for mending clothing." He ducked his chin and lacked only rubbing his toe into the floorboards to approximate an embarrassed little boy.

Caddy's heart skipped and thudded. Did the man not realize what effect his simplest movements and expressions could have on unsuspecting females? "I would be happy to mend for you."

"Then I will be happy to continue administering peace and happiness to your mother as needed." He tapped his fingers on the table. "I should be going, then."

"Oh . . . yes. Shall I see you to the door?"

"I believe I can find my way."

Caddy followed him downstairs anyway, on the excuse she would need to lock the front door behind him.

He turned on the other side of the threshold and inclined his head. "Good morning, Miss Bainbridge."

"Good morning, Dr. Stradbroke."

The early morning sunlight beamed off of his hair, making it appear more golden than brown. Caddy sighed and leaned against the jamb, watching him walk across and down the street.

She wouldn't mind saying good morning to him *every* morning.

CHAPTER FOUR

*O*liver pulled the gunstock away from his shoulder, the echoes of his shot reverberating through his head. He should not have indulged in so much brandy last night.

The partridge flew toward the cover of the tree line several hundred yards away. Beside him, the hunting dog sighed. Oliver repeated the sound, a profound sense of ennui settling over him. In the three weeks he'd been at this house party, he'd hunted partridge, quail, and fox. He'd bagged his share. But what he wanted to hunt was not here at Wakesdown.

"You shall shoot the next one for certain, Mr. Carmichael."

A chill ran across his shoulders and down his arms, and his spine stiffened. He turned and doffed his hunting cap to Edith Buchanan, who looked quite fetching this morning in a gown of ice-blue and silver plaid and a white fur cape and hat setting off her black hair.

"You are always overly generous with your belief in my hunting skills, Miss Buchanan. I fear I am a poor excuse for an aristocrat. I take more interest in the running of my father's estate than in the leisure activities of which I should be fond."

The remainder of the shooters and their followers moved toward the next set of brush, sure to be hiding the partridges set out this morning by the staff.

Miss Buchanan watched until they disappeared over a rise, then turned back to Oliver. "I had hoped for a private interview with you, Mr. Carmichael."

He hated the way she pursed her mouth and seemed to pucker her entire face in what she thought was a simper. He rested the muzzle of the gun on the ground and crossed his hands atop the butt. "And you now have me all to yourself, Miss Buchanan."

Her expression changed from flirtatious to calculating in the blink of an eye. "Let us not dissemble, Mr. Carmichael. I know you do not care for me beyond my fifty-thousand-pound dowry. You know that I wish to marry a man who will inherit a title higher than my father's. This will be my fourth season. It is unlikely that I will have any more luck securing an heir to a title this year than the three years past. However, that will not keep me from trying."

Yes, he had noticed how Miss Buchanan tried to insinuate herself between her American cousin and the viscount several times over the past few weeks.

"I wish to come to an arrangement with you, Mr. Carmichael."

He shifted his weight and tried to appear nonchalant rather than surprised. "Oh?"

"If neither of us has found a better match by the end of the Great Exhibition in October, we shall marry each other." No hesitation, no missishness.

He rather liked her no-nonsense approach to the situation. "You shall become the next Baroness Carmichael in exchange for . . . what? Surely a barony is not as high as you have set your sights."

"No. It is not. However, it may be all I can get. We suit, you and I, despite the fact we feel no affection for each other. You do not need my money, so you will not try to make me believe you have fallen madly in love with me, the way others do. And, should I find an amenable match of higher rank, I know you will not begrudge my breaking our arrangement with protestations of a broken heart."

Cold. Calculating. Cunning. Oliver's left brow raised in awe and appreciation for her ruthlessness. And given her beauty, taking her to wife would be no chore, despite her frigid personality.

He extended his right hand toward her. "Very well, Miss Buchanan, I agree to your terms."

She placed her small, gloved hand in his and gave it a business-like pump. "Of course, you will have the same opportunity—if you find another woman you deem more acceptable than me, you can break the agreement. I shall not hinder you from courting any woman you please, so long as no scandal arises from it."

He inclined his head. "And I make you the same promise, Miss Buchanan. I will not interfere with your search for a husband, so long as no scandal is attached to my name because of it."

Edith wrapped her hand through the crook of his arm. He shouldered the gun and whistled for the dog to follow them. "You will, of course, speak to my father before you leave after the ball."

"As you wish, Miss Buchanan."

The spaniel bounded ahead of them, probably anxious to rejoin his kennelmates whose barks rose over the hill to indicate the direction the rest of the hunting party had gone.

"Once we are both in town, I shall communicate to you which invitations I have accepted. If we are to be engaged in October, it would be best if we are seen together from time to time. And I do so enjoy dancing with you, Mr. Carmichael." She turned that puckered simper up toward him.

He inclined his head again. "I shall await your communiqués with delight, Miss Buchanan. And as you are a superb dancer, I look forward to partnering with you as often as you desire."

At the path that led back to the house one way and farther into the park the other, Edith dropped her hand from his arm. "If you will excuse me, Mr. Carmichael, I have duties to which I must attend. Do enjoy the rest of your hunt."

"Until we meet again." He bowed and brushed his lips over the back of her gloved hand. He held in his shudder until she turned her back, heading toward the house. She would make as fine a baroness as his mother. And she would likely be as reviled and gossiped about as M'lady for her haughty, demanding ways.

If Edith, her sisters, and her brothers were any indication, the next generation of Carmichaels would be the most beautiful and most handsome in the *ton*. And her wealth would go quite far in securing his daughters' futures—once he invested and multiplied it. For if Edith could marry only one step above her on the aristocratic ladder, he would ensure their children would do far better for themselves.

No, he did not *need* her wealth. But he certainly had plans for it. In the meantime, before he tied himself to the harpy, he would spend his last few months of freedom in a more amusing pursuit—that of Miss Cadence Bainbridge. He did, after all, have a bet to win.

Caddy swallowed back harsh words as the bolts of silk crashed to the floor. Nan yelped and jumped from the step stool, trying to lift two at a time and managing only to start unspooling the expensive fabric.

She would never finish Lady Carmichael's alterations this way. She set the blue gown aside and stood to shoo the redhead away from her latest disaster.

"Nan, please go assist Phyllis in the shop." Caddy congratulated herself on the calm tenor of her voice.

"Yeth—yesss, Missss." Nan's shoulders slumped as she left the workroom.

Letty and Alice breathed overly loud sighs of relief.

"She is so clumsy." Letty shook her head. "I do not know how you can stay so calm with her, Miss Bainbridge."

"And the humming!" Alice gave a melodramatic shudder. "Only two or three notes over and over and over."

"Girls!" Caddy stood, all four bolts hugged tightly to her chest. She set the heavy load onto the cutting table. "Remember that you each had your own mishaps and annoying little habits when you came to me four and five years ago. Nan is young and has a lot to learn to get to where you are now."

The two young women began to protest, but Caddy held up a hand to stop them.

She raised her brows toward Alice. "You click your tongue."

Alice turned crimson.

Caddy nodded toward Letty. "And how about losing an entire card of silver needles in the cracks in the floorboards?"

Letty also blushed.

"Nan will learn faster, and lose her clumsiness and annoying habits sooner, if the two of you show her more kindness and understanding, rather than avoiding and ignoring her."

Letty and Alice hung their heads over their stitching.

"Think of the girls who were here when you first came to me and how they helped you learn the job, then see if you can do even better for Nan. I want each of you to think of something you can teach her in the next sennight, and I want her to demonstrate it—without your assistance—next Thursday."

"Yes, Miss Bainbridge," Letty and Alice chorused.

Caddy returned to her stool and picked up the blue gown from the table. The darts she added to the bodice to nip in the waist took tiny, tedious stitches. But despite her frustration with Nan, standing and moving about—lifting the heavy bolts, then scolding Letty and Alice—had done much to ease the ache in her shoulders and lower back.

As she started on the sixth and final dart, the squeaky third step pulled her attention away from the bodice.

Mother came through the door at the base of the stairs into the workroom, Mary on her heels.

"I see you are fully recovered from your . . . bad spell this morning." Caddy couldn't help the waspish tone in her voice. She thanked God that Dr. Stradbroke had suggested taking his payment in trade rather than demanding cash. Caddy did not want to dip into the money she was saving for her trip to London and the Great Exhibition in May. She wanted to be able to purchase the fine fabrics, notions, and decorative items she knew would bring in more customers like the Buchanan sisters and Lady Carmichael. She had budgeted down to the ha'penny for the trip and her purchases and did not want to have to recalculate.

"I do believe that young Dr. Stradbroke is a miracle worker." Mother beamed a suggestive smile at Caddy. "You said he would be willing to consult with me if I allow him to complete a full examination."

"Mother . . ." At the sound of muffled giggling, Caddy glanced over her shoulder and caught sight of two very eager young faces trying to pretend they weren't interested in the current conversation. Caddy stood, set the bodice back on the table, and escorted her mother into the fitting room, closing the door with Mary still on the other side of it. "You know we cannot afford more doctors. I just finished paying Dr. Fieldstone's bill from the last time you truly had a bad spell. The two dresses for Lady Carmichael will bring in enough to pay the mortgage and Mary's and Phyllis's wages and our bill at Howell's, with only a little left over for other necessities."

"You said yourself that Dr. Stradbroke was willing to take his pay in trade—"

"It is not right to assume he will do so again. He, too, has bills he must pay. We cannot impose on his generosity."

"But you have ever so many orders for gowns, with all the fine ladies of Oxford preparing to attend the Great Exhibition this summer."

"Yes, I do—but I must purchase fabric and notions to make those gowns before I get paid for them. Please, Mother, no more unnecessary calls for a doctor." Caddy could not tell her mother about the savings account she had at the bank—the one in which she squirreled away whatever money she had remaining at the end of each month. A day would come when Mother's health was bad enough to require almost constant medical attention. And when that time came, Caddy did not want to end up in the poorhouse because she couldn't pay the doctors' bills. Nor did she want to remind her mother how short her time likely was.

Mother sighed and dropped delicately into the white brocade wingchair. "Very well. I shan't call for Dr. Stradbroke again—unless my need is at the utmost."

Caddy shook her head and returned to the workroom with a strong suspicion she would be seeing Dr. Stradbroke hovering over her mother once again sooner rather than later. Mother's definition of *utmost need* didn't always match Caddy's.

For the next hour, Caddy concentrated on the alterations to the blue gown for Lady Carmichael. With Letty and Alice working on the green gown, she might not need to stay up all night to meet the deadline.

Nan came through the door from the shop, a hopeful gleam in her large brown eyes. "The lady for the afternoon fitting is here."

"Are there any customers in the store?" Caddy stood and hung the blue bodice on the dress form, not looking at Nan.

"Yes, miss."

Caddy smiled to herself over not having to remind Nan to watch her enunciation. She was getting better at doing it on her own. "Then I think you'd best stay in the store with Phyllis until all of the customers are served. I will call for you if I need assistance with the fitting."

"Yes, miss." Disappointment dripped from Nan's whispered words.

She hated knowing she'd caused the child even momentary distress over not getting to do the fun part of the job in exchange for the tedium of helping to keep shop. But Nan was a bit young to be attending dress fittings.

The wife of one of the Oxford college deans sat in stately grace in the wing chair in the fitting room. Caddy pulled away the sheet covering the gold-and-russet plaid silk gown, and the woman gasped in appreciation, rising to inspect the dress closely.

"Oh, Miss Bainbridge, you have outdone yourself with this one. The sleeves—I love how full they are. And the way you used the plaid to create contrasting banding at the edges! The under-sleeves, oh, they're sheer as gossamer. And the flounces." She lifted the top of the four tiers of the skirt. "With flounces so full, I will not need so many petticoats to hold it out."

Caddy endured the woman's raptures throughout the fitting, appreciative of the woman's high esteem for her talent as a designer and a seamstress, but wishing she were more reserved in her expression of it.

"No one in London will have a gown such as this. Not even Queen Victoria." The dean's wife turned to look over her shoulder at the reflection of the back of the gown in the cheval glass.

"Actually, the design came from a sketch I saw last time I was in London, which is rumored to be the style Her Majesty chose for the gown she will wear to open the Great Exhibition." Caddy frowned, not liking the way the bodice strained against the hidden row of hooks down the back. "I may need to let the waist out just a bit."

"No—I do believe my corset laces have stretched. Tighten them and let's see how it fits then."

Caddy did as bidden, unhooking the straining bodice then tightening the laces. Indeed, she was able to reduce her waist a good inch or two. And when she hooked her up again, the bodice fit perfectly.

With no alterations needed—and as this was the third fitting, Caddy breathed a sigh of relief—she assisted her customer out of the gown and wrapped it in the sheet of muslin to be packaged for delivery tomorrow.

The woman's day dress buttoned up the front, so she did not need Caddy's help to re-dress herself. But her constant stream of conversation kept Caddy from excusing herself on the pretense of giving the woman privacy.

"And I saw the most comely man walking up the street as my carriage arrived this afternoon. Never before have I seen a man so tall or brawny in urban dress and not at hard labor in a factory or on a farm. Do you know who he is?"

Caddy's mind instantly conjured an image of Dr. Stradbroke standing in Mother's room, his brawny arms bare to the elbow and crossed, making the well-defined muscles bulge. "I believe you may have seen the new doctor. He has recently moved into the rooms above the apothecary's shop."

"He? Not he and his wife and family?"

"I do not know. I have only seen him in a professional capacity—he has attended Mother twice. I did not think to ask after his personal life." Caddy's stomach gave an odd little lurch at the idea that Dr. Stradbroke might be married. Not that it should matter to her anyway. A confirmed spinster at almost thirty, she had no time for courting. Besides, she'd sworn at a very young age that, no matter how dearly she'd loved her father, she'd never marry a man in a profession that kept him so much away from home. And if any profession was worse for creating absentee husbands than the clergy, it was that of the doctor.

"Well, if he is not married, he soon will be. There are far too many unmarried women in this part of Oxford for him to stay single long. And once they get sight of him, it will not matter if he takes most of his pay in trade and never has two coppers to rub together. For what is deprivation when a woman has that to look at every day?"

Caddy laughed, as she knew was expected, but she quickly ushered her customer out the door with the promise to have the gown delivered the next morning.

The last thing she needed to be thinking of was the handsome doctor. For no matter how "comely" he was or how much she enjoyed looking at him, she'd worked too long and too hard to support herself and her mother to take on the burden of supporting a husband as well.

CHAPTER FIVE

$\mathcal{W}$here is your cousin this afternoon?" Oliver took the teacup and saucer offered him by Edith Buchanan. He enjoyed the irritation that flashed across her face before she composed herself.

"She is up with the dressmaker. Her wardrobe was appalling when she first arrived, so I had to take her in hand and make certain she had garments in which she could be seen in public." Edith spread her skirts—yellow flowers and green vines on an orange ground—to take up most of the settee, including covering half of his leg. If she weren't cautious, the rumor they were intended would be spreading before the house party ended.

"Dressmaker? My mother is always on the lookout for someone who might do as well for her as the one she sees in London. Who is she?" Oliver crossed his legs, effectively freeing himself from the covering of taffeta.

"Her name is Bainbridge. She keeps a shop in North Parade. I know—it is difficult to believe I would patronize anyone from that part of town, but she is comparable in her talent to my mantua-maker in London." Edith swept an open-palmed hand down her torso. "You can see for yourself how well she does."

The gown, though of eye-paining fabric, did seem to be well made and stylish in design. But more important, he'd confirmed that Cadence Bainbridge was here at Wakesdown. How long would she be engaged with Edith's cousin?

Family quarters were upstairs, in the east wing of the house, if he recalled correctly. And Miss Bainbridge would not exit via the main staircase. He was well acquainted with the servants' passages and staircases—they made excellent shortcuts from one part of the house to another. And one never knew whom he might run into. There was one maid, a pretty blonde named Artemis or Andromeda or Athena or something equally ridiculous. . . . She'd rebuffed his advances thus far, but no woman had long been able to resist him once he turned his attention toward her.

If he could slip away, he should have no trouble running into Miss Bainbridge. However, he could not think of a reason to excuse himself from the afternoon-tea gathering, as all guests were expected to stay and socialize until the gong rang to send everyone scurrying to their rooms to change for dinner. He could not even use the excuse several others did of retiring to their rooms early to write letters—Edith knew he'd just visited home two days ago.

As she prattled on about some nonsense, Oliver scanned the room, taking in the groupings. After more than three weeks surrounded by the same people, the pairs did not surprise him.

Ah, he finally saw his escape. "I beg your pardon, Miss Buchanan, but I must speak with Doncroft and Radclyffe." Oliver set his teacup on the low table in front of the settee, bowed, and walked away before Edith could deny him permission to leave.

"Matters progress apace with the Queen of Ice?" Doncroft asked by way of greeting.

"Where were you this morning? Miss Buchanan was quite put out that there was not an equal number of men and women in the walking party. Your absence was greatly remarked upon. I told her you were indisposed this morning due to the richness of the food last night." Oliver glanced longingly at the decanters of spirits on the sideboard, but it would not do to partake without invitation—and in this house, the invitation came only from Sir Anthony and only after dinner.

Doncroft's ruddy complexion darkened.

Radclyffe guffawed, then inclined his head in apology to the young lady who glared over her shoulder at him from the grouping of chairs several feet away. "Donny discovered that the chambermaid who sees to his room is quite . . . friendly with visitors."

Doncroft cuffed the taller man's shoulder. "You make it sound so lurid, Rad. A few kisses stolen in the stairwell, nothing more."

"Because you or she wanted nothing more?" Oliver thought about meeting someone in the servants' stairwell and stealing a few kisses. Someone like Miss Bainbridge would consider herself fortunate to receive the attentions of someone of his status.

"Because that gargoyle of a housekeeper came upon us."

Radclyffe frowned. "I hope you did not cause the young woman to lose her position."

"No—I told the housekeeper it was all my doing, that the girl was not to blame. Though . . ." He sighed. "I do not know that she believed me. I cannot imagine this was the first time she found the chit in such a position."

Oliver glanced over his shoulder. Thankfully, Edith had moved away from the settee and now had her back turned to him, having cornered her sister, apparently reprimanding her for some perceived wrong. Excellent. Now he could escape unnoticed.

He leaned closer to Doncroft and Radclyffe. "I just learned that the seamstress is in the house. I intend to intercept her before she can leave."

"Seamstress?" Radcliffe's boyish face crumpled in confusion.

"*The* seamstress? The one from North Parade whom you intend to seduce?" Doncroft rubbed his hands together.

"Yes. She's seeing to Miss Buchanan's cousin's wardrobe. And I intend to see to her, if I can."

Doncroft gave him a wicked grin. "Yes, yes—go. We shall make excuses for you if your absence is discovered. It is the least I can do since you covered for me this morning."

Precisely what Oliver thought. He glanced toward Edith again and—seeing that she still had her back turned—slipped from the room.

He took the service hall at the back of the oversized entry hall and made his way to the east-wing servants' staircase. He listened for a long moment to ensure no one currently used the stairs before climbing them. Up two flights, he opened the door onto a hallway of closed bedroom doors. He hadn't been in the family wing of the house before, so he could not be certain which was the cousin's bedroom, or even if this were the correct floor.

Moving into the shadow of the tall urn at this end of the hall, he waited. And waited. How long could a dress fitting take?

A door halfway down opened. Female voices spilled into the hallway. Oliver straightened and moved forward a bit, ready to intercept the seamstress.

Edith glanced around the room. Ever since voicing her idea of an arrangement to Oliver, she'd tried to keep him close to make sure he upheld his end of the bargain—that he did not do anything to shame her.

She'd known him long enough to know his penchant for outrageous flirting . . . and for backroom meetings with women of certain reputations. No more. Not if she was going to tie her name to his.

Not seeing him at the settee where she expected him to rejoin her, she looked for his two friends—Doncroft and Radclyffe. Each handsome in his own way, but neither one as wealthy or as high ranking as Oliver, she'd effectively ignored the two of them for the past three weeks.

He was not with them either. In fact, he wasn't anywhere in the room. How dare he depart without begging her leave? Even if she were not his intended fiancée, she was still hostess of the house party.

Well.

Clamping her back teeth together, Edith twitched her skirts to unbunch her petticoats, turned, and found a perfect target.

He'd entered late—not having been with the walking party— and he had not yet come over to speak to her to make his apologies. Edith turned her toes in as she walked across the room, making her skirts sway like the bell they resembled.

She stopped several paces away from where he stood observing the other guests. She dropped into a deep curtsy, wishing tea did not call for the higher-cut neckline of an afternoon gown. "Good day, Lord Thynne."

The viscount inclined his head. "Miss Buchanan."

"I hope you found employment enough to keep you from boredom today." Edith reached her left hand up and twined her fingers in the delicate gold chain holding her mother's locket.

She did not care for the piece, but she liked the air of sentimentality it gave her. And it was the appropriate length for this bodice.

"Yes, thank you. Miss Dearing showed me the water garden, fountains, and pond."

Edith forced a smile. Hearing that he'd chosen to spend the morning with her cousin confirmed her suspicion that there was more than a mild flirtation between the viscount and the penniless American woman. "Did the garden designer join you? I understand that my cousin has formed quite the . . . friendship with him."

Perhaps it was beneath her to hint that her cousin was carrying on inappropriately with her father's hireling, but Edith couldn't help herself.

Thynne showed no adverse reaction. "Yes, she has learned quite a bit from Mr. Lawton about his plans for the grounds. In fact, I have asked him to draw up a proposal for redesigning the gardens and park at Greymere Hall."

Edith almost stamped her foot, but stopped herself by shifting her weight and digging the nail of her thumb into her palm. "How lovely."

Lord Thynne launched into a boring recitation of all the changes he hoped to make to his home, both inside and out. Edith leaned forward, widened her eyes a bit, and nodded occasionally.

From the corner of her eye, she saw Doncroft and Radclyffe watching. The two leaned their heads together for a whispered conversation, then Doncroft left the room.

She controlled her smile of satisfaction. No doubt Doncroft left to warn Oliver that Lord Thynne was flirting with her.

"If you will excuse me, Miss Buchanan. I have an engagement to keep with your father." Thynne inclined his head again and, without waiting for her permission, walked out of the sitting room, leaving Edith standing alone, in full view of all her guests.

Dorcas's laugh rang out and Edith's skin crawled at the sound of it. She marched over and insinuated herself between her sister and the three men standing near her chair, looking down on her with undisguised appreciation.

"Do excuse us, gentlemen." Edith wrapped her hand around Dorcas's forearm and squeezed. Dorcas let out a small squeak, but one look from Edith quelled her from complaining about the firm grip. "I need to speak with my sister."

Dorcas pulled her wrist from Edith's grasp, but followed her meekly out into the entry hallway. Edith could not believe she needed to speak to her sister again this afternoon about her inappropriate behavior.

"What is it this time?"

Edith spun around at the exasperation in her sister's voice. Dorcas stood there, arms crossed, looking quite put out.

"I saw you openly flirting with those men. Laughing aloud. You aren't even *out* yet. You should not be carrying on conversations with them at all. I warned you about your inappropriate behavior during the walking party this morning."

"*My* inappropriate behavior?" The organdy flounces of Dorcas's pink dress quivered and fear whitewashed her face. "Unlike you, Sister, I do not actively seek to flirt with the men. I cannot help it if they choose to come to me after they—" Dorcas's face flamed dark red.

Edith set her fists to her hips, fury building in her stomach. "After they what?"

"After they walk away from you." Dorcas's eyes widened and she seemed to have trouble catching her breath.

Edith found breathing hard too. Never before had her sister spoken to her like this. "I beg your pardon?" She enunciated each word as if it were separate from the others.

Moisture pooled in Dorcas's eyes, but she swallowed and took a step forward. "I am not the only one who has noticed, Sister, that the men may pay obeisance to you, but they do not stay by your side long. I am also not the only one who has noticed that many of them choose my company over yours."

Edith wanted to slap her. Wanted to tear her hair out of the perfect coils and ringlets. Wanted to scratch at the fear-filled blue eyes gazing at her from the pretty, heart-shaped face. "You know nothing. You are a simpering fool who will never be able to keep a man's interest long enough to elicit a proposal from him. You would do well to keep your mouth closed and follow in my footsteps."

She turned and started up the stairs, unwilling to let Dorcas have the upper hand in this argument.

"Follow in your footsteps?" Dorcas's voice echoed in the hall, followed by her light footfalls on the stairs. "I have watched you these many years, Edith. And what I have learned is that if I want to catch a husband before I'm a bitter spinster from whom desperation flows like the Thames, all I need to do is the exact *opposite* of what you do." Dorcas lifted her skirts and ran up the stairs.

Edith gaped after her sister. Bitter? Desperation? How dare she, the impudent child!

She squared her shoulders, lifted her skirts, and ascended the stairs in a slow, deliberate pace. Did they all talk about her and call her a desperate, bitter spinster when her back was turned?

She would show them. Before the season ended, she would be at the altar—and she fully intended to become Lady Thynne, not Mrs. Carmichael. Her American cousin might have caught the viscount's attention, but she would never keep it. Not if Edith had anything to do with it.

Caddy sent Alice down to the waiting cab with their sewing kits and stayed to help Miss Dearing's maid remove the pinned gown. She wrapped the silver-and-green silk in white muslin while the maid helped Miss Dearing dress for dinner in another of Caddy's creations. The deep purple satin brought out the coppery highlights in the American's hair, and Caddy congratulated herself on choosing the color for her.

"I shall bring the gown out for a final fitting a few days before the ball, Miss Dearing." Caddy stepped forward and adjusted the lace along the scooped, off-the-shoulder neckline of the dinner dress.

"Thank you, Miss Bainbridge. I look forward to it." Miss Dearing extended her right hand.

Caddy reached out and shook it, amused by the American's unusual ways. No woman of Caddy's acquaintance, including her clients, would ever have considered shaking hands with her. But she liked the idea that Miss Dearing, an heiress to a railway fortune if the rumors were to be believed, saw Caddy as an equal. Someone to be respected and proud to be acquainted with—not someone to be hidden away, shunted off through servants' passages and back doors.

She gathered up the bundled gown and departed, taking a moment in the hallway to get her bearings and remember the direction to the service stairs.

With the bulky bundle over one arm and using her free hand for balance against the wall, Caddy sidestepped down the narrow, steep stairs, watching her footing carefully. With Mother's illness—real or feigned—Caddy could not afford to incur any additional medical expenses by falling and breaking an arm or leg. Nor could she afford to be out of work while she recovered. Best to be overly cautious.

She was almost to the lowest level when someone came barreling up the stairs from below. The passageway would have been just wide enough for two to sidle past each other, but not with the additional bulk of the gown.

Caddy pressed herself against the wall, ready to apologize for blocking the way. But the man who stopped on the half-landing below did not look like a servant. Not in a silk waistcoat, fawn breeches, tall boots, and a perfectly tailored hunting jacket.

"Well, who have we here?" He came up two steps until he stood directly below her. "I've not seen you around before."

Caddy dipped her knees into a curtsy as best she could, given her awkward balance and the narrow space. "I do apologize. If you will let me pass, I will be out of your way directly."

He stepped up onto the same level as Caddy. He didn't tower over her the way a certain handsome doctor did—no, he was mere inches taller than she. And she could smell the spirits on his breath mingling with the nearly overpowering scent of his cologne. She took shallow breaths, trying to keep from gagging over the effect of the combination in such a confined area.

"Let you pass? No, I do believe I will keep you here with me so I can get to know you better." He looked her up and down. "You're not wearing the usual afternoon gray gown of all of the other maids, so either today is your day off or you're new and haven't yet received your livery."

Caddy straightened. "I am no maid. I am Miss Buchanan's seamstress, and as such, I know you will be a gentleman and let me pass."

Thick brows hooded blue eyes, and the man leaned closer. "Me? A gentleman?" His arm snaked around her waist, pushing the bundled gown out of the way. "Not until I have to be, which is after my father dies and I inherit the title and estate. Not until I am called *Sir* will I need to behave like a gentleman."

He lowered his head toward her. Caddy turned hers, and his lips landed just beside her ear. He chuckled, his hot breath searing fear into her soul.

"Mr. . . . I am sorry, I did not catch your name." Caddy struggled to keep her breathing slow and even so as not to let him know how much he frightened her. Fear only made men like him feel more powerful.

"Doncroft." He kissed the side of her neck just below her earlobe. "Reginald Doncroft."

"Mr. Doncroft." Caddy felt for the edge of the step with her toe. If she could get below him, she could likely escape. "I am flattered by your attention; however, if it were to get out that I had an assignation in the back stairs of Wakesdown Manor, I would lose the custom of the Buchanans and with it much of my livelihood. You would not want that to happen to me, would you?"

His grip around her waist loosened. That was it, her chance. She stepped down, pulling the bundle around so that it formed a barrier, albeit a weak one, between them. "Good day, Mr. Doncroft." She turned and ran down the remainder of the stairs, not slowing until she reached the bottom and stepped out into a footman's path.

"I beg your pardon." She sidestepped and swept the gown out of his way to keep from upsetting the large tea tray he carried.

Footsteps clattering on the stairs behind jolted her as if she'd just sat on a pin, and she hurried out through the kitchens to the waiting hackney.

Thomas Longrieve reached for the bundle—but instead, his hands settled on Caddy's shoulders. "Are you unwell, miss? You look as if you have the devil himself on your tail."

Caddy calmed her breathing and smiled at the cab driver. "I am fine, thank you." She stole a glance at the door and, seeing a shadow of movement, thrust the wrapped gown into the coach and climbed in behind it before Thomas could assist her. Alice looked askance at her late arrival, but Caddy shook her head and climbed in so they could be on their way.

She shuddered thinking what might have happened had Mr. Doncroft come across Alice in the stairwell. Though only fifteen, Alice had the look of a woman three to five years older, and she enjoyed flirting with the young men who made deliveries for the greengrocer and the apothecary.

Once back at the shop, Caddy sent Alice inside with the gown. She pulled several coins from her pocket and pressed them into Thomas Longrieve's rough palm. "Thank you for letting me hire you for the full day. I know you could have made much more than what we agreed on from your regular fares in the city."

He looked down at the money and tried to hand half of them back to her. "This is far too generous, Miss Bainbridge."

She stepped back from him, refusing to take the money back. "I had a good day today, Thomas. Please, let me do the same for you."

The cab driver, probably only ten or fifteen years her senior, swallowed hard and wrapped his thick fingers around the coins. "Bless you, miss. With the new baby . . . well, this is much appreciated. And you know if you ever need anything, you only need to send word by my boy Johnny and we'll do whatever we can for you."

"I know, and I appreciate it. Good night, Mr. Longrieve."

He tipped his tall hat to her. "Good night, Miss Bainbridge."

Caddy gave him the brightest smile she could muster then waited until he'd climbed up on his high seat and driven away before entering the shop.

Upstairs, she joined her apprentices, Phyllis, Mother, and Mary at the kitchen table for dinner, which Mother had held for their return. Though she tried to keep conversation over meals light and polite, it was about time the girls learned the danger inherent in being a seamstress and visiting the homes of their clients.

"Not every man is like Mr. Doncroft," Caddy qualified after telling the girls bluntly of what had happened at Wakesdown. "But in our position, we must be cautious that we do nothing to encourage the men of a house to believe we are in any way interested in their advances. We must protect ourselves, yet we must do so with diplomacy and decorum. If we cause the man offense, we are likely to lose the business of his wife or daughter. Remember, it is for his money we work."

"So we are to let a man do as he wishes to us?" Nan, sitting beside Caddy, leaned closer and looked up at her with wide brown eyes.

"No." Caddy pushed loose strands of red hair back from Nan's freckled face. "You are never to allow a man to take liberties with you." She looked at Alice, Letty, and Phyllis to ensure they understood her words. "I would rather lose money than to see any of you harmed because you felt you must not give offense. But try, first, to politely and diplomatically extract yourself from the situation."

Filled with dinner and with food for thought, the girls left the table to return to their work. Before Caddy could rise, Mother leaned over and rested her hand on her arm. "I hope if Dr. Stradbroke importunes you with a kiss, you don't decide to be polite and diplomatic with him. You should kiss him back."

Heat flared in Caddy's cheeks. "That is quite enough of that kind of talk."

Mother grinned and sat back in her chair.

For the rest of the evening, Caddy could not get the vision of what might have happened if Neal Stradbroke had been the one to catch her in the stairwell. No, she likely wouldn't have been polite or diplomatic. And she probably wouldn't have turned her face away from him.

CHAPTER SIX

*W*hat's that you're whistling?"

Neal glanced to his side. "Was I whistling?"

Johnny Longrieve puckered his lips and blew out a good imitation of the song that had been stuck in Neal's head for two days.

He tousled the boy's hair. "Very good."

"What's it called?"

"'Springtime Brings on the Shearing.' I learned it from a shepherd when I was a bit younger than you."

"Will you learn it to me?" The young face littered with a few days' beard growth shone with expectation.

Neal shifted his medical kit to his other hand, resisting the urge to correct the boy's grammar. "Why aren't you in school, Johnny?"

The boy shrugged. "My da didn't see the need, but I'm too old now anyway. I got my numbers—adding and subtracting—and I can write my name. But I'm to take over driving the hackney cab when Da is too old. I'd be with him today, taking Miss Bainbridge out to Wakesdown, 'cept I had messages to carry this morning. I only go with him whenever no one needs me to deliver nothing."

Heat prickled the back of Neal's neck at the image that formed in his mind at the mention of the seamstress's name. He tried to shake it off, not liking how two brief meetings with the woman had so affected him.

"Do you want to drive your father's cab?" Neal started walking again.

Johnny, taking two steps for each of Neal's, shrugged again. "Don't matter. It's what I've got to do, 'cause it's what Da told me I'd do."

Neal grunted, understanding all too well. After all, his own father had been teaching him the trade of a surveyor until . . .

"Although, I'd love me to be able to read, and to learn others to read. Maybe have a school for boys like me so they don't have to drive cabs or clean chimneys or do what their fathers and grandfathers did."

Neal paused on the stoop of the small, low-slung tenement of his next patient. "How much would you like to learn to read? How hard would you be willing to work?"

The boy's eyes, which always looked too old for the young face, lit up. "I'd do anything."

"Good. Then ask your father's permission to visit me in the early evenings, after your chores are done and if your mother gives you leave. I may not always be in, but if I am, I will teach you to read."

Johnny leapt up, arms raised, and whooped.

"But if I hear you are not keeping up with your responsibilities at home, the lessons will end. Understand?"

The dire tone of Neal's voice had no effect on the young man's excitement.

Neal hid his amusement. "Off with you now." He waited until Johnny trotted off a few yards before turning and knocking on his patient's door.

After lancing some boils at one home, setting a child's broken arm in another, and mixing a concoction to help soothe the sore throats of a family of nine, Neal checked in on a few more families in Jericho, then headed back to North Parade. He traversed the distance quickly. Along the way, he returned the greetings of the people he'd come to recognize over the past several days of plying his trade in the poor area not quite a mile beyond his chosen neighborhood of residence.

He stopped at the greengrocer before going home. Setting his bag on the floor, he leaned back on the counter, crossing one ankle over the other, observing the customers milling about.

Unusually, Mrs. Howell was not in the shop. Mr. Howell, though, came over as soon as he saw Neal, greeting him with a handshake.

"What's the news?" Howell asked, mimicking Neal's pose.

"Nothing to report. A few minor cases, but nothing to be concerned about. How is Mrs. Howell?" Neal's gaze followed an older man who hobbled between baskets containing fruits and vegetables straight from the hothouses of several nearby estates. The way the man favored his feet led Neal to believe he suffered from gout.

"She is well, thank you. I shall tell her you inquired. She is visiting with Mrs. Bainbridge at the moment."

Neal's interest piqued. "Did Mrs. Bainbridge come here alone?" Though she lived only a few dozen yards from the store, Mrs. Bainbridge should not be walking alone in her condition.

"She walked with her nurse's arm for support. She was a bit out of breath, but once she sat for a few minutes, she seemed to regain her strength easily enough. She managed the stairs just fine." Howell straightened and acknowledged one of his customers with a nod. "Please excuse me, Doctor."

Neal continued leaning against the counter, but he glanced over his shoulder at the door he knew hid the stairwell to the family's quarters above the shop.

Howell headed back his direction, and Neal pushed himself upright. "Do you think the ladies would mind if I called on them? I should like to pay my respects to your wife."

"The missus would appreciate that, I am certain."

Another exchanged handshake, and Neal picked up his bag and went upstairs. He set the kit on the floor in the hall outside the sitting room, then knocked on the door.

"Yes?"

"Mrs. Howell, it is Neal Stradbroke. May I come in?"

"Oh yes, please do."

He pushed the door open. Mary, the nurse, looked up at him from a straight chair beside the door, then went back to reading her book.

Mrs. Howell rose and ushered him into the room, offering him the chintz-covered armchair beside Mrs. Bainbridge. Their hostess regained her seat on the settee across the low tea table from them.

"May I offer you a cup, Dr. Stradbroke?" Mrs. Howell reached for the teapot.

"No, thank you, ma'am. I cannot stay long. But I could not stop in without greeting you. And you, also, Mrs. Bainbridge, when I heard you were here."

Cadence's mother beamed at him. She did indeed look much better than she had just yesterday. "Why, such a compliment, Doctor. I am honored."

He let the ladies engage him in small talk, carefully avoiding giving specific details of patients or their diagnoses. As both were potential patients of his, he wanted to assure them he would not betray any confidences.

The small porcelain clock on the side table showed he'd been here fifteen minutes. When Mrs. Howell paused in her tale of her grandchildren's latest escapades, Neal cleared his throat.

"If you will excuse me, I must take my leave." He rose, took Mrs. Howell's hand, and brushed his lips across the papery skin. She needed to drink more water and possibly use a hand cream to restore her skin's moisture.

"If you do not mind, Dr. Stradbroke"—Mrs. Bainbridge pushed herself up from the chair, holding onto the arms until steady—"I would beg your arm home. I fear I quite overtaxed Mary on the walk here."

Neal glanced at Mary in time to see the middle-aged nurse's brows rise.

"I shall be pleased to escort you home." He offered her his hand. "Good afternoon, Mrs. Howell."

"Good afternoon, Dr. Stradbroke. Mrs. Bainbridge." She saw them to the top of the stairs.

Neal descended sideways, holding Mrs. Bainbridge's hand and ensuring she didn't take a spill. At the bottom, she let him assist with her cloak, then tucked her hand through his elbow.

He matched his steps to hers, letting her set the pace. The March wind had a bite to it, but the sun had shone long enough to warm the air tolerably this afternoon.

"Are you from Oxford, Dr. Stradbroke?" The feathers and flowers on Mrs. Bainbridge's bonnet waved in the breeze.

"No, ma'am. I came here from Winchester. I lived with my grandmother on a farm there."

"But that is in Hampshire County." Confusion laced her voice, and her brows pinched together when she looked up at him.

"Yes, it is."

"You do not have a Hampshire accent. I cannot place it precisely, but you sound more as if you are from the midlands or even the north part of the country."

Panic rushed in hot and cold waves through him—as it did whenever the topic of his origins arose. He could not lie to her, but he could not let anyone discover the truth either. He'd already learned what that revelation could do to a medical practice. He needed to pay tribute to his grandmother's tutelage by remembering to use the accent she'd taught him instead of the one he'd learned as a child.

"Perhaps it is because I have traveled much of this country and spent time with many of its residents that I sound as if I could be from various regions." Not a lie.

Mrs. Bainbridge seemed satisfied with that explanation. "That is likely. Mr. Bainbridge, before we were wed, went to Scotland on a tour before taking orders. When he returned, he amused all of us by speaking with a Scotch burr for weeks. I would imagine that Caddy—Cadence—would be like that. She's always had his gift of mimicry."

"Mr. Bainbridge was a rector?" He remembered his earlier visit where Caddy told him her father had died four years ago.

"Yes. He had a church just north of here in Tackley. 'Twas but a poor parish, so Caddy knew from a young age that she must fend for herself. But because of her father's connections, she was allowed entry into a fine school in Oxford. She sewed clothes for her classmates to earn her own pocket money, and many of them have remained loyal customers these many years."

Yes, Miss Bainbridge struck him as the kind of woman who could make her own way in life. He caught a sigh before it escaped his lips. Women who could make their own way in life rarely saw the need for love or courtship or marriage. At least, that's what his grandmother taught him.

Of course, he hardly knew the woman. No need to be thinking about her in such terms anyway.

As if his mind had the power to conjure her, Miss Bainbridge alighted from Johnny's father's cab just outside the shop. She took a bundle from Alice, who climbed down behind her.

Caddy caught sight of them when she turned to pay her fare, and her face drained of color. She shoved the bundle into Alice's arms, hoisted her skirts, and rushed toward them.

"Mother, are you unwell? Dr. Stradbroke, what happened?" She reached for her mother's free arm, wrapping her hand around the thin wrist, but Mrs. Bainbridge shook her off.

"Nothing is wrong. I visited Mrs. Howell, as I told you I would. Dr. Stradbroke called in just as I was ready to leave, and he graciously offered to escort me home."

Not quite how he remembered it happening, but he did not contradict her.

Miss Bainbridge's blue eyes bored into him as if mining for the truth. He pressed his lips together and adopted a devil-may-care expression. At least, he hoped he did.

Caddy opened the front door of the shop, then held it open for Dr. Stradbroke and her mother to pass through in front of her. She sent Alice to the workroom with the dress, but couldn't tear her eyes away from the spectacle of the doctor assisting her mother out of her cloak. The gentleness he exhibited was incongruous with his massive size. He towered over Mother by a foot at least, and his broad shoulders and heavily muscled arms contrasted with her frailty, giving her a waiflike appearance.

He held the woolen double-cape toward her, but instead of taking the garment, she wrapped her tiny hands around his large ones. "Doctor, I cannot thank you enough. Will you not stay and take tea with us? I am certain Agnes will have laid out plenty of food. Caddy and her girls work so hard all day, they need more than just a morsel at teatime."

Neal glanced over Mother's head and caught Caddy's eye. If the burning in her cheeks was any indication, he no doubt saw the blush that glowed from her face. He seemed to want her to make the decision for him, but she would not oblige. She tried to keep her face impassive and will her cheeks to cool.

"Thank you for the invitation, ma'am, but I must be getting home. I have been out on calls all day, and I promised young Johnny Longrieve to tutor him in reading in the evenings. As the only doctor in the immediate vicinity, it is better if I am home should anyone need me." He laid the cloak over the cutting table, made a slight bow to Mother, then moved toward the door. "Miss Bainbridge, will you see me out, please?"

Caddy's breath caught in her throat. She nodded and moved toward the door—but he accelerated to get ahead of her and open it before she could.

She waited until it closed behind them before whirling on him. "I knew something was wrong. How ill is she?"

Dr. Stradbroke held up his free hand, his gaze sympathetic. "There is no cause for immediate fear. Your mother's heart is weak. But I believe a daily regimen of fresh air and exercise may be beneficial in her case. She is not to exert herself, however. No more than a stroll, and not alone. She may go as far as the green-grocer, but no farther, and only if she has promise of a quarter hour's rest once she arrives there. She should stay indoors in foul weather, especially when it is cold. Of course, this daily exercise should not interfere with any treatment her regular doctor has prescribed. I will call on her again next week and see how she feels."

Caddy listened in fascination. He was such a young man to be so serious and so knowledgeable—surely no older than she, who still had almost two years until she turned thirty. And handsome. She hadn't failed to notice how every woman on the street slowed or paused to get a good look at him. Being seen with him, deep in conversation, filled her with a strange sense of pride. She wasn't certain why—he could do nothing for her or her business. Perhaps it was the interest he'd taken in Mother's case. Yes, that must be it.

"Miss Bainbridge?"

"Sorry. I was . . . thinking. So, a daily walk to the greengrocer, and you will call in a week to see how she fares?" Caddy forced herself to pull her gaze away from the infinite blue pools of his eyes. She wanted to touch the thick, blond-tipped lashes rimming them to see if they were as soft as they appeared. And that strange lilt to his speech, which she could not identify, made her want to keep him engaged in conversation as long as she could.

What was wrong with her? She'd seen many a handsome man in her life, and she'd never allowed one to affect her this way. Why now? And why Dr. Stradbroke? "If she seems weaker in a day or two, have her send word to me." He shifted his large black leather bag from one hand to the other. "But I do not think she will."

Caddy nodded, swallowing hard, forcing herself to view this man dispassionately. She had no room in her life for that kind of distraction. "Thank you, Doctor."

He inclined his head. "My pleasure." He started across the street, whistling as he made his way toward the apothecary's building.

She paused, her hand resting on the doorknob, fighting the urge to watch him walk away. Before entering the shop, she took a deep breath and prayed God would settle her mind and allow her to focus on the work she needed to do.

With Lady Carmichael's gowns finished and delivered, Caddy turned her attention to the green-and-silver ball gown she'd promised Miss Buchanan's cousin for tomorrow night. It required few alterations, but she needed to work on the monthly inventory with Phyllis tomorrow. That task would have to wait until after she'd gone to the bank in the city and deposited the cash she'd received for Lady Carmichael's two gowns—material and labor—along with a generous bonus for her speed in finishing the gowns. She might not like Lady Carmichael, but she did appreciate the woman's patronage.

Long after she'd said good night to her mother and seen the apprentices off to bed, Caddy sat in the workroom, all of the candles and lamps lit while she worked on taking in the bodice of the green-and-silver ball gown.

Hours into the dark of the night, her neck and back ached, but she finally finished. She hoped Miss Dearing would be pleased with the dress. The design was plain, but with a fabric such as this—a green vine pattern on a silver silk tissue—ornate styling would overwhelm the wearer.

After carefully setting the bodice in the box with the skirt, Caddy put out the lamps and snuffed the candles, leaving only one lit to carry upstairs with her.

A crash sounded from the store. Breaking glass. She groaned. Obviously something too heavy had been placed on an upper shelf and the bracket had given way, smashing whatever was below. She hoped it was not the notions display case, with its expensive curved-glass front.

Cupping her hand in front of the candle's flame, she stepped into the shop to see if she could determine how much damage she would be faced with in the morning.

Halfway across the store, an excruciating pain exploded across the side of her head. White stars blazed in her eyes, then all went dark. She was falling . . . falling . . .

CHAPTER SEVEN

$\mathcal{E}$xhausted from everything that had happened in the past thirty-six hours, Neal opened his mouth for another wide yawn—but movement inside Miss Bainbridge's dark shop stopped him. He stepped behind an old elm tree and peeked around it. The glass panes in the front door were shattered—someone had broken in!

The door swung open and a cloaked figure ran down the street. Neal tore away from his hiding place, intent on giving chase—but quickly realized he'd never be able to catch the criminal. Instead, he ran into the shop, hoping no harm had come to anyone.

He stepped cautiously in the darkness, not wanting to grind the broken glass under his feet into tiny shards, which would make cleaning up nearly impossible.

Dress figures stood to his right and left, displaying ready-made gowns through the front windows to passersby. A few feet in front of him was the high table where he'd seen the store clerk cutting fabric for customers. On either side of that table were display cases—one with buttons and hooks and all kinds of decorative items, the other for ribbons and flowers and feathers. On the other side of the table and cases, lining the back wall, were shelves up to the ceiling containing bolts of fabrics. All looked exactly as it had on his previous visits.

He made his way toward the counter at the end of the room, behind which was the door to the workroom and the stairs up to the family's private area.

Seeing a faint glow coming from behind the counter, he quickened his step and rounded the end.

A candle lay on its side, sputtering, having rolled out of its holder. The flame came perilously close to a pile of fabric on the floor. He dropped his medical kit and reached for the brass holder. Its light revealed the pile of fabric on the floor to be a person.

Holding the candle high, he reached for the woman's shoulder and rolled her onto her back. His breath caught in his throat.

"Miss Bainbridge!" After straightening her head, he pressed two fingers to the side of her throat. A low, steady pulse met his touch, and he let out a relieved puff of air. He brushed her hair away from her face, but a clump stuck to her right temple. Warm dampness coated his fingers, and when he looked at them in the wan candlelight, they were dark.

Head wound.

She groaned and raised a hand to her head. "What . . . happened?"

Pressing against her shoulders to keep her from trying to sit up, Neal adjusted his position from crouching to sitting on the floor beside her. "Hush. You're going to be all right."

Her eyes flew open. "Dr. Stradbroke! What are you—? Oh. I remember hearing . . . and when I came in . . ."

"Did you see who did this to you?" Assured she was not going to try sitting up again, Neal released her shoulders and reached for his kit, holding the candle over it to find what he needed.

"There's a lamp up there." Caddy waved her hand to indicate a place above her on the shelves lining the wall behind the counter. "Third or fourth shelf."

Neal rose, found the lamp, and used the candle to light it. The additional illumination brought Miss Bainbridge's injury into shocking relief. Blood covered the right side of her face from a gash that looked like it reached from the far corner of her eyebrow up into her hairline.

"You are most likely going to require stitches. If so, I will need a far brighter light, boiling water, and bandages."

"And needle and thread, I suspect—which I can certainly provide you with." Her smile melted into a grimace.

Neal couldn't help smiling back. Even injured, she didn't lose her sense of humor. "Do you mind if I examine you for other injuries first?"

"No, I don't mind." She closed her eyes, and even in the dim light, he would have sworn the cheek not covered with blood flushed.

To avoid further embarrassment, he averted his gaze as he checked her shoulders and collarbones for displacement, lifted and moved her arms, wrists, hands, and fingers, then moved down to her feet and lifted and moved her legs, letting his senses of touch and sound judge her mobility and her reaction to movement.

He moved back to her side. "Do you hurt anywhere other than your head?"

"No. I don't think so."

"Good. I want you to place your hands on my shoulders. I am going to raise you up—do not try to help. Let me do all the lifting." Placing his hands on her waist, he waited until the slight weight of her hands settled on his shoulders.

A few more inches, and he'd be embracing her. The thought sent heat rushing up the back of his neck, and he hated himself for it. He had nothing but respect for Miss Bainbridge, and he did not want the pleasant acquaintanceship he'd begun with his new neighbor to be spoiled by unrequited attraction and juvenile reactions.

"Ready?"

"Yes."

He got his feet situated under him for balance, then pushed up with his legs, holding her steady with his upper-body strength.

For a woman who looked to be of average build, he was surprised by how light she felt. Nowhere near as light as her mother, but not as substantial as he'd been prepared for.

He kept his hands on her waist until he was certain she had her feet under her. "I am going to hand you the lamp to carry. I will keep my arm about your waist for support, if you do not object."

"I don't object." Though darkness hid her face, he could hear a smile in her voice. His explanations of his methods were sometimes amusing to his patients, but one of the first things he'd learned from his mentor was to err on the side of caution and give too much instruction and information rather than to risk ruining his reputation by offending a patient's sensibilities.

With his bag in his free hand, he let Caddy lead him through the workroom and upstairs to the kitchen. By the time he helped her into one of the ladder-back wooden chairs, he could feel her trembling from the exertion.

"Let's try to get that bleeding stopped." He pulled a soft muslin pad from his bag and pressed it gently to her temple. "Apply pressure."

Her fingers brushed his as she placed her petite hand where his larger one had been.

After stoking the fire, he pumped water into the largest pot he could find and put it on the stove to start boiling. "This may take a while. Shall I rouse Mary?"

Miss Bainbridge's drooping head snapped up. "No." She winced. "Please do not waken anyone. Mother is a light sleeper, and Mary sleeps in a room adjoining hers with the door open. If Mother hears any commotion, she will worry herself ill again."

Was she not concerned about her reputation? What would people think when word got out that he'd been here with her alone? "What about your maid?"

"Agnes already gets little enough sleep as it is. I'll be fine. I have always been stronger than I look." Her eyelids drooped and she started to slump forward.

"Very well." He sighed. "Then you are responsible for keeping yourself awake while I gather all the supplies I need." He checked his kit. "I do not have enough bandages with me. Do you have clean muslin I can use? Towels to wipe up the blood? And additional candles or lamps?"

He followed her directions around the kitchen and the shallow alcove in the hall beyond. While the water heated, he handed Miss Bainbridge the muslin and a pair of shears he'd found in a drawer and set her to cutting strips for bandages.

When a bit of steam came off the water, he scooped some into a bowl, set it on the table, and soaked one of the towels. In the now well-lit kitchen, he had a better idea of just how much blood she'd lost.

"I'm going to pull this away now." He took the padding, soaked through with bright red blood, and eased it away from her head. The cut underneath still seeped, but the pressure had slowed the flow of blood. He washed away the sticky, drying blood from her neck, chin, and cheek before dumping the water, getting fresh, and starting on the injury with a clean cloth.

She drew in her breath through gritted teeth, but she made no other noise and did not move other than an occasional wince.

"The edges look smooth, which will be helpful in stitching it closed."

She sighed. "So I will need stitches?"

"I am afraid so. I will use as few as I can and make them as small as possible."

The iron pot rattled with the strength of the boiling water. Neal washed his hands and instruments with soap, setting each on one of the clean cloths from his kit.

"Can you do it with me sitting here, or should I lie on the table?"

Neal considered for a moment. "It will be easier if you lie on the table." He stepped back, giving her room to maneuver. She stood, turned, and sat on the edge of the table. Placing her feet in the chair she'd just vacated, she eased herself back into a prone position, still holding the muslin pad in place.

He lifted her head and placed a folded towel beneath it, then set the four lamps he'd found around her, creating a halo-like effect. He smiled at the fanciful notion.

"What?" The light made her lashes cast long, dark shadows under her eyes.

"Just admiring the living icon of Saint Cadence Bainbridge."

She frowned. Then a slight smile relaxed her features. "My mother would be the first to tell you that I am anything but saintly."

Neal cocked a brow as he moved his instruments into easy reach and into the order in which he would need them. "I find that hard to believe."

"When I was a child, I provided the fodder for many of my father's sermons—honoring one's parents, obedience, discipline, diligence . . . all lessons that he taught on Sundays after I'd shown him the opposite throughout the week."

Neal took a moment to gaze down at the woman on the makeshift operating table. He had a hard time picturing Cadence Bainbridge as a disobedient child. She was so self-possessed, so confident. "It seems your father's words took root."

"Only because my parents spent many hours each day on their knees praying over me." Caddy's eyes fluttered closed. "I will never deserve it."

"I think your mother would disagree." He understood now why she took such good care of her mother—a sense of obligation born out of love. "I am ready to begin if you are."

"Are you going to put me to sleep?"

"No. With a head injury, that would be dangerous. I am sorry, but you will feel every bit of what I do.

Eyes still closed, she gave a brief nod. "We should start, then."

"This is going to sting." He opened the bottle of alcohol, pulled the muslin pad away from the still-bleeding injury, and poured the liquid over the cut.

❧

Caddy's back arched, and she breathed through clenched teeth. The liquid fire set the throbbing injury ablaze, increasing her pain tenfold.

"I am so sorry. But it is the only way to clean the wound and guard against infection." Neal's deep voice cut through the pain and darkness. Soft fingertips touched her cheek, and she realized he was wiping away the tears that slid from her eyes.

He pressed more cloth to her temple and she fought the urge to knock his hand away, to scream, to sob—anything to get the pain to go away.

"Take a deep breath." Neal pulled one cloth away and used another to wipe up the excess alcohol—and the tears that still traced down her cheeks.

Air stuttered into her lungs.

"And another one."

The next breath came a little more easily.

"Now, close your eyes and try to think of something else."

"What?" Caddy flinched when Neal moved her head—then realized he needed to angle it so he could have a clear view of the cut. Her right cheek rested against the towel.

He pushed back the strands of damp hair that had stuck to her face, then wiped it one more time. "What do you do when you are not sewing clothes for others?"

"I . . . teach the women in the poorhouse the skill of dressmaking." She trembled in anticipation of the first bite of the needle, which she knew must be coming soon.

"Saint Cadence indeed." The smile in his voice made Caddy's shivers increase—though this time not from more pain.

"My father believed that teaching someone a skill went much further in feeding his or her family than giving alms." When would he start? What was he waiting for?

"I think I would have liked your father very much."

Caddy opened her mouth to ask Dr. Stradbroke when he planned to get on with stitching her wound together when she felt the first sting of the needle.

Pain gathered in the back of her throat, but she would not release it as sound. Taking shallow breaths, she tried to think about the days spent at the poorhouse surrounded by women and girls of all ages, experiencing their joy as they finished an apron or a bonnet.

"M-my apprentices . . . come from the p-p-poorhouse." Hot tears streaked down her nose and across her cheek onto the towel below, even though she tried to force them to stop. "Three now work as seamstresses for one of the finest couturiers in London."

"How long do they apprentice with you?" He leaned so close she could feel the warmth of his breath on her neck.

"Three to five years, depending on how quickly they learn the necessary skills."

"Have you seen the machines that sew?"

Caddy winced and released a small gasp at a fourth bite of the needle.

"You're doing well, Miss Bainbridge. Just one more after this one."

Trying to keep her focus off the ever-increasing pain, Caddy went back to his last question. "I have seen illustrations in books and magazines, but I have not seen one in person." She worked to regulate her breathing so she didn't sound like she'd just run down the street. "I read there will be demonstrations of these sewing machines at the Great Exhibition. I hope to see at least one."

Neal made no response.

"Do you plan to attend the Exhibition?"

"I . . . I am not certain I will." He stilled her head with a large hand on her chin. "Last one."

Caddy held her breath as the needle once again pierced her forehead, her stomach rebelling against the pain.

She heard the clip of his scissors. "There. Now you can breathe again."

The skin of her neck cooled, indicating he'd moved away. Opening her eyes, she watched him fold a strip of muslin into a pad, which he pressed to the cut. He lifted her head and wound a long strip around her head to hold the pad in place.

"You will need to change this daily. Keep the wound dry and clean. I will take the stitches out in a couple of weeks."

Caddy allowed him to help her sit up. "A couple of weeks?" The servants' ball at Chawley Abbey was but a week from now.

"Yes. But after a week, you can stop wearing the bandage, so long as the bleeding has stopped. You should be able to hide the scar with your hair or a hat, and the bruising should have faded by then. No powders or cosmetics, though, as those could cause infection." He pulled the chair from under her feet and assisted her up, resting his hands on her waist until she'd found secure footing.

"Fret not—I am not so vain as to use cosmetics." The warmth of his hands almost made her forget the pain in her head. "Might I go to sleep now?"

He released her and watched her closely. "You seem steady. I do not think you are in danger of falling into insensibility. But if you begin to feel feverish, or if the cut does not seem to be heal-ing—if you see red streaks or any discharge—I want you to send Mary or one of the girls for me immediately." He held up his hand when she started to argue. "I am serious. Head injuries are not to be trifled with."

As he stood over her giving directions and warnings, he gave the appearance of a towering guardian angel. A warm glow that had nothing to do with infection or illness stole through her.

But she could not stand here with him all night. Exhaustion weighed on her, and she craved the comfort of her bed. "How much do I owe you, Doctor?"

He paused in packing his tools back into his kit. Caddy was certain he would name a price that would make her choke.

"As before, I would like to take payment in trade. I have a larger pile of mending than I originally thought."

Caddy released a relieved breath. "I would be pleased to do that for you."

He finished packing his instruments and lifted the bag as if it weighed nothing. "Then I shall call later this week—to bring the mending and to check your injury."

She moved to follow him to the door, but he stopped her, laying one of his large, soft hands on her shoulder. "No need to see me out. Go get some rest. This afternoon, I shall send the constable so you can give him your statement and he can begin looking for the culprit who did this to you."

Ah, yes. In all the focus on her injuries, she had forgotten what caused them in the first place.

$\mathcal{B}$efore taking the stairs up to his flat, Neal peered into the makeshift henhouse in the back garden. Matilda and Sheila slept, heads tucked against their chests, in the nests he'd made for them atop two empty crates he'd begged off Mr. Howell.

Weary to the bone, he trudged up the stairs and unlocked his door. In the country, no one thought of locking doors. But with the supply of drugs he kept, not to mention the expensive surgical equipment he couldn't carry with him, he left nothing to chance. And, as he'd just experienced firsthand, living this close to the area known as Jericho made North Parade a target for the less savory types. The Eagle Ironworks and the traffic on the canal seemed to draw riffraff into the area who preyed on the good, hardworking people who made their homes here. Neal had chosen North Parade because of its proximity to Jericho after hearing of the need for a doctor to minister to the needs of the working-class suburb of Oxford.

After dropping his kit on the kitchen table, he crossed to the front room and pulled the curtain back. Across the street, a light flickered in the shop windows of Bainbridge's. He crossed his arms, frowning. He should have known she wouldn't have gone to bed to get the rest she desperately needed.

Of course, she now had a front door with panes broken out of the window.

Neal returned to the kitchen and took up the pouch of nails and hammer he'd purchased to build the chicken coop, then jogged back downstairs. He found the few extra planks of wood he hadn't used yet, tucked them under his arm, and made his way back across the street.

Caddy gasped and raised her broom over her head when he entered.

Neal backed up against the door. "Miss Bainbridge, 'tis I, Neal Stradbroke."

The broom wavered, then lowered. "Doctor? What—?"

"I came to patch up the hole in your window. If you would lend me your lamp . . ."

Caddy put the broom down and carried the oil lamp over, holding it so it cast a glow on the door.

After several attempts to hold the board in place and nail it at the same time, Neal pulled the extra nails out of his mouth. "Miss Bainbridge, if you would be so kind—"

She reached out and held the board in place with her free hand. "I was wondering when you would get around to asking for assistance."

He glanced at her, surprised to see the amusement in her gaze. "I suppose I am accustomed to working with assistants—nurses— who know when to offer help without being asked."

The angle and depth of the doorway meant tight quarters. Neal tried his best to maintain distance and avoid physical contact with Miss Bainbridge . . . no matter how much he wished otherwise. He tapped the first nail in—and he felt her cringe at the noise.

"Are you ill? Feeling faint?" He was ready to set down the carpenter's tools and ply the trade for which he'd trained.

"No. I just hope that Mother and the others will sleep through this."

He should have guessed. The more time he spent near her, the more he realized that she never thought of herself before others. "If the break-in did not wake them, I doubt this will."

It took all three boards to cover the two panes that had been broken out, and by the time Neal started tapping the last nail in, the sky had lightened considerably.

Caddy shifted from foot to foot, biting her bottom lip.

Ignoring the need for quiet, Neal pounded the last nail in. Any time now, their neighbors would be rousing, setting about their morning routines before opening up shop for the day. And if he was seen leaving Miss Bainbridge's at dawn . . . he did not want to imagine the gossip that would start. Of course, they could assume he'd come here to see Mrs. Bainbridge again. But he did not want to risk the daughter's reputation over the hope they would.

As soon as the head of the nail was flush with the wood, he opened the door. "Will you be all right if I—?"

"Yes, yes. Thank you. I don't know what I would have done without your assistance." She leaned out the door and looked up and down the street.

"You need your rest. Please, try to get some sleep." He reached to tip his hat, then remembered he wasn't wearing one. "Good . . . morning, Miss Bainbridge."

A smile stole over her features, hiding her frown. "Good morning, Dr. Stradbroke."

Swinging and spinning the hammer in his hand, Neal whistled quietly as he jogged across the street and up the stairs to his flat.

He went straight to the front room and pushed back the curtain to gaze across the street. The lamp he'd left her with made enough of a contrast inside the dress-and-notions shop that he could see Miss Bainbridge's feminine silhouette still moving about—no doubt having gone back to sweeping up the glass, since he'd interrupted that task.

He watched until the dawning light outside made it impossible to see even her shadow moving inside the shop. Letting the curtain fall, he did something he hadn't done in years. He prayed, asking God to watch over Miss Bainbridge.

At the first stirrings from upstairs, Caddy stashed the broom in the small supply closet behind the counter, doused the lamp, and dashed up to her bedroom. Girding herself with a deep breath, she opened the blinds and turned toward the small, round mirror over her washstand.

She groaned and turned away from the reflection. Papa had been fond of sensational stories of the American frontier, which he'd read aloud to her until one particular story gave her nightmares for weeks. The dream about being scalped still came occasionally. After seeing the strips of white muslin wrapped around half of her head, she had a feeling that night terror would return.

The bedstead creaked when she sank down onto the edge of the mattress. Explaining the injury didn't worry her nearly as much as telling Mother the thief had made away with the strongbox that contained the week's earnings—including the large sum she'd been paid at Chawley Abbey. She'd considered taking it straight to the bank, but she made her deposits once a week, and she saw no need to change that pattern.

Had the burglar known her schedule? Had he been watching her and known she'd delivered two fancy dresses on Friday and been paid for them?

Who would have such intimate knowledge of her business?

She lay back on the bed, head throbbing. A few minutes' rest and then she would face the day—and the curious stares and questions she knew she would encounter.

A monstrous shadow engulfed her, hitting her head again and again with a pounding rhythm that would not cease. She tried to pull away, but it was as if she were bound, unable to move, unable to run.

A distant voice called her name. She tried to respond, but she could make no sound.

Something warm and heavy covered her shoulder, pulling her away from the shadow. A familiar yet foreign scent filled her nostrils. Spicy, laced with a hard-edged medicinal aroma—and an unmistakable undertone of a hard-laboring man. Through the dark, she lifted her hand, her fingertips meeting the hard, square jaw covered with a day's growth of beard. She sighed in relief.

He was here. "Neal."

"Wake up, Miss Bainbridge. You are dreaming."

No. She wasn't dreaming. That was his voice—his deep timbre sending shivers down her spine. But she needed to see him to be sure. The left side of her head fought against her will, but she dragged her eyes open and blinked a couple of times to clear her vision.

Neal Stradbroke hovered above her, his hair—a mix of blond and brown locks—falling forward over his forehead. Her fingers rasped against his new growth of beard. Dark shadows circled his eyes, and he looked like he could use a good, long nap.

"You came to rescue me."

The skin around his blue eyes crinkled as the corners of his lips twitched up. The movement of his cheek under her hand sent a bolt of lightning down Caddy's arm. For a moment, she allowed herself to enjoy it—and then she realized what she was doing and where they were. She let her hand drop to the mattress at her side.

If anyone saw them alone together in her bedroom . . .

"Is she coming around, Doctor?" Mother's voice trilled from behind him.

Caddy closed her eyes and let her breath out slowly, trying to still the embarrassment that wanted to race through her chest and climb into her face.

"Yes, ma'am, I believe she is." Neal's voice came from farther away.

Caddy peeked through her lashes and saw that he'd straightened. One large hand rubbed the back of his neck as if it pained him.

She pushed herself up. The room spun, and she grabbed for the post at the foot of the bed. Her hand came in contact not with carved wood, but with muslin covering a warm, solid mass. His arm. Mortification coursed through her.

Dr. Stradbroke grabbed her elbows and assisted her back into a prone position. "You should stay in bed for today. You need rest in order to recover from the blow you took."

"Blow? She took a blow?" Mother's voice sounded even more shrill than normal. "What happened?"

Caddy closed her eyes and checked the bandage to ensure it had not shifted and revealed the extent of her injury to Mother.

"Mary, will you see to Miss Bainbridge?" Neal's voice moved toward the door as he spoke. "I will accompany Mrs. Bainbridge to the kitchen." After a bit of rustling, the floorboards creaked out in the hallway, and then footsteps faded away toward the stairs.

Caddy opened her eyes. Mary stood at the side of the bed, chewing her thumbnail. "It's a right fix you've gotten yourself into, miss. You know Ma'am will not rest easy until she learns every detail of what happened."

"The doctor can tell her about it better than I can. He was awake for the entire ordeal, whereas I . . ." Caddy touched the bandage again.

"Let's get you into a nightgown, shall we?"

Caddy moved slowly, allowing Mary to help her disrobe. She'd never felt such relief at having her corset removed. As she returned to the bed, coverlet drawn to her chin, pillows plumped behind her head, Caddy promised herself that she would make sure Mary received a raise in pay. The middle-aged woman's nursing skills were nothing compared to her ability to coddle without coming across as coddling. As soon as she was able, she would go to the strongbox and—

The intruder! Caddy sat bolt upright, heart pounding—which made her head throb all the more. She started to throw off the covers, but Mary restrained her with strength surprising in a woman so small.

"Miss Caddy, you cannot get out of the bed. You heard the doctor. You need your rest."

"I have to know—have to find out—" But the dizziness and nausea wouldn't allow her to rise, and she sank back against the pillows again. "Mary, I need to see Phyllis, please."

"I shall fetch her—but only if you promise to stay put and don't try to get up again."

"I promise." Caddy let her eyes drift shut. She was on the verge of sleep when footsteps brought her back to consciousness.

The shop girl entered, eyeing Caddy's bandage warily. "The doctor told us what happened."

Caddy made a mental note to thank him next time she saw him—even though words would never be enough to express her gratitude for his assistance through this ordeal. "Will you please check the strongbox and see if last night's trespasser found it—and if so, how much he made away with?"

Phyllis pressed her lips together as tears welled in her brown eyes. "I'm sorry, miss, but the strongbox is gone."

Mr. Howell had warned her that she needed a safe, but Caddy hadn't listened, feeling that a locked strongbox would be deterrent enough. The small cast-iron chest weighed at least twenty pounds. But now it, and all the money in it, were gone. The quarterly rent. Mary's and Phyllis's wages. The bills she had planned to pay with the income from the gowns for Lady Carmichael and Miss Dearing. The apothecary and grocer bills.

Panic wrapped around Caddy's windpipe and cut off her breath. In less than a month, she planned to go to London—not only to attend the Great Exhibition and see fabrics and colors and patterns from around the world, but to acquire as much as she could for the shop. All the money in her small private account, saved for this purpose, would now have to go to covering the expenses the strongbox money had been meant for.

She cleared her throat twice before she found her voice. "Thank you, Phyllis. That will be all."

The nineteen-year-old looked as if she wished to say more, but left silently.

Caddy lay staring up at the rough planks of the ceiling between the heavy beams supporting the floor above.

Where was God in this?

She'd been raised to believe in an all-powerful, all-knowing Creator who loved and protected His children. But her parents' religious devotion made her feel constrained as she grew up, and when she went off to finishing school, she mocked their beliefs to the other girls. While working her apprenticeship at a shop in London, she'd been exposed to people with different ideas than she'd heard in the country parishes her father had served in as rector all her life. Intellectuals who tried to prove the existence of God through reason. Atheists who tried to do just the opposite. She'd met people from every religious order imaginable, along with those who claimed no religion at all.

She'd felt mature and worldly stepping away from the faith of her father and mother. Until she struck out on her own, opened the seamstress shop, and tried life as an independent woman.

Loneliness had driven her back to her father's church. Ten years after they sent her away to school, Caddy realized how empty she'd been inside. She'd embraced each new idea that had come her way, but none of them filled her with contentment the way listening to her father's homilies and to her mother's gentle hand at the pump organ.

Father. He'd had an apt Scripture verse for everything. She didn't have to think very hard to know which one he would have applied to her current situation.

"And we know that all things work together for good to them that love God, to them who are the called according to his purpose."

The words from the eighth chapter of Romans had become a familiar refrain during the months before his death—that along with his pleas for Caddy to take care of her mother, who, even then, had not been strong.

How did being robbed work for her good? Or was she not one of the called? Perhaps God had not forgiven her for the years of cynicism and mockery.

Twin tears trailed from the outside corners of her eyes and into her hair. She had no choice but to ask God to help her—and trust Him to do so. Because this was a situation she could not handle on her own.

CHAPTER NINE

$\mathcal{O}$liver crossed his arms and slumped low in the pew. As his mother did, the Buchanans insisted their houseguests attend church with them every Sunday. And, if possible, the rector of the Wakesdown church was even older and more long-winded than the one in the Chawley parish.

He exchanged a wry grimace with Doncroft, assuming he, too, secretly cursed Radclyffe for using the excuse of a visit home as an escape from the boredom of sitting in the cold, drafty sanctuary for a couple of hours—meaning neither Oliver nor Doncroft could do the same.

Heaving a sigh, he stood with relieved poppings of his joints as the last hymn started. Next week, after the ball on Saturday night, he doubted anyone, even the family, would feel much like getting up early to do their religious duty.

He and Doncroft slipped out the back and set their feet on the road to Wakesdown before they could be waylaid by anyone.

"What news of the seamstress?" Doncroft shrugged out of his cloak.

Oliver did the same—not just because the early April sun made the black wool unbearable, but also to have a moment to form his answer. "My campaign to make her fall madly in love with me begins tomorrow. Now that the house party is in its last week, I believe I will have more freedom to leave Wakesdown without so many questions as to my movements."

"And North Parade is between here and the club. I am certain that Radclyffe would be more than happy to provide cover by going there with me and waiting for you to join us. After you visit your paramour, of course." Doncroft's expression turned salacious.

Oliver almost ran his fingers through his hair—but stopped short of ruining the artfully arranged riot of curls his man had affected this morning. A shadow nibbled the edge of Oliver's good mood—a shadow as foreign to him as if it came from the deep recesses of Africa. No—he'd felt this before. As a child. When he'd done something he'd been expressly forbidden to do and had been discovered.

Was it . . . could it possibly be guilt?

No. He had no reason to feel guilty. He did not intend any harm—it was all in good fun.

Shaking off the morose thoughts, he cuffed Doncroft's shoulder. "No, my good man. Not paramour. Dupe is a more apt description. For I would never lower myself to taking someone of her low birth and status as my mistress. Even I have some standards."

Doncroft chuckled, though the sound contained little mirth. "Yes, you must be cautious when it comes to such things. If you follow through on your plan to marry Miss Buchanan, you will be one of the most henpecked of husbands in all England. And I do not think she would stop short of physical displays of her displeasure with a husband found keeping a mistress."

After tossing his cloak to hang over his shoulder, Oliver jammed his hands into his pants pockets and raised his shoulders as if to protect himself from the imaginary strangling hands of his potential wife. "I am the soul of discretion." He shot a sharp glance Doncroft's direction. "And I expect my friends to be also."

Doncroft guffawed. "Like *Les Trois Mousquetaires*—'*un pour tous, tous pour un.*' I have not forgotten my vow."

Seven years ago, Doncroft had bought French periodicals with the serialized installments of Alexandre Dumas's story of Athos, Porthos, and Aramis and brought them into the rooms they shared their first year at Oxford. Enthralled by the adventure— and the personalities of the characters—they had adopted the musketeers' "one for all, all for one" motto, swearing to remain friends no matter what happened. In fact, for some time, each had identified himself by his favorite musketeer's name. It had been quite some time since Oliver had signed correspondence to his friends as Aramis. Perhaps it was time to reread the story and see if he could learn how his hero would conduct himself in a situation such as this.

"Your French pronunciation is as deplorable now as it was back then." Oliver shoved Doncroft, catching him off guard and making him flail and dance to keep from tripping off the edge of the road into the shallow, water-filled ditch.

Oliver enjoyed the levity and ease of the company of one of his closest and oldest friends . . . while it lasted. Back at Wakesdown, he did his best to avoid the other guests—especially Miss Buchanan.

After an early tea, the ladies returned to their rooms to rest until dinner. Oliver, tired of being cooped up like a chicken inside the house, escaped to the grounds, exploring parts of the garden currently undergoing renovation and restoration. Beyond a pond with a fountain in the center, he stepped up onto the porch of the folly—at least he assumed the small building was a folly, with its Greco-Roman temple design and set so far out in the park.

But he could not enter the building to discover its true purpose. The door was locked, and most of the windows were covered with bramble vines.

With a bit of work, it would make an excellent clandestine meeting place for a young couple—if the woman could escape her chaperone.

A northerly breeze brought a chill to the air. Oliver took the main path back toward the house. He nodded greetings to Lord Thynne and the Buchanans' American cousin who strolled in the Italianate terraced portion of the garden nearest the house. The pretty blonde maid trailed behind them. He tried to catch her eye, but she kept her gaze downcast and scurried after Lord Thynne and Miss Dearing.

Ah, well. He needed to focus his efforts on discovering how to work himself into Miss Bainbridge's good graces anyway. One conquest at a time. Besides, Doncroft was right—Oliver did not dare risk allowing Miss Buchanan to catch wind of his amorous pursuits, even if they were only for entertainment and nothing serious.

After a few years of marriage, he was certain she, too, would discover the necessity of such extramarital activities and become adept at her own flirtations and assignations. Once that happened, they would be truly happy together.

Much to his pleasure, Miss Buchanan pleaded a headache and took a dinner tray in her room, sending her apologies to the guests.

No one seemed to mind her absence. In fact, conversation around the dinner table flowed more easily, and laughter came more freely, than when the eldest daughter of the house presided at table, because everything did not have to revolve solely around her and her interests. As soon as they were married, he would put a stop to that.

Monday morning, while most of the gentlemen went out hunting, as usual, many of the ladies decided a jaunt to Oxford's High Street for shopping was in order. Though Edith used Miss Bainbridge's services, she would never visit North Parade when trying to maintain a sense of superiority over her guests. Which meant he could visit with impunity.

As soon as he could escape from the breakfast room, Oliver had his horse saddled. Doncroft and Radclyffe met him at the stables to wish him luck and to plan their meeting at the club afterward.

The drizzling rain turned to a downpour by the time Oliver reached North Parade. The ride gave him time to consider what he would say to explain his presence at a dressmaker shop, since this time he had no missive from his mother.

Only a few hardy souls dashed in and out of the shops along the narrow street, shoulders hunched and heads covered for some protection from the deluge. A modest black carriage sat outside Miss Bainbridge's shop.

After tying his horse to the plain iron post outside, Oliver let himself in. The shop girl looked up from the table in the center of the room, where she stood cutting fabric for a customer, and nodded toward him. "I will be right with you."

He lifted his head slightly. "I had hoped to meet with the proprietress. If you will inform Miss Bainbridge that the Honorable Mr. Oliver Carmichael is here, I am certain she would wish to wait upon me herself." How could she not? He knew how much money M'lady had parted with two days ago for the gowns that she would wear to the Great Exhibition.

Both the shop girl and her customer seemed to recognize the Carmichael name, as they exchanged only the briefest glance before the girl hurried off and disappeared through a door behind the counter at the end of the room.

Caddy tried to concentrate on the rows and columns of numbers in front of her. Her head did not throb nearly as much as it had Saturday and Sunday, but it ached enough to keep her from being able to give her full concentration to the task at hand. Of course, the task at hand served only to remind her of what had happened Friday night. She had enough work booked over the next several weeks to keep her and her three apprentices working well into the night every day. While that income would allow her to pay her bills, it would not replace the money she had saved for the trip to London and the fabrics she had hoped to purchase there.

The bell on the front door chimed; Caddy closed the ledger. The constable had come by on Saturday afternoon, as Dr. Stradbroke had promised. But Caddy had been so groggy she hadn't understood half of his questions. He'd promised to return first thing Monday morning to take her statement.

Phyllis entered, a worried look on her face. "Mr. Oliver Carmichael's here, miss." She pulled her full bottom lip between her teeth.

Oh, dear. What could he want? "I shall come out and see to him. Thank you, Phyllis."

Caddy pressed both hands against the top of the small table that served as her desk and pushed herself to her feet. She waited until the room stilled before she let her hands drop to her sides. Turning, she caught sight of herself in the small mirror that hung over the bureau she used to store some of the more expensive notions and accessories. She bore a strong resemblance to the wounded soldiers returning from the Napoleonic war in the paintings they'd seen at school. She couldn't allow Mr. Carmichael to see her in such a state and have him carry the tale back to his mother, who already seemed to question her competency.

"Next time I see you, Dr. Stradbroke, I will apologize for what I'm about to do." She untied the knot in the muslin and unwrapped it from around her head. Then she carefully removed the folded pad of fabric covering the stitched cut, working it away with small movements when it stuck in a couple of places.

From the third drawer, she pulled out a finely knitted snood. She collected her long, thick braid into it, pinning it at her crown. She finger-combed the front of her hair down over her forehead, creating soft wings that swept down to cover her ears, then tucked the strands into the snood.

For once, her straight hair worked to her advantage. Except for the faint shadow of a bruise surrounding her eye, Mr. Carmichael should not be able to see her injury. And the dark gray skies outside meant a dim shop interior, so hopefully he would not notice the bruise.

She removed her apron and hung it on the hook on the back of the office door, took a deep breath, then walked out into the shop.

Mr. Carmichael stood at the floor-to-ceiling shelves displaying bolts of silks. Did his mother want to commission another gown?

He turned when she was still several feet away. Caddy extended her right hand.

"Mr. Carmichael, what a pleasure." Speaking and smiling at the same time moved all the muscles in Caddy's face. The pain of the stitches pulling against her flesh sent a wave of icy discomfort down her spine, and perspiration rose on her upper lip and forehead. She did her best not to let her pain show.

"Miss Bainbridge, the pleasure is mine." He took her hand in his, but instead of a businesslike shake, he raised it and brushed his lips against her knuckles. Her *bare* knuckles, since she did not wear gloves while working. "I trust you are well? And your mother?"

"We are both well, thank you."

Caddy pulled her hand back and resisted the urge to use it to wipe the beads of sweat threatening to drip down her face—from his flattery or the nausea her headache gave her, she wasn't certain. "How may I help you today?"

He looked as if he would prefer to engage in a longer conversation, but with a sigh, he turned to the shelves of fabric. "Last time I was in here, I saw a few silks I would like to have sent to my tailor for waistcoats."

The few tailors who worked in Jericho occasionally sent men to Caddy's store for fabric. Most of their customers had no need of the fancy goods Caddy stocked. But occasionally one wanted a brocade or inexpensive silk for a wedding waistcoat. So the occasional male customer was not unusual.

However, she had a hard time believing she carried anything in her little shop that was better than the goods at Oliver Carmichael's tailor—probably one on High Street who catered to the aristocracy and to deans and professors at the colleges. "I would be happy to have the fabrics cut and sent over for you. Which ones would you like?"

He chose five fabrics in greens and yellows, all with an excess of embellishment. He would not let Caddy pull the bolts and carry them to the table, but did it himself.

Phyllis moved to the main counter with her customer to finish the sale. Caddy unrolled a few yards of the first fabric.

Before she could reach up and brush it away, a droplet rolled down her forehead and dripped onto the dark green silk. Fortunately, it plopped on the end of the fabric, so she quickly trimmed a few inches off under the guise of creating a straight edge. She swept the trimming into the basket by her feet before he could see the dark spot.

Another bead of sweat trickled down her spine, even as she shivered slightly from the chill in the room. Her legs trembled, and she longed to sit down.

Blinking to clear the fog from her eyes, Caddy measured carefully, then set weights on the corners to keep it still while she cut. She finished, straightened, and turned away just as another droplet ran from her forehead down the bridge of her nose and dripped to the floor. She swayed and grabbed the edge of the high cutting table.

"Miss Bainbridge are you—?" Mr. Carmichael grabbed her shoulders. "You're bleeding!" He pushed her hair back from her forehead.

Caddy did not protest when he pressed his own white lawn handkerchief to the wound, nor when he wrapped his arm around her waist and herded her toward the workroom.

"You, there. Get Miss Bainbridge a glass of water and bring some clean muslin. Your mistress is injured." Oliver's high-handed manner made Phyllis jump and move faster than Caddy had ever seen.

She might have laughed if she didn't need to concentrate on keeping her knees from collapsing with each step. She did not want him to accompany her upstairs, but without his assistance, she wasn't certain she would be able to make it. She motioned him toward the door to the stairwell.

Like Dr. Stradbroke two nights ago, Mr. Carmichael was patience itself as he waited for her to take each step at her own pace. Not blessed with Dr. Stradbroke's height and bulk, however, Mr. Carmichael did not engender in Caddy the same sense of safety or comfort the doctor's help had given her.

In the sitting room, Mr. Carmichael supported Caddy under each elbow as she lowered herself onto the settee. She pulled his handkerchief from the cut, and it came away bright red, saturated with blood.

"I am so sorry. I will replace this, I promise." She pressed the fabric to her head when she felt another trickle beginning.

"Do not fret over it. A handkerchief is nothing in comparison to your injury. What happened?" He perched on the edge of the armchair adjacent to the sofa and leaned forward, bracing his elbows on his knees.

"Someone broke into the shop late Friday night. I heard the noise and went to investigate, thinking a shelf had fallen. The intruder knocked me senseless, resulting in my injury."

"Have you seen a doctor?"

"Yes. Dr. Stradbroke . . . attended to me and stitched the wound." She could not risk anyone finding out he had been here with her alone, and stayed most of that night, even though nothing untoward happened.

"It does not appear he did a very good job. I shall send our family physician to tend to you."

Before Caddy could argue, Mary edged past Oliver and bent over her. Tilting Caddy's head back, she sponged gently at the wound, rinsing her rag frequently in the bowl of hot water she'd brought with her.

Oliver sat up, then leaned back against the cushions. "Did your attacker make off with anything?"

"Oh, nothing important." Caddy spoke through gritted teeth, eyes closed, from the pain of Mary's ministrations.

Mary snorted. "I wouldn't call the iron strongbox and all of your money *nothing*." She pressed a folded cloth to the cut and secured it in place with a clean strip of muslin wrapped around Caddy's head.

"Including what you were paid at Chawley Abbey for my mother's gowns?" Oliver jumped to his feet. "You must allow me to make restitution, Miss Bainbridge."

"I could not accept it, Mr. Carmichael." Caddy touched the bandage and sighed. So much for not letting Mr. Carmichael know what had happened. She shot Mary an incensed look, then tried to rise to see him out.

Mary pushed her back down on the settee, surprisingly strong for someone so small. "You need to rest, miss."

Heavy footfalls on the stairs signaled the arrival of the constable. Caddy straightened her skirt and touched her fingertips to the bandage again. She hated the way it called attention to her infirmity.

But instead of the constable, Phyllis rushed into the room, followed closely by Neal Stradbroke.

Caddy closed her eyes and groaned quietly. The last thing she needed was to try to explain in front of Mr. Carmichael why she'd removed her bandage and caused her wound to bleed. But Mr. Carmichael, upon seeing Dr. Stradbroke, regained his seat in the chair nearest her, apparently determined to stay.

She shifted her gaze from gentleman to doctor and back. Never before in her life had she been in such a situation—in a sitting room with two handsome, eligible men.

But rather than enjoy the experience and allow herself to be flattered by the concern in Dr. Stradbroke's blue eyes or Mr. Carmichael's protective body language, all Caddy wanted was to go to her room and sleep. And to pretend none of this had ever happened.

CHAPTER TEN

*N*eal wasn't certain who the short, curly-haired fop in the sitting room was. But the way the man hovered over Miss Bainbridge gave rise to a very unpleasant sensation in his gut.

Ignoring the jealousy and the other man, Neal turned his attention to Miss Bainbridge. Eyes closed, head resting on the high back of the sofa, and a complexion that had turned an alarming shade of gray.

He took the glass of water from Mary before the other man could, then stepped between him and his patient. "Take a sip of this." Neal bent down to support her head with one hand cupped at her nape. The netting holding her braids felt rough compared to the silky texture of her hair.

His skin tingled—as it had done the night of the robbery every time he'd touched her. Then, he had written it off to knowing his ministrations would cause her additional pain. Now . . . he did not want to think about what it meant.

Miss Bainbridge blinked twice before her eyes focused on him, then realized what he was doing. She leaned forward and took a sip of water, holding her hand under her chin to catch any spillage.

After setting the glass on the side table between the sofa and the chair occupied by the stranger, Neal knelt on the floor in front of Miss Bainbridge. He lifted her left hand and pressed two fingers to the inside of her wrist just under the plain cuff of her long sleeve.

As he timed her pulse, he got a good look at the underside of her hand. Her fingertips and palms bore signs of needle pricks and fine-line scars from scissor cuts. She not only worked hard, she had been doing it for many years.

His admiration for her rose even further. His grandmother had lived independently, taking care of herself for thirty years after his grandfather's death—including the years after she'd taken Neal in. He helped out however she would allow, but he'd always known she was in charge and not to be questioned or gainsaid. Her business acumen and ability to make a small farm turn a pretty penny had enabled her to send him to Eaton and on to Oxford to study medicine without his having to work to support himself or pay tuition.

It hadn't been until after she died that he'd learned the true source of the income he'd always thought had come from the farm.

Shaking himself from the upsetting line of thought, he returned his attention to Miss Bainbridge. "Would you like to tell me what happened?"

"I was in the shop, assisting a customer, when I became dizzy. Mr. Carmichael was kind enough to help me up the stairs." She gave a wan smile over Neal's shoulder toward the gentleman in the chair.

A huff behind Neal made him turn. Nurse Mary stood there, arms crossed, incredulity painting her broad features. "She was being vain, Doctor, and I've no shame in calling her out on it. You told her to rest, to stay off her feet, as much as possible. You told her to keep the bandage on until you came to remove the stitches. But she didn't want this here 'fine gentleman'"—a sneer entered her voice at the epithet—"to see that she was injured. So she took the bandage off. Likely took part of the scabbing off with it too. Had blood dripping down her face, she did."

"Mary, that is quite enough."

Neal looked back at Caddy to find that her face had gone from gray to red. She might be embarrassed by Mary's betrayal, but at least she had some color back in her cheeks. He lifted the edges of the bandage. "It seems to have stopped bleeding. You bandaged her, Mary?"

"I did. And if it happens again, I'll not only bandage it, I'll hog-tie her to keep her from repeating the offense."

While Miss Bainbridge's expression indicated she was quite put out with her mother's nurse, the corners of her lips twitched as if she fought a smile. Her full lips looked pillowy soft . . . and he wondered what it would be like to kiss them.

No, no. He couldn't think things like that about a patient. No matter how pretty and accomplished she was.

"Well, Doctor? What is your prognosis?"

The nasal, masculine voice came from the person Neal had been to this point successfully ignoring.

Neal stood and straightened his plain, brown linen waistcoat. Mr. Carmichael stood also, but his stature fell short of Neal's by half a foot at the least. "My prognosis is the same as it was when I last saw Miss Bainbridge. She has a wound to the temple brought on by a blow to the head. She is likely concussed in addition to the cut, which will take some time to heal. But if she continues to go against my orders"—he shot her an accusatory glance over his shoulder—"the cut will not heal as quickly, and she will have to wear the bandage much longer."

Miss Bainbridge had the audacity to smile at him. A faint one, but a smile nonetheless.

Footfalls on the stairs drew everyone's attention to the sitting room door. One of Miss Bainbridge's apprentices showed the constable in.

"Ah, I see we have a full house." The man crossed the room and extended his hand to Neal. "I thought I might see you here when I heard the whispering downstairs about Miss Bainbridge suddenly taking ill again." The constable's mustache twitched as he spoke, the bushy piece hiding his mouth from view.

"Yes, but she will now be following my instructions and resting, so there should be no more incidents like this." Neal arched a brow at her. "Will there?"

"No, Doctor, there will not. I will be the model patient and follow your orders to the letter." But the expression on her face—one that indicated a secret pleasure—made him believe otherwise.

"And—Why, you are Mr. Carmichael, heir to the Baron Carmichael of Chawley Abbey, are you not?" The constable gave a shallow bow.

If possible, Mr. Carmichael grew even more imperious. "Yes, my good man. Now, what do you intend to do to find the ruffian who injured Miss Bainbridge?"

The aristocrat's haughty tone seemed to set the constable ill at ease. "I must get some details from Miss Bainbridge first. Until I know what happened, I will be unable to begin an investigation."

"Whatever you need, Chawley Abbey's resources are at your disposal, be it manpower or funds to grease palms."

The baron's son unceremoniously shouldered Neal out of his way, then bowed to Caddy, lifted her right hand, and kissed the back of it. "Miss Bainbridge, should you need anything at all, send a message to me at Wakesdown Manor—I am staying there until Sunday."

The smiles and secretive pleasure Neal had seen in her expression melted away under the aristocrat's attentions. He couldn't help but notice how she pulled her hand back from Carmichael's grasp when he held it overly long.

"Thank you, Mr. Carmichael, but I could not dream of imposing on you in such a manner." Miss Bainbridge looked uncomfortable with Carmichael hovering over her so.

"I assure you, it would be no imposition." He backed up a pace, tossing his head so his hair flew about. Neal supposed that must be something women appreciated seeing. Mr. Carmichael took his hat from the table just inside the sitting room door. "Until next time, Miss Bainbridge. Constable—remember, my resources are at your service." He barely spared Neal a glance. "Doctor."

Neal inclined his head, but Carmichael's back was already turned as he exited the room.

The constable turned to Miss Bainbridge. "I am sorry you were taken ill again today. Shall I leave and return later?"

"No, please. I am feeling well enough to answer your questions." She motioned for him to sit in the chair recently vacated by Carmichael.

The constable gave a sidelong glance toward Mary, who hovered near the door. "Miss Bainbridge, may I request that we speak privately? The doctor may stay to ensure that you do not take ill again." The constable raised his brows toward Neal, conveying with no words his wish to question Neal as well.

Neal nodded toward Mary, then closed the door behind her after she left. He returned to them and sat in the chair opposite the knee-high tea table from Miss Bainbridge. "Thank you for your discretion, Constable. While nothing untoward happened, if word got out that I was here for hours alone with Miss Bainbridge . . . well, I do not want her reputation to suffer."

"Yes, as you mentioned at my office." The constable pulled a leather-bound journal from a pocket inside his coat, and the nub of a pencil from another, and faced Miss Bainbridge. "Rather than trying to fill in the gaps on what you told me Saturday, please start at the beginning and recount everything you can remember from that night."

Caddy leaned her head back and closed her eyes. "It was late. I had just finished a gown and was about to . . ." Her face heated at the thought of saying *go to bed* in front of Neal Stradbroke, as it called to mind the embarrassing scene from Saturday when she'd awoken to find him hovering over her. "I was about to turn in for the night when I heard a crash from the shop. I was afraid one of the shelves had been overloaded and fallen onto one of the glass display cases, so I went down to investigate. When I entered the shop . . ."

She stopped, fighting against the pain in her head, and opened her eyes. "I am sorry, I cannot recall."

"You went behind the main counter to retrieve a lamp."

Her gaze snapped to Dr. Stradbroke. "I did? I . . . yes, I did." Locking gazes with the doctor made Caddy's face hot, so she turned her eyes back to the constable. "It was dark, and I needed to see if the shelf had fallen. But before I could get to the lamp, there"—her heart pounded and she swallowed hard—"there was a dark figure. And then I was struck in the head. That is all I remember until . . ." She sneaked a glance at the doctor, unsure how much he had told the constable about their unchaperoned time together.

"I believe this is where your part of the telling comes in, Doctor." The constable did not look up from the notes he scribbled.

Dr. Stradbroke cleared his throat and leaned forward, elbows braced on his knees. "I was coming home from Jericho, walking east on North Parade. I had just passed Howell's when I saw a cloaked figure run out of Miss Bainbridge's shop."

The constable looked up. "Which way did he go?"

"In the opposite direction from me."

The constable dropped his pencil. "Are you certain?" He leaned over to retrieve the writing utensil. "He did not run west, toward Jericho?"

"No."

"Does that make a difference?" Caddy was alarmed at the change in the constable's demeanor at this revelation.

"It changes the scope of my investigation. I was prepared to spend my time in Jericho . . ." He looked at Dr. Stradbroke again. "Did he start toward you, then change direction once he saw you?"

Neal shook his head. "No. I was hidden in the shadows. He ran east apurpose."

The constable appeared disappointed. When he turned and noticed the scrutiny with which Caddy watched him, his eyes softened, and his mouth seemed to turn up into a slight smile under its thick fringe of fur. "Not to worry, Miss Bainbridge. I will find the criminal. It just might take a little longer than expected. Now, Doctor, go on."

Caddy listened with a mixture of fascination, shock, and mortification as the handsome man explained how he'd found Caddy on the floor, the dropped candle so close that her skirts could have gone up in flames and burned her to death.

"I do not believe the thief delivered the blow to Miss Bainbridge's head, though."

If raising her brows weren't currently so excruciating, Caddy's would have shot up in surprise. "You don't?" She touched the bandage covering the scar that seemed to belie his words.

"No. From the nature of the wound, its location, and where I found you when I arrived, I believe you might have lost your balance or tripped and fallen, hitting your head on the sharp corner of the counter."

Caddy closed her eyes and tried to remember. She'd entered the shop and gone for the lamp. And then . . .

"He rose up from behind the counter. I . . ." Her eyes popped open. "I was so startled that I leapt back. My skirt caught on something, I'm not certain what. I tried to catch the edge of the cabinet to keep from falling. But I miscalculated in the dark, and I hit my head on it instead." She gazed at the doctor in wonder. "How did you know?"

He shrugged. "I suspected and deduced." He turned back to the constable. "I tended to Miss Bainbridge's wound and then departed for home, as I told you before."

"Yes, quite so." The constable wrote a bit more, then looked up at Caddy again. "What was taken?"

"The strongbox."

"What was in it?"

Caddy's mouth went dry. Admitting how much money she'd left vulnerable like that in front of an officer of the law was one thing—but in front of Neal Stradbroke?

She whispered the amount, but a grunting groan from across the tea table indicated the doctor had heard clearly enough.

"I planned to take it to the bank the next day." As if that were any excuse for leaving the money in the strongbox—the location of which anyone who came into the shop could know.

The constable made more notes. "Is it generally known in the neighborhood that you keep such amounts of money about?"

"No. And I would not have had it then except we were so late returning from Wakesdown that the bank was already closed."

"Then you must have been targeted by someone who knew you had the money. Can you think of who that might be?"

Had this been her fault? Was she somehow to blame for the break-in? "No. Except for the butler at Chawley Abbey who paid me, I spoke to no one about it. Not even Alice, who was with me."

The constable muttered to himself and continued writing in his leather journal.

Caddy dropped her gaze to her clasped hands. She could not look across the low table at Dr. Stradbroke—she did not want to see the pity, or accusation, she assumed would be reflected in his bright blue eyes.

"Did you go straight from Chawley to Wakesdown?"

Frowning, she dragged her gaze up from her hands back to the constable. "Yes, the schedule of my appointments did not allow for time to stop at the bank."

"How did you get from one place to the other?"

Caddy opened her mouth, then closed it, an outlandish possibility suddenly clouding her mind.

"What is it?"

She finally returned her gaze to Dr. Stradbroke. He sat on the edge of his seat as if ready to jump up and run off after whomever she might name.

Not wanting to put voice to her suspicion now, she shook her head.

"Miss Bainbridge," the constable prompted, "if you know something, you must tell me."

"It is only a whim of the mind caused by my injury. I know noth—"

Dr. Stradbroke launched himself from his chair, hopped over the tea table, and sat beside her on the settee. He wrapped his large, soft hands around hers, which were still clasped together.

A jolt of electricity shot up Caddy's arms and stole her breath from her chest.

"Please do not be afraid, Miss Bainbridge. The constable will ensure your safety, and I will provide whatever protection I can through vigilantly making my presence known in the community." He looked down and released her hands as if he'd just realized he was holding a stone plucked from a roaring fire. He slid several inches down the seat until the side of his leg did not press against her skirt.

"But I know nothing that could help the constable." The untruth of her statement kept her from making eye contact with either of the men. "If that is all, I do believe I need to rest for a while."

Caddy stood, hands folded at her waist, eyes downcast. The two men also stood, though both seemed hesitant to leave. She crossed the room and opened the door, then turned and bent her knees in a polite curtsy. "Constable. Doctor. Thank you for your assistance."

Heart hammering, she walked as calmly as she could to her bedroom, trying not to conjecture about what the men thought of her abrupt departure. Collapsing onto her bed, Caddy squeezed her eyes closed and prayed.

She prayed not for healing or deliverance from pain, nor about what she would do to survive the loss of the money. She prayed she was wrong—that the person she suspected had nothing to do with the robbery. Because if she was correct, justice in this instance would not bring resolution. It would only bring more suffering.

CHAPTER ELEVEN

*H*e had not taken the hint.

Edith stood at her bedroom window, fuming. She'd sat up here, alone, for more than a whole day, waiting for Oliver Carmichael to come and pay his respects and give her his best wishes for a quick recovery from her indisposition.

Instead, he'd spent last evening below with the party guests, no doubt entertaining flirtations from all the other girls since Edith was out of the way. And today he'd been away from Wakesdown all day.

Her maid bustled about in the dressing room, packing Edith's trunks in preparation for the removal to London in a week's time. Each little noise pulled at Edith's nerves like an archer stretching a bow. Until finally—

"Enough!" Edith flung open the half-closed door to the room that contained all of her clothing, shoes, and accessories. "Stop what you are doing and leave. I need quiet."

"Yes, Miss Buchanan." Jones curtsied and fled from the suite. She was the fifth lady's maid Edith had employed in the last three years, and the most recent to be likely to lose her position for not meeting Edith's expectations.

As soon as the door clicked shut, the small porcelain clock on the dressing table chimed. Four thirty. Time for Edith to dress for tea. If she decided to go down.

Noise from outside drew her to the window again. As a child, she'd chosen a suite in the east wing on the courtyard-side of the house so she could see guests as they came and went. She parted the sheer curtains and peered down in time to see Oliver Carmichael dismount his horse, along with his friends Doncroft and Radclyffe.

She breathed a relieved sigh, then pulled the cord to recall Jones to help her dress for tea. No doubt the three men had been to their club in town—a club that admitted only men, which meant her fears that he had been visiting a paramour, or even calling upon another lady, were unfounded. She chided herself for doubting him. After all, they had formed their arrangement mere days ago. If she could not trust him to keep his side of the bargain for so short a time, she should break the agreement.

But absenting herself and hoping he would come to her had been a mistake. She had not yet made him fall in love with her. That would be the only enticement that would make him forsake the pleasures of a house party or the company of his friends to seek her out.

The maid entered, and Edith led the way back into the dressing room. "I am over my illness, and I want to look my best to show it." The gowns that had already been packed were those she had worn several times during the house party. She shuffled through the ones still hanging. "Ah, here it is."

Jones nodded. "We will need to tight-lace you for that one, miss."

"Then best you get on with it." Edith returned to her bedroom, untied the belt of her dressing gown, which she had not changed from this morning, unbuttoned it, and then shrugged out of it. She turned her back to Jones, hands pressed to the sides of her corset. She could feel it gap in the back when she pushed on it. "Do it up as tight as you can. I want to look as though my health has returned yet I am still in a fragile state."

"Yes, miss."

Edith took hold of one of the newel posts at the end of her bed to give her maid leverage. At intervals in the process, Edith measured her waist with her hands. "Tighter, Jones. Tighter."

When finally satisfied, she could barely breathe, and the corset's boning dug uncomfortably into her ribs, but instead of pain, it gave her confidence. "Get the tape measure."

Jones complied and brought the narrow, stiff, marked cloth, which she wrapped around Edith's waist. "Seventeen inches, miss."

Edith smiled at herself in the standing mirror. The magazines mandated eighteen inches. Most of her guests, even with tight-lacing, could not get their waists down to that size. Her cousin Kate's was an ungainly twenty-four inches when tight-laced, but the American was so tall, the thickness was not as noticeable as it would be on someone of Edith's petite stature.

And it was that petite stature that gave Edith the ability to meet—and exceed—the standard of fashion. Well, her stature combined with her ability to endure and adapt to the discomfort tight-lacing caused. She pursed her lips, reveling in how the expression displayed her high cheekbones and the smooth planes of her face. She'd been blessed with thick black lashes surrounding large eyes with a natural upward tilt at the outside corners, so she had no need of cosmetics to give them definition or draw attention to them.

Yes, she was most definitely a natural beauty. And today, she would use that to her advantage. She perched on the stool at her dressing table. "I do not want curls or bows today, Jones. I want simple and elegant."

Jones went to work, and when Edith took the small mirror to view the back of her coiffure in a double reflection, she decided she would not sack the maid just yet. The front was simple, certainly, with the shiny ebony hair parted in the middle and combed smoothly over her ears. The chignon in the back, however, was an intricate design of interwoven tendrils and braids, similar to a Celtic knot. Anything but simple, and most definitely elegant.

Edith set the hand mirror on the table and rose. "Now, my gown."

When she had first seen the dress, she'd deemed it too plain for herself and considered allowing Dorcas to have it. But Dorcas, with an entire new wardrobe for her presentation and first season, had no need of another gown, so Edith kept it. And now she was happy she had. The brocaded cream silk took on a golden shimmer when the light hit it. A few shades darker than her skin, it set off her paleness to perfection, made her blue eyes appear bigger and brighter, and created a bold contrast to her black hair.

Jones laced the afternoon bodice so that it fit snugly to Edith's torso. White gauze undersleeves, buttoned above her elbows, covered what the wide pagoda sleeves of the dress fell away to reveal. The heavy skirt, with its deep box pleats surrounding a tiny waistline, created its own fullness, needing few petticoats under it to affect the perfect bell shape. The lace at the rounded neckline was high enough to be demure without being so high as to make her look prudish.

The evening bodice she would change into before dinner was even more exquisite. Though Edith hated to admit it publicly, Miss Bainbridge was an excellent couturier.

She looked like a bride—no, like a queen. She raised her chin even higher, displaying her swanlike neck to full advantage. She would outshine stout little Queen Victoria in this gown.

Now it was time to go down and win the heart of her own prince. Well, future baron. And if, while she was working on Oliver, she happened to catch the attention of a certain viscount currently courting her cousin . . . that was simply the way the world worked.

Certain she was the last to arrive, Edith paused outside the sitting room, fingered the thin gold chain that held the ivory cross pendant she wore, then dropped her hands to clasp at her waist. A deep breath. A raised chin. An extended neck. Yes. She was ready.

The room went silent when she swept in, her gait measured and confident. She caught sight of Oliver Carmichael from the corner of her eye. He took a step forward, but she did not look at him. Instead, she moved to the table holding the tea services and food.

Several female friends surrounded her when she gained the table, gushing over the beauty of her dress and how happy they were to see her hearty and hale again. Edith continued to act as if she had no idea Mr. Carmichael was in the room, directing her focus on the women who seemed intent on basking in her reflected glory.

Oliver bided his time. He knew what Edith was doing—he'd been the target of too many other young women's schemes not to recognize her game. She hoped that ignoring him would make him vie for her attention, force him to display his plumage and try to out-preen all the other peacocks in the room.

When a young buck—an heir to great wealth and property, but no title—approached Edith, Oliver turned his attention back to Doncroft and Radclyffe.

Doncroft watched Edith over Oliver's shoulder. "She seems to be trying to make you jealous of the attention she receives from others."

"It would appear so." Oliver shrugged. "She may do as she pleases. It is she and not I who needs this marriage. She well knows I can find a younger, richer wife in a trice during the London Season." He grunted a chuckle. "Her sister Dorcas is a choicer morsel, given her age and pliable nature."

Radclyffe's left brow raised, and Oliver would have sworn his friend took offense at his objectification of the middle Buchanan sister. "Oh-ho—do I sense an attachment forming?"

Radclyffe tried to school his expression, but it was too late. "I regard Miss Dorcas Buchanan very highly. But I am the poor third son of a viscount. There will be many others of higher rank and wealth competing for her affection once she is in London."

Oliver thought to tease him further, but a change in Doncroft's demeanor made him turn to sweep his gaze over the room at large.

Edith had taken her accustomed seat on a narrow settee—just wide enough for two to sit comfortably—and had invited one of the other men of the party to take the seat with her.

"Are you going to allow that?"

Oliver turned back to his friends, his head cocked to the side. "What is to allow or disallow? I am not her fiancé, nor her brother or father. She has made it clear that she intends to snub me today. I am ever an agreeable gentleman and accede to her wishes."

When his two friends continued to gaze at him in surprise, Oliver laughed. "I will not let her dictate my actions today, because I do not want her to believe she can continue to play these games once we are wed. If we do indeed marry. I have watched my father bow to my mother's whims and wiles my entire life. I do not intend to do the same when I choose a spouse. My wife will bend to my dictates. Not the other way around."

Doncroft joined in Oliver's amusement at the idea, but Radclyffe continued frowning.

Oliver cuffed him on the shoulder. "Go. Seek out your lady-love. Let her soft voice and simple ways salve your conscience."

Radclyffe needed no further prompting. He straightened his waistcoat and crossed the room to the other black-haired Buchanan beauty of the party.

Aye, Dorcas Buchanan was sweeter and more pliable than her older sister. She had the same bridal legacy as Edith—fifty thousand pounds—and beauty to equal, if not surpass, the elder sister's. But Oliver had known the two women since childhood, and of the two, Edith was more likely to understand and accept a more open arrangement to a marriage . . . especially once he was secure in having an heir. The middle sister was too pure, too sweet, to understand the need to seek pleasures and comforts elsewhere.

She was better off with someone like Radclyffe. He served as the moral compass for their band of three, having kept them from outright debauchery many times when they were at university and since.

If only the youngest sister were not so young. From what Oliver had seen and heard of her, she was a right little spitfire—and, were she a few years older, would give Doncroft a merry chase.

Alas, however, she was yet a girl of the schoolroom, still with her governess. Mayhap, in four years, when Florence debuted, if Doncroft had not married by then—and had reformed his ways a bit—Oliver could have his two closest friends as his brothers-in-law.

If he married Edith Buchanan.

Doncroft wandered off to flirt with the more vivacious of the young women. Oliver kept to the perimeter of the room. Yet he did not want Edith to think he was brooding. So he found the one person sure to make her pay attention.

He paused in his approach and bowed to the stocky, blond-haired man standing in the small cluster of guests. "My Lord Thynne," he greeted the viscount before speaking to each of the others in turn. "And Miss Dearing. How lovely you look in blue."

Edith's American cousin held her hands loosely at her waist. Oliver raised up on his toes just a bit so that he was of a height with the obnoxiously tall woman. Lord Thynne did not seem at all concerned that the woman he courted stood a few inches taller than he.

"Thank you, Mr. Carmichael. I do not believe I have seen you about today. I hope there were no problems that drew you away from Wakesdown."

"No, Miss Dearing. I . . ." He couldn't admit to his true purpose for leaving the estate. "I had some errands to see to in town."

"Ah. Well, I know you were missed." She nodded toward where Edith sat.

He refused to turn to look.

Lord Thynne leaned close to whisper something in Miss Dearing's ear, inclined his head to her and the group surrounding them, then left the sitting room. Within a few moments after his departure, Oliver found himself standing alone with Miss Dearing. He supposed he could not blame the others—after all,

Miss Dearing was not titled and, if the rumors were true, not wealthy. She was American, and she was not formally betrothed to the viscount, meaning she had nothing to offer those who wished to know Lord Thynne for their own advancement in society.

Oliver shifted his position so he could see Edith from the corner of his eye. Her lips had pulled together in the petulant pucker he found both annoying and endearing. "I hope, Miss Dearing, you will save at least one waltz for me on Saturday."

"I . . ." She glanced toward the door Lord Thynne had exited through, but then shook her head and smiled at Oliver. "I would be happy to, Mr. Carmichael." She set her teacup on the sideboard behind her. "I have not heard you speak much when the subject of the Great Exhibition is raised. What are your thoughts on the event?"

Other than the fact that it would bring everyone into London for the summer and allow him a freedom of movement and anonymity he had never experienced before? Other than the idea that he would spend this summer sewing his wild oats before settling down to a marriage of negotiation and tolerance with Edith Buchanan? "I am quite looking forward to it. With the exception of a yearlong tour of Europe after graduating Oxford, I have not traveled much. The Exhibition will be as if the world is coming to us."

He paused, appraising her expression. "You look surprised, Miss Dearing."

"I have found that members of the aristocracy for the most part do not look on the Exhibition favorably."

Oliver's leg muscles trembled with the effort to keep himself up at her height. He finally gave up and lowered his heels back to the floor. "Ah, yes. I have heard your uncle express his feelings that the Exhibition will be the ruin of London and of English society. I believe you will find it is the *older* members of the aristocracy who are against it. Those of us of the younger generation embrace change and invention. And that is what the Exhibition is all about, is it not? A display of the advancements and innovations taking place throughout the empire."

"And other parts of the world as well." Her blue eyes glittered with humor.

"I look forward to the displays from the Americas. I long to visit that part of the world and see all the things I have only ever read about." He slew his gaze to his right and gauged Edith's current temper. If the bright patches of pink shining on the apples of her cheeks were any indication, he'd pushed her almost to her limit.

The grandfather clock in the far corner softly chimed six o'clock, the earliest time one could politely leave an afternoon tea. Oliver lifted Miss Dearing's right hand. "I have enjoyed our tête-à-tête, Miss Dearing. And I look forward to our waltz on Saturday night."

He bowed and walked casually from the room, smiling to himself at the sight of Radclyffe towering over Miss Dorcas Buchanan, and the young woman's rapt expression as she gazed besottedly up at him.

Five steps out into the entry hall, he slowed, waiting, listening.

Light footsteps and the brush of skirts on the gleaming marble-tiled floor brought a smile to his face, but he eliminated it and continued walking toward the grand staircase that dominated the soaring space.

"Oliver." Edith's voice was a hushed whisper.

He turned, acting as if she'd startled him. "Miss Buchanan?"

Her icy blue eyes sparked with fury. "How dare you—in front of me and all my guests . . . and with my own cousin!"

Oliver raised his hands in front of him, palms facing her. "My dear, I have no idea what you are on about."

One of her delicate hands balled into a fist and slammed into his chest. "Flirting shamelessly with my cousin when you are promised to me."

One look over her shoulder told him they were about to lose their privacy. Oliver took hold of her upper arm and led her to the billiards room.

"You are hurting me!" Edith tried to jerk her arm away, but Oliver did not let go.

"No, I am not. It's your pride that is wounded, not your arm." He closed the doors and turned the brass key in the lock, then tucked it in his waistcoat pocket.

Edith gasped. "What are you doing?"

"We need to have a private conversation, and I do not want you storming out before I have had my say."

Rather than play the cad and watch her chest heaving as she tried to breathe in that ridiculously tight dress, Oliver meandered about the room, admiring the furnishings and decor. "You are holding a few misconceptions that I would like to relieve you of." He fingered the crystals hanging from a sconce and watched the rainbow reflections dance on the thick rug under the billiards table.

"And pray tell, what are those?"

He stopped on the opposite side of the table, braced his hands on it, and leaned toward her. "First, I am not your fiancé, nor am I *promised* to you. Our arrangement is that if—*if*—neither of us is engaged to be married to someone else before the end of the season, we will marry."

Edith opened her mouth to speak, but one raised eyebrow from Oliver stopped her. She pursed her mouth closed.

"Second, if you continue to act the harridan and harangue me for not continually paying court at your feet, I will nullify the agreement. I said I would marry you if neither of us is engaged at the end of the season. I did not say that I would not be actively participating in the social activities here and in London that could lead to my finding someone else to marry. If you think to entice me to marry you by this behavior"—he waved a hand her direction—"then we should part company now as acquaintances and think no more of a future together."

He marched around the billiards table and took her by the shoulders. "Do you understand me, Edith?"

She nodded, eyes wide. Yet it was not fear he saw in them. Just this once, Oliver decided to give her what she wanted. He leaned down and claimed that oft-petulant mouth with his, drawing her to him until she wilted in his arms and responded, her lips moving and angling under his.

As her arms started to encircle his neck, he broke the kiss. He went to the door, unlocked it, and opened it, then turned back to Edith. "I expect you to abide by what I have said." With a nod of his head, he turned heel and walked away, smiling to himself. But it was not kissing Edith that put him in such a fine mood.

Instead, he imagined doing the same with Cadence Bainbridge—taking her by surprise with a passionate embrace. But Miss Bainbridge would take a bit more wooing before then. And he knew exactly what to do next.

CHAPTER TWELVE

$\mathcal{N}$eal crossed his arms on top of the framed wire-mesh chicken coop and leaned over to watch Sheila and Matilda scratch and peck at the pan of mash he'd just placed in there for them. Two eggs in three days was not much of a yield, but he enjoyed the daily reminder of life on his grandmother's farm.

The cage rattled when a large gray tabby cat jumped from the fence onto the frame forming the top of the coop. Neal stretched out one hand and the stray cat came toward him, bumping its forehead against his palm. "I know they look delicious, but they're not for you, Rascal. There is a bowl of scraps for you up on the landing, though."

As if perfectly understanding the words, the cat gave one last longing look at the chickens, then hopped lightly off the coop and trotted up the steps to the landing at Neal's door.

This had become their daily habit: Neal greeting the cat at the chicken coop and then the cat going up and eating the scraps Neal put out for him.

He was about to go inside and get some dinner for himself when a rattle at the gate made him stop. Johnny Longrieve slipped into the garden and was about to run up the stairs when he noticed Neal standing at the chicken coop. The lanky young man bent over, bracing his hands on his knees, his breath coming in short pants. "You have to come quick, Doc. There's been an accident at the ironworks. Lots of people hurt."

Neal took the stairs to his flat three at a time, stepping over Rascal when he reached the landing and flinging open the door. For the second time today, his heart pounded in alarm. But this time, he was certain the case would not turn out to be as benign as his visit to see Miss Bainbridge.

He wished he could have gotten some rest before being called out again. He knew his limits; three days with no sleep was the extent of his stamina, and he was going on two days now. Skipping dinner wouldn't help matters. But if people's lives were at stake, his stomach could wait.

He got his horse from the livery, hauled Johnny up behind him, and galloped off.

Upon arriving at the mill, Neal learned that one of the boilers had exploded. Half of it went through the roof and landed several hundred yards to the north; the other half went a similar distance in the opposite direction. Since the incident occurred during a shift change, most of the workers had been crowded near the doors, putting them at a relatively safe distance. Neal shuddered to think of the carnage he would have encountered otherwise.

After tending to a number of broken bones, bruises, burns, and lacerations that would all heal with time and proper follow-up care, Neal finally left at nearly midnight, famished and barely able to keep upright in the saddle.

After returning his horse to the livery, Neal exited into the alley in back. He was about to round the corner and head home for some much-needed sleep when a figure in a dark cloak slipped through a gate halfway down the alley. Unlike three nights ago, the man came toward Neal's direction.

He was not going to get away this time.

❦

Caddy sat bolt upright in bed, heart throbbing wildly in her chest. She was not certain what had awakened her—until she heard it again. The clattering sound came unmistakably from the shop below.

Not again. She had no money in the shop now, but she was not going to allow anyone to trespass on her property. She picked up the narrow, square piece of lumber Neal had brought to patch the door. Its yard-long length gave it enough weight that if it were well swung it would be a good weapon. And this time, Caddy had surprise on her side.

She edged down the stairs, keeping her back pressed to the wall, the lumber held before her like a cricket bat. She'd played the game quite a bit as a child with the boys who attended her father's day school, and by the time she gave it up at fourteen years old to go off to school herself, she could out-strike any of them. It had been quite some time since she had done so, but she knew she could if she must.

At the bottom of the stairwell, she eased the door open and slipped as silently as possible into the shop.

Caddy regulated her breathing and tried to still her trembling hands. She swept her eyes to and fro among the cabinets, cases, and shelves, trying to make out a shape that should not be there.

A scratching sound. A howl. A crash. And then—something bumped into Caddy's ankle.

Moving her makeshift weapon into her left hand, Caddy bent and felt around in the darkness about a foot from the floor. She gasped and jerked back when she touched something warm and furry. How had an animal gotten into her shop? Setting the piece of lumber on the counter, she reached for the lamp and lit it, then turned and found herself looking at the most beautiful gray tabby cat she had ever seen.

"Where did you come from?" Caddy reached her hand out to allow the feline to familiarize itself with her scent. It took two steps, then bumped its head against her palm. "You haven't seen anyone else skulking about in here, have you?"

The cat jumped up on the counter, landing with grace despite its large size. It mewed several times as if trying to answer her. It let her scratch it behind the ears for a moment, then it jumped off the counter and dashed out of sight. Caddy grabbed the lamp and set off after it. The last thing she needed was for the animal to get in its mind that bolts of fabric would make good scratching posts. She hissed softly through her teeth, trying to catch the cat's attention and get it to come back to her. Instead, it released a howling meow. She lifted the lumber and lamp and followed the cat's calls through the storeroom to the back door.

"Is this how you got in?" Caddy set the lamp on a shelf and reached to open the door, surprised and quite upset to discover it was not locked. She was not certain which of the girls had been last to leave, but apparently she needed to have another conversation with all of them about making sure the doors were locked at night. She pulled the door open, and the cat dashed out.

The way he swerved going through the door made Caddy look down.

She gasped. Her strongbox sat on the narrow door landing.

Caddy glanced around the small back garden, but other than the gray cat disappearing over the fence, she saw no movement. She snatched up the box and closed and locked the door. Unable to carry both the heavy box and the lamp, Caddy doused the light and left the lamp on the shelf in the storeroom. She would put it back where it belonged tomorrow. With both arms wrapped around the chest, she climbed the stairs, winded from the additional weight. Her legs felt weak when she reached the top.

In the kitchen, she set the strongbox on the table and lit the lamp that hung over it. She was about to return to her room for the key when she realized the lock had been broken. She slid the latch and the lid swung up, revealing the contents of the box.

She sank into the nearest chair, eyes filling with tears. Though no longer in the neat bundles she'd sorted it into in preparation for making her deposit, it looked as if most if not all of her money was there.

A folded piece of paper sat on top, and once she could breathe again, Caddy lifted it out. It looked like a page torn from a journal, old and worn, brown around the edges with what looked like water damage. The note was scrawled in rough hand, almost illegible.

When Caddy read it, a new raft of tears filled her eyes. The apology was brief and simple, the plea for forgiveness touching. With no name signed to the note, Caddy was uncertain whom she needed to forgive. But whoever it was, he had her forgiveness and her gratitude.

Taking the strongbox into her bedroom, she emptied the contents onto her bed and began counting. She counted twice just to be sure. Only five pounds was missing. Before the return of the strongbox, five pounds had seemed a vast sum. With its return, though she wished the money had not been taken, she hoped whoever had done this had put the funds to good use.

Caddy bundled the money by like denominations, separating the coins and paper. She then removed the sham from one of her pillows, put the money into it, wrapped the cloth around the bundle, and laid it on the mattress beside her.

Several times during the night, Caddy startled awake, certain she had heard someone moving about in her room. But as soon as she came fully awake, she realized it was only her anxiety-induced dreams that made her think so.

As soon as the first rays of dawn peeked through the lace curtains covering the window over her bed, she rose and dressed. She pulled her hair out of the single long braid, brushed it as best she could around the bandage covering half of her head, and re-braided it. She twisted it into a heavy knot and covered it with a snood before tying on her broad-brimmed poke bonnet. The part of the bandage that covered her forehead was still glaringly apparent, but at least the rest of it was hidden.

In the kitchen, she picked up the basket the maid usually carried to the greengrocer.

Agnes looked at her askance from stoking the fire in the broad hearth, but Caddy offered no explanation. She slid the heavy pillow sham into the basket, tucked her reticule in alongside it, and departed for the long walk to the bank.

Once away from the shop, she realized it would have been better to call for a cab to drive her. But she wanted to make sure she was at the bank as soon as it opened to deposit the money into her account. Besides, everyone in North Parade, and probably everyone in Jericho by now, knew she had been robbed. So who, upon seeing her, would think she had anything on her worth taking?

She walked south for two miles along the main road into the northern reaches of Oxford. The longer she walked, the more signs of life she started to see. Street vendors waved or called greetings. A trickle, then a steady stream, of horses and carriage filled the streets with their clatter. Shutters, doors, and windows whooshed open as residents welcomed the new day and shop-keepers opened for business.

She was unaccustomed to walking so far, and the basket seemed to get heavier and heavier. The brightening sky glared into her eyes, making her constant headache worse. But she kept moving, one foot in front of the other, minute after minute, yard after yard, until finally she saw the bank ahead.

If the clerk thought it odd that Caddy had her money wrapped in a colorfully embroidered pillow sham, he gave no indication. Caddy kept a few coins back to pay for a cab home, but she reveled in watching the clerk write the amount of her deposit on her receipt. While there, she had him draw up checks for the bills she had been afraid she would not be able to pay.

After tucking the checks into her reticule and putting that back in the basket, she thanked the clerk, then stepped outside. She scanned the busy street to try to find Thomas Longrieve and his cab, but when she could not find him, she hailed another and climbed into the carriage with a sigh of relief.

It was with light steps and a lighter heart that she dismounted the coach minutes later in front of her shop. She paid the driver, then reached in the basket to pull out her key for the front door. But when she turned the key she realized the door was already unlocked. She knew she had locked it when she left. Eight o'clock was too early for Phyllis to have unlocked it for the day. The mystery marred Caddy's happiness over the return of the money, but that was forgotten when she reached the kitchen and saw three men sitting at the table with Mother and Mary.

Dr. Stradbroke stood as soon as he saw her. Caddy's smile faded when she realized how grave his expression was. She dropped her bonnet to the table and glanced at the other two men. The constable and—she grabbed hold of the back of the closest chair. "Mr. Longrieve?"

The cab driver would not look at her. Her heart sank. She did not want to believe that someone she trusted so much could have stolen from her. But his guilty countenance testified against him.

The constable kindly but firmly asked Mother, Mary, and Agnes if they could have privacy, and the three women reluctantly left the room.

The doctor pulled out a chair and motioned Caddy toward it, but she held up her hand to stop anyone from speaking before she did. "Why, Mr. Longrieve?"

Mr. Longrieve dropped his head into his hands—the chain hanging from his manacled wrists making an insulting jangle. "Ever since the baby come . . ." He fell silent.

Caddy sank into the closest chair. To her surprise, instead of regaining his seat, Neal took up position standing behind her.

"If you had but asked, I would have been happy to loan you the money."

Longrieve's shoulders slumped even more. "You're so kind and generous to me already, miss, I could not bring myself to ask for more."

Caddy considered him for a moment, then shook her head. "No. I refuse to believe it. You are not the kind of person who would do this."

The cab driver's back shuddered with his ragged breath.

Caddy leaned forward and touched his elbow. "Who are you covering for?"

Mr. Longrieve shot her a furtive glance, then dropped his head again. "No, miss, I did it. I broke into your shop, hit you on the head, and took your strongbox."

Caddy took in a breath to protest once more—to use his words about hitting her in the head to prove his innocence, given what Neal had helped her remember—but a large, warm hand on her shoulder silenced her.

Did Neal Stradbroke know something he wasn't telling?

The constable stood with a sigh. "He asked to see you before I took him in, Miss Bainbridge. Now he has, and he's confessed, so we'd best be going."

Caddy stood, her head still swimming enough that she reached for the back of the chair for balance. Her hand landed atop Dr. Stradbroke's. He pulled it away only to circle his arm around her waist and cup her elbow for support.

"What will happen to him?"

The constable smoothed his hand over his bushy mustache. "Transportation to Australia, most likely. There's a labor shortage—men are needed to build roads and bridges to the gold fields in the southeast, so the judges have been handing out sentences of seven years of penal servitude for almost any offense. Robbery, along with the grievous injury to you, miss, will earn that much at least, possibly more."

Beside her, Dr. Stradbroke stiffened. Obviously he wasn't any happier than she with the idea of Mr. Longrieve being condemned to such a terrible fate. "What if I testify on his behalf? After all, he did return the money."

The constable snapped his head around. "He did?"

"Yes."

"Not all of it," Mr. Longrieve added. "Some of it was already spent before I . . . before I made the decision to bring it back."

Caddy wanted to scream at the man to tell the truth, to admit who had really committed the crime, but Dr. Stradbroke's grip on her elbow tightened.

"I will testify on his behalf, as well."

She looked up at the doctor, unsure if he'd spoken or if she'd imagined the deep, soft voice. She'd known Mr. Longrieve for years; Neal could not have known him but for a couple of weeks at the most. Why would he put his own reputation on the line for a stranger?

The constable shook his head. "It's nice of you both to want to help. But he has confessed to his crime. The judge will not likely invite witnesses to the stand before passing sentence."

"We will be at the trial nonetheless," Neal said, more to Mr. Longrieve than the constable. "Miss Bainbridge and I will speak on your behalf if we are allowed."

Caddy nodded her agreement. "Please tell your family that if there is anything they need, they are to come to me, no matter what it is."

"Or to me. I will call on them every day to make certain they are keeping well and want for nothing."

She appreciated Neal's offering what she could not do—especially considering the number of orders she had pending.

The constable led the manacled man from the room, and for a moment, Caddy sagged into Neal's supporting arm. She glanced up at him, wishing she did not have to face all of life's problems alone. She wanted to have those strong arms wrapped around her, to bury her face in his broad chest, to feel the comfort of his kiss against her forehead.

Straightening, she strengthened her resolve. She knew so little about him, he was nearly a stranger. Oh, she admired him—not just for his attractive physical appearance, but for his kindness and gentleness, his intelligence, and his gentle humor. Yet there was something about him that made her uneasy. Something he seemed to be hiding.

"Thank you, Miss Bainbridge, for taking his side. I know how hard the baby's illness has been for his family. I have offered to give them free medicine, and to take my payment in trade—for laundry services once his wife is back on her feet—but he would have none of it. He insisted on paying me—first with two of his last remaining chickens, and now with coin since he has nothing else to give me."

Caddy lowered herself back into the chair. She rubbed the side of her forehead that wasn't covered with cloth. "I have known Mr. Longrieve for years. When I was in financial straits, he offered me his services with the same conditions you offered—I provided mending for his wife's laundry to pay his fare whenever I needed to deliver a garment or pick up a shipment at the depot. That's been years ago, but I will never forget their kindness." She looked up at the doctor. "I know he did not do this."

"I am of that mind too. But to prove it . . ." He pounded one fist into the other palm. "Transportation." He spat the word, and his hands curled into fists. "How will his family survive if he is sent away for the rest of his life?"

"The rest of his life?" Caddy's breath caught in her throat. "But the constable said seven years."

Dr. Stradbroke paced the kitchen. "Convicts who are sent to Australia are not allowed to return to England. So it might as well be a life sentence." He stopped at the window and looked out into the street, but Caddy wasn't certain he actually saw anything. "Australia is . . ."

When he said no more, Caddy picked up the thought. "I have heard stories about that place. Mr. Longrieve will be fortunate if he is not murdered by the marauding bands of convicts who live there." She shuddered.

Dr. Stradbroke's back stiffened. "Not everyone who lives in Australia is a convict. And most of the men who have worked out their sentences have settled down. Many have even managed to reconnect with their families to start new lives."

"You are too kindhearted, Doctor." Caddy started to rub her forehead again but stopped when the motion pulled painfully against her stitches. "But we must do all we can to keep Mr. Longrieve from such a fate."

Dr. Stradbroke returned to the table and picked up his cloak, which had been draped over the back of one of the chairs. "I will look in on the Longrieve family later today and send you word if they need anything."

"Thank you. If you learn when the trial is to be, please let me know immediately."

"I will. Good day, Miss Bainbridge."

"Good day, Dr. Stradbroke."

Caddy frowned as she watched him leave. He couldn't know the Longrieve family well—he had been here less than a month. Then why was he so upset over this? He wasn't the one who'd been robbed and injured.

She would let him have his secrets . . . for now. Once Mr. Longrieve was safely back at home with his family, Caddy would set her attention to finding out what the doctor was hiding. After all, he was spending far too much time under her roof for her not to know everything about him.

CHAPTER THIRTEEN

*N*eal tried to shake off his anger at Miss Bainbridge's words, but it dogged him like a shadow all the way to his flat. Australia was a terrible place. Anyone who came from that country was no better than a thieving murderer. Nothing good could ever come from those shores.

He could not bring himself to accept such casual prejudice against the place and its people.

He stripped off his outer clothes and boots, then fell onto the bed in his pants and shirt, falling asleep almost instantly. He awakened to the afternoon sun shining through his thin curtains. He lay in bed relishing the luxury of lingering awhile until a faint scratching sound caught his attention.

Tripping over his boots and rubbing his eyes, Neal stumbled through the bedroom and kitchen and opened the main door.

Rascal the cat marched in, tail raised, meowing as he circled the room before jumping onto the table.

The early spring air outside was warm, with a gentle breeze, so Neal left the door open. "I guess you're wondering where I was this morning."

The dark feline eyes stayed fixed on him as he moved about the room, setting water on to boil for tea, then slicing bread and covering it with cheese, which he set on a tin plate on the spider-stand over the hearth to toast. He tossed the cheese rind to Rascal, who sniffed it and then eyed him balefully.

"No cream. Sorry. Used the last of it yesterday."

Rascal sneezed, then hunkered down on the table to gnaw on the rind.

Neal drank his tea and ate his toasted cheese accompanied by the low, vibrating purr of the cat. After feeding the chickens— barring Rascal from the gate with his foot—he returned to his rooms and dressed. He had to shoo the cat out of the flat before leaving.

The horse needed little guidance to get to the Longrieve home in Jericho, since he usually started his daily rounds by calling on Mrs. Longrieve and the baby. This afternoon, however, he was not greeted by an ebullient teen eager to discuss the latest reading project he'd conquered. Neal tied the horse slowly, wishing he did not make his visit under such tragic circumstances.

Mrs. Longrieve opened the door at his soft knock, her face haggard and pale. She stepped back and invited him in wordlessly. He followed her lead and said nothing, crossing the cramped room to the crate Mr. Longrieve had fashioned into a cradle for the baby.

Though the infant slept, she did not look peaceful. Neal lifted her and carried her out into the sunlight. Her nearly translucent skin had a yellow tint to it, and when he pried open her mouth, her gums were pale.

The baby squirmed and began a plaintive whimper—as if she did not have enough energy for a proper cry. He cradled her to his chest and ducked back into the narrow row house.

"Johnny's out trying to earn money for food." Mrs. Longrieve took the baby from Neal, draped a blanket over her shoulder and the child, and began nursing. "It's hard for him, it is, with so many younger boys what will take fewer coins to carry messages the same distance."

"What about driving the cab?"

"The constables took it—to be sold to pay our debt for the theft."

Neal crossed his arms. "All but five pounds were returned. The cab must be worth much more than that."

Mrs. Longrieve's shoulders slumped. "They said we'd have to sell the cab, and our horses, to pay for a lawyer and court fees."

"We will see about that. I will go to the constable to see what can be done. Once your husband is exonerated, he must have a way to support his family."

"But we have nothing to pay the legal expenses with."

"Do not worry—I will take care of it." Neal picked up his kit. "When you next see Johnny, send him to find me. I have an errand for him."

"Yes, Doctor. How much do I—"

"You owe me nothing. I came to check on my friend's family, nothing more." He stepped outside and donned his hat. "Good day, Mrs. Longrieve."

Moisture brimmed in the gaunt woman's eyes. "Good day, Dr. Stradbroke."

The horse, accustomed to being left tethered at the Longrieves' home for a nosebag of oats and a nap while Neal made his rounds on foot, tossed its head when Neal untied the rope and led it out into the street to mount.

"Come on, ol' chap." Neal ran his hand under the long chestnut mane, then patted the muscular neck. "We have work to be about."

The animal waited until Neal was mounted before turning to try to bite the toe of Neal's boot. With dexterity gained from years of training farm horses, Neal controlled the animal and headed off to the constabulary office.

Oliver stood back and watched as the Chawley Abbey carpenter set the second pane of glass into the rebuilt sash in the front door of Miss Bainbridge's shop.

"I am so relieved the money was returned." He patted the breast pocket of his coat. "I had come fully prepared to reimburse you for the cost of M'lady's gowns."

Miss Bainbridge reached up and touched the wing of hair that did little to conceal the bandage covering half of her forehead. Her smile looked weary. "I appreciate your generosity. But now I will not have to forego my visit to London and the Exhibition."

Oliver turned toward her, his attention fully caught by her words. "You intend to visit the Great Exhibition?"

"Yes. I understand there will be displays of fabrics and fashions from all over the empire. I would be remiss not to attend." She finished rolling fabric onto a wooden bolt, then reached overhead to slide it in between others on a shelf, like books.

Oliver gazed at the rows of shelves containing dozens and dozens of bolts of fabrics, from the most vulgar cottons and muslins to exquisite silks and linens. Only someone of high intelligence and business acumen could have built a business that attracted rich and poor alike. He could think of no other shop his mother patronized that also counted residents of Jericho as customers. In fact, she usually shunned those types of places.

He supposed that because M'lady did not have to set foot inside the shop, she did not have to admit that Miss Bainbridge counted some of the poorest residents of Oxfordshire among her clientele. And M'lady usually looked better in the elegant but understated gowns Miss Bainbridge made for her than the ostentatious creations from her London dressmakers.

"And it will be a chance to see what all the ladies of London are wearing, will it not?" Oliver leaned on the high table in the center of the shop where Miss Bainbridge had just cut a measured length of the cotton duck she'd just re-shelved.

A slight pinch formed between her fine, dark brows, but it quickly disappeared. "Yes, of course."

Now she sounded like she was humoring him. That wouldn't do. "I am certain, though, that you find other ways to keep abreast of the latest styles. Through . . . magazines and such."

"And such." She flinched when the bolt of fabric beside the one she pulled out came out and started falling toward her forehead. Quick as lightning, she caught the rogue bolt and pushed it back in place before it could cause her further harm.

She carried what must be a heavy load to the table and began unrolling the coarse indigo fabric. It landed with a hollow thud on the table each time the flat board rolled over as she measured several yards of the stuff.

Oliver reached across the cutting table to feel it—it was as rough as it looked. He wrinkled his nose. "What on earth is this used for?"

"This is denim. It is quite durable, so workmen from many professions rely on it for clothing that will hold up to all kinds of difficult work." She glanced beyond him toward the door, and Oliver turned. Though the carpenter's pants were brown, they did seem to be made from the same type of heavy twill material.

"All finished, Mr. Carmichael." The carpenter put the last of his tools back into the wooden case he carried and stood, taking one last swipe at the two new panes of glass with a white handkerchief.

"Very good. Please wait outside at the carriage for your payment."

"Thank you, Mr. Harrison," Miss Bainbridge called after the carpenter, who had obeyed Oliver with a quickness he hadn't realized the man possessed.

Outside, the workman turned and doffed the cap he'd just returned to his head, bowing to Caddy through the newly repaired window.

"How much do I owe you for his time and the supplies?" Caddy crossed to the end of the room and reached under the counter for the strongbox Oliver knew had been returned there.

"Nothing. It is my pleasure to be able to offer you this small token of service. I am aware of what my mother pays for her gowns in London, and how much she paid you, and you do not charge nearly enough." He leaned toward her with a grin. "Especially since I know how difficult my mother can be."

"But I must—"

He straightened and held up a hand as if to defend himself from her words. "No. I will not accept payment. And if I discover you undercharging my mother for her next commission, I will be very unhappy."

Pink tinged Miss Bainbridge's cheeks. Finally, he'd evoked some kind of emotional response from her.

"Now, when you come to Chawley Abbey for the servants' ball next week—"

The chime on the door sounded, and Oliver turned to chide Harrison for returning without permission. But his voice caught in his throat at the sight of the two men who entered the shop.

Both had the physical build of dockworkers, though they wore clothes that indicated higher social strata than that. Each had curly dark hair—though not styled curls like his own—and seemed in need of a barber's services. One had thick mutton-chop side-whiskers; the other had a goatee sprinkled with silver here and there, making Oliver guess them to both be a good ten years older than himself.

"We're looking for a Miss Bainbridge." The taller of the two men, the one with blue eyes, spoke. Oliver frowned, trying to place the accent.

"I am Miss Cadence Bainbridge. How may I help you?" She stepped around the counter and toward the two men. Oliver wanted to interpose himself between them, to put up a show of protecting her from the rough-looking men. But the shorter of the two still had almost a head in height and several stones in weight advantage over him. No need to provoke them.

"We've been told," said the stockier, dark-eyed one, "that a Dr. Neal Stradbroke has been seen coming and going from your shop."

⁂

Caddy's heart pounded in her chest. These men were looking for Dr. Stradbroke? Why? They looked dangerous, despite their fine suits. "And who are you?"

"My apologies, miss." The taller man with light eyes and a goatee stepped forward. "I am Hugh Macquarie and this is Russell Birchip. We . . . uh . . ." Mr. Macquarie gave his companion a sidelong glance. "We have business with Dr. Stradbroke, and we were told you knew him and where he might be staying."

Caddy crossed to the cutting table and resumed measuring the denim to give herself time to formulate an answer. Mr. Carmichael seemed a little too interested in what these two strangers might have to say about Neal Stradbroke. And these two strangers were a little too interested in finding Neal Stradbroke.

The need to protect him from whatever they might want struck with an almost physical force. She marked it down to the fact that he'd been so kind to Mother and generous with his time and services.

But the way her heart raced whenever she saw him had nothing whatsoever to do with Mother.

"I . . . have not seen him since early this morning." She straightened the bi-folded fabric and withdrew the heavy shears from the pocket of her apron. "I believe he calls on patients in Jericho during the day."

She didn't miss the smirk on Oliver Carmichael's face at the name of the lower-class suburb. She cut through the heavy fabric, secured the shears in her pocket again, then started folding the four yards of cloth.

The light-eyed man regarded her with narrowed eyes a moment, then reached into his interior coat pocket and withdrew a card. "When you see him next, please let him know that we stopped in and asked for him."

Caddy took the card and tucked it into another pocket in the utilitarian sewing apron without looking at it. "If I see him, I will be certain to mention it. But I do not know when that will be."

Both of the strangers inclined their heads before exiting the shop.

"Well . . . that was interesting." Oliver Carmichael propped his elbow on the cutting table and slouched toward her, watching the two men pass up the sidewalk through the front windows. "What do you suppose they wanted?"

"I suppose they will tell Dr. Stradbroke when they find him." She slipped her hand into her pocket and ran her finger along the smooth edge of the calling card. "Is there anything else I can do for you today, Mr. Carmichael?"

He straightened as if reminded why he was in her store in the first place. "Thank you for allowing me to be of assistance to you." He took his hat up from the main counter, tipped it to her, and crossed to the door. "Good day, Miss Bainbridge."

"Good-bye, Mr. Carmichael."

He opened the door, but backed up several paces before exiting, sweeping his hat hurriedly off his head.

Miss Edith Buchanan marched into the shop, chin raised, eyes piercing, nostrils flaring. "Why, Mr. Carmichael! What a surprise to find you here—in a seamstress's store in North Parade. When you left today, you told me you were going to your club."

"I . . . er . . . I heard of Miss Bainbridge's misfortune. I offered her the services of Chawley's carpenter. And when she accepted, I came to supervise the work."

Caddy straightened the fabric remaining on the bolt, keeping her eyes pinioned to the drama unfolding near the door. Oliver Carmichael and Edith Buchanan? She supposed, given what she knew of each of them, they were fairly well matched.

"Oh, I see." Miss Buchanan's voice squeaked.

Caddy lifted the heavy bolt and returned it to the shelf, turning her back on the spectacle the two were making of themselves.

She took her time finding the bolt of unbleached muslin she wanted next.

"So you knew you were coming to Bainbridge's shop when you left Wakesdown, but felt you could not tell me?" The shrill edge of Miss Buchanan's voice grew sharper.

Caddy set the thick bolt onto the table softly, not wanting to draw attention to herself by thumping it down the way she usually did.

Oliver leaned closer to the black-haired beauty, lowering his voice. But Caddy still heard him. "I considered it of no consequence. If I had told you of my duty here, you would have wanted to know what happened, and I thought the story might be too upsetting for you."

Caddy held her breath to keep from snorting in derision. She had been around far too many wealthy men over the past ten years not to recognize his scheme. He obviously planned to court Miss Buchanan—and with her beauty and purported wealth, what man wouldn't? But he thought he could sow some of his wild oats with Caddy while he waited for the courtship to end and the marriage to begin.

She would not be party to his game, though. No man would use her like that. Not again.

"I appreciate your concern, Oliver, but I am made of stronger stuff than you think."

At Miss Buchanan's use of his Christian name, Caddy looked over just in time to see her reach up and pat his cheek.

"Now, please be so kind as to wait for me outside. I have business with Bainbridge, then I will be riding back to Wakesdown with you, since it is now too late for you to join Radclyffe and Doncroft at the club, and I told Dorcas to go on home without me."

Caddy raised her brows in astonishment—not over Miss Buchanan's high-handed speech, but at Mr. Carmichael's immediate compliance.

The door had barely closed behind him when Miss Buchanan strode over to the cutting table.

"How may I assist—?"

"The gown I ordered last week? Cancel that. I, too, heard of your misfortune and"—she stared unabashedly at Caddy's bandage—"I am convinced that your health is too uncertain for me to rely on you to get the garment finished in time for it to be fitted to me properly before we leave for London. I will simply go to my dressmaker there and have her make it."

Before Caddy could protest, provide assurances that she could finish and fit the dress on time, or mention that she'd already cut the fabric and started piecing the gown, Edith Buchanan turned on her heel. Her flaring skirts knocked over a rack of ribbons. But she didn't appear to notice as she strode through the door, chin once again in the air.

Caddy's knees buckled and she grabbed the edge of the table. While losing one commission for a gown was not devastating, she'd been counting on Edith wearing it in London and having women there admire it enough to ask after the dressmaker.

If only she had a ball to attend on her visit to London. The pieces she'd cut could be altered for her taller, larger frame.

A ball . . . Caddy straightened and began pulling the muslin from the bolt. She had agreed to attend the servants' ball at Chawley Abbey next week. She'd assumed she'd wear the same gown she'd worn to the last dance she had attended—one to celebrate a schoolmate's wedding three years ago.

But if she could finish the gown, so long as nothing happened to ruin it at the servants' ball, she could sell it afterward—as secondhand, of course—and not have to take a complete loss on the expensive fabric.

And she never knew—if it turned out as well as she imagined, she might take it with her to London and wear it to the Exhibition and see what kind of interest it drew.

CHAPTER FOURTEEN

$\mathcal{T}$he men who'd been injured in the accident at the ironworks seemed to be healing well after three days. Neal packed the tincture of silver nitrate back into his bag and accepted the basket of baked goods pressed into his arms by his last patient's wife.

With the men unable to work until the burns and lacerations on their hands and arms healed, most of them had been reluctant to accept Neal's ministrations—until he worked out trade arrangements with each.

And once he made sure the wives knew he was a bachelor and living alone, the offers to provide him with baked and canned goods—and even a few to come to his flat and cook full meals for him—had been gratefully accepted.

He juggled his kit and the basket until he felt convinced he was in danger of dropping neither, then let himself out of the tiny, dark front parlor.

The gray glare outside made his eyes water—either that or the smell of the fishmonger next door. He paused a moment, letting his eyes adjust, before heading back toward the Longrieves' home.

He supposed the families of the ironworkers knew he would be sharing the food with Mrs. Longrieve, Johnny, and the baby, which was why they were overly generous with the quantity. He loved that about small, working-class communities like Jericho—and like the village in which Grandmamma had lived. They looked out for one another. *"When you cannot afford meat to fill your crying children's bellies, you cannot afford to judge others,"* she'd said.

Something he'd found true while she was alive. But after she died, when the truth of Neal and his parents had become known, the judgment had come swiftly and fiercely.

He shook the bad memories off like a dog who'd fallen into a mud pit, the physical action bringing him back into the present. In Jericho, no one knew anything about him other than what he shared with them—and they did not bother to pry.

At the Longrieves' home, the baby was sleeping—now looking much brighter and more robust since Mrs. Longrieve's diet had improved—and Johnny was out running messages for the solicitor Neal had retained to represent the injured workers in their suit against the ironworks.

After pressing the basket of baked goods on her—her weak protest falling easily to the aroma of the yeasty goodness inside—Neal exited the small house and secured his kit to his horse's saddle.

"Doctor!"

He turned at the familiar voice. "Constable." He glanced over his shoulder at the shabby house, then crossed the street to meet the constable so their voices would not carry to Mrs. Longrieve. "What news?"

"The trial begins Monday morning, nine o'clock." He ran his hand over the bushy mustache. "I still believe it is a waste of time for you and Miss Bainbridge to attend."

Neal crossed his arms. "I will not allow this to be a show trial. I will do what I can to make certain he receives a fair hearing."

The constable shrugged. "Do as you wish. But be prepared that the sentence will be harsh and swiftly arrived at."

Neal shook hands with the man, then mounted the horse and headed back to North Parade.

After stabling the horse, instead of going straight home, he walked down to the seamstress shop. Miss Bainbridge would want to know about the trial date being set, and he had promised he would tell her.

Phyllis looked up from the cutting table and graced him with a crooked-tooth smile before turning her attention back to the shears she used to cut through what looked like expensive silk fabric.

Nan came through the door from the workroom, and a broad smile spread across her freckled face. "Good afternoon, Dr. Stradbroke." She slurred the *s* in his name as a much younger child might, and her cheeks brightened.

"Good afternoon, Nan. Is Miss Bainbridge in?"

"No. She goes to the poorhouse at Oxford Castle on S-Saturdays, to give the women dressmaking lessons." Nan twisted the end of her russet braid around her fingers.

"Oh. Please tell her I called in—no, actually, I believe I should give her this news as soon as possible. Is she at the poorhouse now?"

"Yes." Nan's tone indicated wariness at his intention of going there.

"Thank you." He inclined his head to Nan, then to Phyllis and her customer, and went back out into the street. Going into the women's area of a debtor's prison could bring rumors and speculation down on even the most pious bishop; however, the idea of Caddy Bainbridge risking not only her reputation but her virtue every time she set foot through the prison gate made him spur his horse into a trot.

He'd seen the old Norman castle-turned-prison a few times since arriving in Oxfordshire, but he'd not yet had a reason to call in—they already had doctors who supposedly saw to the needs of the inmates. However, it would not hurt to make himself known to the proprietors.

Half an hour after arriving—and after examining the turnkey's carbuncle—Neal made it into the innards of the prison. Most of the inmates met him with eyes vacant of any emotion but despair, while a few eyed him with avarice and speculation, as if calculating how much money he might have on him.

He followed the turnkey's directions to get to the room where Caddy held her lessons. He climbed rickety stairs to the third level and watched his footing down the narrow corridor to the room at the end.

Stopping in the doorway, Neal looked around. Taking up this entire level of the castle's tower, the round room's windows let in light from all angles. A well-worn table in the center held a large basket that had lace and ribbons and fabric draped over its sides. Around it sat at least two dozen women and girls bent over projects, needles and scissors glittering in the warm spring sunlight.

Caddy Bainbridge moved from person to person, praising the work, making corrections sound like suggestions, as she taught each one techniques to make her sewing better.

When every one of the women in the room had noticed him and looked his direction, Caddy finally turned around. Her cheeks reddened, and she drew in a deep breath.

Neal had a similar reaction at seeing her. She wore a plain gray dress covered in a large apron, and her hair had been pulled into a neat knot at her nape, which was mostly obscured by a lacy day cap that did its best to cover the majority of the bandaging wrapped around her head.

Seeing her here, working with the people Grandmamma would have called "the least of these," captured his heart thoroughly and irrevocably. He'd admired her before. Now he had to admit that he was definitely falling in love with her. She represented everything he'd always wanted in a life companion: smart, good humor, and a heart for those less fortunate.

But he could not entertain such thoughts—not yet. He must get to know her better, find out if she would accept him for who he really was, not just for what he seemed to be.

"Please, do not let me disturb your lesson." He set his kit down on the floor and leaned against the wall near the door.

Caddy excused herself from the young woman she'd been helping and crossed the room to Neal. The layer of dust on the old stone floor swirled about the hem of her skirts as she walked, and halfway to him she paused to sneeze.

He straightened, ready to offer her his handkerchief, but she pulled one from the cuff of her sleeve before she reached him.

"Is anything wrong?" She kept her voice low, probably because she knew every ear in the room was trained on them.

"I stopped at the store to see you, but Nan told me you were here. I saw the constable a little bit ago." He looked up and smiled at a few curious faces, then lowered his voice even more. "The trial is set for Monday. Nine o'clock. I have already seen Mrs. Longrieve. I will call on her Monday morning and hitch up the cab. We will stop by for you on our way into town."

Caddy's brows pinched with her frown. "I shall be ready when you arrive. Do you think . . . ?" She seemed to wilt before she could finish the question.

"That is why we are going. To do whatever we can to ensure Thomas is allowed to go home." Neal reached out and plucked a piece of brown thread from her sleeve near her shoulder. His fingers tingled from the brief contact with the warmth he felt through the soft wool.

Caddy closed her eyes and swallowed hard, her cheeks reddening again. Neal controlled his smile, assuming she also reacted to the all-too-fleeting contact.

"I . . ." She glanced over her shoulder. "I am almost finished here. Do you . . . would you mind waiting and riding back with me? I have stayed longer than usual, and it will be dark soon."

"It would be my pleasure, Miss Bainbridge." As soon as she turned, Neal bit the inside of his cheek to keep from giving voice to his pleasure over her request. He swallowed back the *hurrah* and instead leaned against the wall again, watching as Caddy instructed her pupils how to finish off the pleats they were fashioning.

Once finished, each of the women packed her project away into a bag—probably one of the first items Caddy had them make—and left. While Caddy put on her bonnet, Neal placed the unused fabrics into the basket, then he set his kit on top, and carried it out for her.

She retrieved the horse she'd hired from the livery, and he assisted her in lashing the basket behind the saddle before doing the same with his bag on his horse. When he turned to offer her assistance up, he found her already mounted and watching him with an expectant expression. With a grin, he swung up into the saddle and led the way away from the castle.

Out in the street, he kept his horse at a moderate walk, wanting to extend the amount of time he had her to himself.

"Do you truly believe the judge will allow anything to be said on Mr. Longrieve's behalf? The constable seemed to think the trial would be a formality, that his sentence was already decided the moment he was arrested."

"I hope when they see that you, the victim of the crime, are there to speak on his behalf, they will show mercy and not convict him." Neal noticed how the light and shadows caused by the setting sun ahead of them defined the angles and curves of Caddy's face and figure. For a shopkeeper, she sat a horse well, as if born to the saddle.

"I've prayed every day since he was arrested that they do not send him to Australia. If that is to be his punishment, they'd be better to condemn him to death."

Neal's stomach dropped and heat climbed up into his cheeks. "You cannot truly believe that he would be better off dead than transported to Australia."

Caddy's usually soft chin hardened and jutted forward. She looked at him, eyes flashing. "I do indeed. Everything I have heard and read about that place is horrifying. It is the realization of hell on earth. I would not wish such a fate onto my worst enemy."

"Have you ever met anyone who has been to Australia?"

She looked affronted. "Of course not! The only people who go there are criminals and murderers."

Neal turned his gaze forward, teeth clenched, trying to find words that would educate and not accuse. "Perhaps you have not heard everything there is to know about it. Did you know that settlers have been going there for more than fifty years? Good, hardworking people, starting farms and businesses, creating cities, and bringing civilization to the untamed land."

He looked over in time to see Caddy shaking her head. "I am amazed at your capacity to see the good in others, Doctor. Even on the far side of the world, you defend those who are indefensible."

He could not put voice to the amazement he felt at her inability to set aside her prejudice against people she knew nothing about outside of rumor and innuendo. Yet he could not muster the same anger he'd felt toward the people in Grandmamma's village when they'd spoken many of the same insults about Australia and the people who lived there. Instead, what had been a tiny flame now flared into a blazing fire of desire to make Caddy change her mind—not through words of persuasion, but by making her fall in love with someone born on the far continent.

By making her fall in love with him.

Caddy pressed her lips together in frustration. Obviously, Dr. Stradbroke hadn't liked what she'd had to say about Australia, but she couldn't lie about how she felt. Everyone she knew agreed with her.

As silence fell between them, Caddy began to regret being so forward with her opinions. She did not understand why, but Neal had obviously taken offense to something she had said. Rather than angry, though, he looked disappointed. Perhaps if he would be more forthcoming about himself, she would have a better idea of what to say and what not to say around him.

The silence grew uncomfortable, so she cast around for another topic. "When do you think you can take the stitches out?"

Neal turned to look at her almost as if startled to find her still beside him. "Oh, another week perhaps." He reined his horse closer to her as they turned into a narrower street filled with more traffic.

An apology tripped to the end of her tongue, but not knowing what to apologize for, she kept it in. There must be something they could talk about. She knew from experience he did not like speaking about his past. She also knew that he had gotten more than an earful about her own past from Mother on his several visits in his capacity as doctor to both of them. No use in cutting a cloth that was already tattered.

"You ride into town every week to the castle to teach those women how to sew?" Neal's forehead pleated with what looked like consternation. "It is rather dangerous, do you not think? Anything could happen to you while you're there."

His concern for her safety ebbed up to replace her anxiety over his earlier disappointment. "I worried about it in the beginning, yes. But the jailors and turnkeys knew me from when I would visit with my father many years ago. They have ensured my safety."

"Your father took you to the poorhouse with him?"

"He did not want to, in the beginning. But I begged and pleaded until he allowed me to accompany him. I think part of the reason he gave in eventually was that he got bored making the two-hour ride into town and then back home by himself."

Neal cocked his head like a dog trying to understand a new command. "Your father's parish was outside of Oxford. The poorhouse would not have been under his purview. So why would he have been visiting?"

"We lived in a very poor parish. At any given time, at least one person from our congregation was in debtor's prison. In fact, it was one of those parishioners who taught me to design and sew dresses during our weekly visits. She had been a seamstress in London, married, and moved to her husband's farm. But after he died, she had no way to earn a living, since no one out in the country needed her skills. I would sneak copies of *Godey's* in to her, along with pencil and paper, and she would show me how to design a pattern based on the styles in the fashion plates."

"What happened to her?"

"My father helped her sell the farm, which allowed her to pay off her debt and move back to London, where she became a seamstress again. I served at her shop as an apprentice for three years after I left school. Then she loaned me the money to open my own shop. She would not allow me to repay her monetarily; instead she asked that I pick up the work she had been doing at the castle—teaching any woman there who wanted to learn how to make a living with needle and thread."

"Are you still in correspondence with her?"

"Oh, yes. I will be staying with her when I go to London to see the Great Exhibition."

At the mention of the Exhibition, Neal's expression once again closed and he turned his face forward. Frustration gathered in Caddy's chest. Just when it seemed like they were getting somewhere, he shut down.

Suddenly, Neal turned and looked at her again. "You said you did your apprenticeship after you left school. Where did you attend?"

"The Oxford College for Young Ladies." At Neal's raised brows, she knew she need not explain the exclusivity the school generally applied to the pupils it admitted. "My father and the headmaster were childhood friends and attended Oxford together. That is how I got in."

"Did you like it there?"

Caddy sighed, hating to admit the truth, given how hard her father had worked not only to get her into the finishing school but to keep her there. "No. However, it was a good education, and even at a young age I was quite aware of what a blessing the opportunity was. And I count some of my former classmates among my most loyal customers. If it had not been for them taking pity on an old school chum, my shop might not have stayed open a full year." She hesitated, then forged ahead with what she really wanted to say. "Where did you go to school?"

"Here, at Oxford. But once I finished my education, it was easier to get my start in the north, where there are fewer doctors. Manchester. York. Big cities with large populations of people who have little to no means to pay for a doctor's care but still need to receive it."

"Surely you required some form of payment. After all, you must be able to pay your way in life as well."

Neal's mouth melted into a smile. "Oh, I have plenty. You see, I discovered after my grandmother's passing that money had been set aside for me. Other than rent and medical supplies, I rarely find myself in need of anything I cannot get in trade for my services."

Tingles climbed up Caddy's arms at the warmth in Neal's gaze. "Yes, I find that those who give the most tend to be those who have the least to offer, yet they do so with a joy and generosity that's hard to find in most people of means."

His smile broadened. "I knew you would understand. My grandmother called them 'the least of these.' It came from one of her favorite Scripture verses."

"It's from Matthew chapter twenty-five, verse forty. 'And the King shall answer and say unto them, Verily I say unto you, Inasmuch as ye have done it unto one of the least of these my brethren, ye have done it unto me.' It was one of my father's favorites as well."

Caddy's heart ventured into treacherous territory. She liked Neal, she enjoyed his company, and she could not deny the close connection she had felt with him since the day she met him. But he was holding something back. Hiding something. He seemed unwilling or unable to be completely honest with her. At twenty years old, she had made the mistake of giving her heart to a young man she could sense was not being completely honest with her. Eight years later, she still regretted it. She would not allow herself to go through that again.

"Mother said you come from Hampshire County. Is that right?"

"I lived there with my grandmother from the time I was twelve."

She could sense him tightening up, pulling away again, but she pressed on anyway. "From the time you were twelve? And your parents—"

"It was a long time ago, and I prefer not to speak of it."

Rather than sadness, an edge of anger roughened Neal's voice. She wanted to know as much about him as he knew about her—who his parents were, what they had done, why he had ended up living with his grandmother. But she could wait. He seemed settled into the neighborhood, as if he planned to stay for quite a while. She had plenty of time to find out everything there was to know about him.

Both horses seemed eager to return to the livery stable at the end of North Parade—a good thing, since she and Neal had been too involved in conversation to pay attention to where they were riding. And in Oxford, one narrow street looked very much like another. When they finally turned onto North Parade Street, Caddy's knees ached from using them to stay in place on the sidesaddle, and her head pounded in rhythm with the horse's hooves.

She stifled a yawn behind her hand and was about to thank Neal for escorting her home when she saw two figures loitering on the street in front of her store. Two burly men whom, as she drew closer, she recognized as the two who'd stopped in the shop several days ago.

"Oh, Doctor, I forgot to tell you. Those two men"—she motioned toward them—"came by looking for you the other day. I did not know where you were at the time, so I could not help them, but I did say that I would let you know." She pulled her gaze away from the strangers when Neal made no response. His expression had turned stony, his shoulders stiff. In fact, his whole body and demeanor had shifted, as if he were prepared for a physical altercation with the two men.

Her instincts had told her the two strangers were not to be trusted, but she had not imagined Neal would have such a visceral reaction to them.

The two men broke off their conversation with each other at the sound of the hoofbeats on the cobblestone street. Rather than menacing, though, she was surprised to see them looking happy when they recognized Neal. He obviously did not return the sentiment. He inclined his head toward them in acknowledgment of their greeting, then rode beside Caddy all the way to the end of the street and the livery stable.

Once they had dismounted and Caddy's basket and Neal's medical kit were removed from behind the saddles, the livery apprentice took over leading the horses into their stalls. Walking beside Neal back toward her store, where the two men still stood, Caddy opened her mouth several times to say something, anything. But nothing came to her, so she stayed quiet.

"Good afternoon, Miss Bainbridge." Both men tipped their hats to her.

"Good afternoon, Mr. Birchip, Mr. Macquarie. May I be of assistance?"

The burly men shook their heads. "No thank you, miss. It is the good doctor here with whom we have business."

Caddy pressed her lips together to keep herself from asking what their business with Neal Stradbroke was. From his expression and stiff stance, he would not appreciate her curiosity.

Mr. Birchip opened the door for Caddy. She stepped across the threshold, then turned back one last time. "Thank you, Dr. Stradbroke, for seeing me home."

She wanted to ask what it was these two dangerous-looking men wanted with him, but she held her peace. If he wanted her to know, he would tell her. But she wanted him to want her to know.

He touched the brim of his hat. "Good day, Miss Bainbridge." He turned and walked toward the apothecary shop, and the two men followed him. Through her recently repaired shop door, Caddy watched him and the two strangers disappear behind the row of buildings housing the apothecary shop and Neal's apartment.

Setting the almost empty scrap basket under the cutting table for Phyllis to begin refilling, Caddy considered various ways to try to discover who the two men were and what business they had with Neal.

She shook her head. Not Neal. Dr. Stradbroke. She had no right, no permission, to think of him by his Christian name. Yet her heart yearned for the day when she would have that right. But that would not happen until he decided to open his heart and be completely honest with her.

CHAPTER FIFTEEN

ℰdith narrowed her eyes at the sight of her cousin Kate entering the room, not in the atrocity of a yellow gown Edith had commissioned for her to wear tonight, but in a concoction of silver and green that made Kate look like a fairyland creature. Edith's gown of peacock blue and jewel-bright green, trimmed with sparkling gold ribbon and lace, now seemed overstated and garish in comparison.

Unlike the last ball, Kate and her brother were not the guests of honor, so they had not joined the Buchanans in the receiving line as the majority of guests arrived. Which meant the gallery, serving as a ballroom, was already quite full when Kate made her entrance. And what an entrance it was. With the orchestra warming up in their corner in preparation to begin the dancing, Kate promenaded down the length of the room, and everyone turned to watch her progress.

"Good evening, Lord Thynne."

At her father's words, Edith turned from her group of friends in time to see Viscount Thynne enter the room. She'd never thought him much of a looker, but in his black evening suit with white waistcoat and cravat, he presented a stunning figure, short and stocky though he was. Edith's breath caught in her throat. She dropped into a deep curtsy, aware that her gown showed her figure to full advantage.

"Good evening, my lord." She lifted her eyes to gaze at him before beginning to rise.

He inclined his head first to her father, then to her. "Sir Anthony. Miss Buchanan. Miss Dorcas."

Edith raised her fan and lowered her chin as she waved it coyly before her face. But Lord Thynne's eyes slid away from her to scan the crowded ballroom.

She didn't have to guess what made his expression change from one of boredom to one full of warmth. He excused himself and made his way down the length of the room to the other end where *she* stood. He bowed to Kate, then lifted her hand to kiss the back of it before tucking it under his elbow and leading her around the room to speak to the other guests—who bowed and curtsied to Kate as if she were the Queen of Sheba.

Edith fumed. She should have been the one making a grand entrance. She should be the one people paid obeisance to. And she should be the one the viscount gazed upon with affection the way he looked at Katharine Dearing.

Edith let a tiny bit of her anger manifest in a stamp of her foot, which she camouflaged by turning on her heel, fully prepared to leave the ballroom. Her nose and chin bumped Oliver's cravat.

"How long have you been standing there?"

Oliver's hands encircled her bare upper arms to steady her as she stumbled back. "Long enough to know that you were about to create a scene needlessly. Have you forgotten that it is you, and not your cousin, who is to lead off the ball tonight? That you are the hostess and everyone will be looking to you as a leader in fashion and manners of Oxfordshire society? Your cousin may have caught their attention for a moment, but you are the one who has, and will continue to have, lasting influence on the people gathered here."

Oliver's words swirled around Edith and washed away much of her jealousy toward her cousin. Not all of it, but enough.

Oliver let his hand slide down her left arm, then he raised her hand and kissed her knuckles. She could feel the heat from his breath through the silk of her glove, and a thrill of excitement raced up her arm and made her light-headed. She hated that he could make her feel this way. Hated that a few flattering words and a simple touch could distract her so easily. She wanted to be jealous; she wanted to ignore the heat running through her and savor her bitterness. Her envy sparked her creativity into devising ways she could separate her cousin and the viscount and try to win Lord Stephen for herself.

Instead, she found herself taking Oliver's proffered arm and allowing him to take her out into the middle of the room to lead off the dancing.

Watching Kate and Lord Thynne stroll back up the length of the room, Edith eyed Kate's gown critically. Looking beyond the fabric, she realized Kate's dress had a much plainer style than her own. The skirt, though possibly as full and gathered as Edith's, was not held out to its full advantage by petticoats and crinolines the way Edith's was. And as she had already noted on numerous occasions, Kate's waist would never be as tiny as her own. Her cousin's hair was an indecisive burnished brown, nothing like Edith's spectacular mane of shiny black tresses, which set her pale skin and blue eyes off to perfection in a way Kate could never hope for.

By the time she'd finished dancing the first set with Oliver, Edith's plan of action was completely formed. She would take a leaf from her cousin's book when it came to gaining Lord Thynne's attention. She would simply ignore him. She would stop trying to flirt with him, stop trying to draw his attention away from Kate. If she had a good time and laughed and flirted with the other men, he would grow tired of the mouse at his side and see what a good time could be had with Edith. And by doing so, she might just punish Oliver for the way he had been treating her recently too.

Edith laughed and danced and flirted and tried to pretend she had completely forgotten that Kate and Lord Thynne were in the same room with her. And it worked just fine . . . until she saw the two of them walk over to her father.

Sir Anthony looked as if he were about to melt with excitement from whatever Lord Thynne said to him. It appeared he was about to call for silence, until Kate laid a hand on his arm and said something else to him. Father's face crumpled like that of a toddler whose favorite toy had been swiped away by an older sibling.

Acrid jealousy climbed up into the back of Edith's throat. She need not hear the words to know what had been said. Lord Thynne had proposed, and Cousin Katharine had accepted. But for some reason, Kate did not want it announced immediately. For that, at least, Edith was grateful. Until the engagement was officially announced, she still had a chance. A slim chance, but a chance nonetheless.

"Do you think your father will hold a ball in their honor once we are in London?" Oliver's breath once again sent a shiver down her spine, but this time it was not one of pleasure.

Edith wanted to lash out at him, but she could not afford to alienate Oliver at this point. Right now he seemed to be her only ally.

"If my cousin wishes to marry a viscount, how could my father do anything but show Lord Thynne the highest courtesy?"

"And yet . . ." Oliver arched his right brow in a sardonic expression that made Edith's stomach burn.

"And yet?"

"I think you still intend to see if you can win the viscount for yourself. Am I wrong?"

She considered contradicting him, but that would be a flat-out lie. "Why should I not? Do not I, the daughter of a baronet, deserve to marry a titled man more than my penniless cousin?" As soon as the words were out of her mouth, she regretted them. Aside from the affront to Oliver's status as merely the *heir* to a title, she had not wanted to let him know that her American cousins were here because their father had lost all his wealth and needed them to marry English money. Nor did she want anyone to know that Lord Thynne had chosen a woman of no means and no pedigree over the daughter of a baronet with a fifty-thousand-pound dowry.

She hooked her arm through his. "At least I am pursuing someone of higher social standing than myself, unlike you, chasing after my seamstress."

His arm stiffened under hers, and the last vestiges of mockery left his face. She tapped his wrist with her fan and laughed at him. "Remember, we agreed we would not interfere with each other's pursuits so long as neither of us does anything to shame the other."

He caught her free hand and twirled her around into the mazurka just starting. "And do you call your following me to Miss Bainbridge's shop noninterference?"

"I call it protecting my reputation. I have recommended Miss Bainbridge's services to many among my acquaintances. If it became known that she is a woman of loose morals, that would reflect badly on me. So I must insist that you stop visiting her shop, that you no longer have anything to do with her."

Oliver inclined his head, which Edith took to indicate a grudging acquiescence of her request.

And yet . . .

❧

After foisting Edith off on another undeserving young man, Oliver slipped out of the gallery and made his way to the card room. As he suspected, Doncroft was well into his cups and had a large pile of coins on the table before him. He finished the hand, downed the rest of his brandy in one gulp, and scooped his winnings into his coin purse, which he stuffed into an inside pocket of his tailcoat.

"I am surprised to see you here," Doncroft slurred. "I thought for certain Miss Buchanan would have you leg-shackled by now. I suppose Radclyffe is out wooing the delectable Miss Dorcas."

"I do believe he was partnered with her for this set, yes. Shall we go cheer him on?"

"Lead the way."

It did not take Oliver long to notice that drink had turned Doncroft's charmingly boyish smile, which usually made women flock to him, into a salacious leer that made them raise their fans and hide their faces from him. This was no good. "Come, old man. I have changed my mind. Let's step outside for a smoke."

"Capital idea. My father returned from the West Indies this week and brought with him some of the best cigars I have ever tasted. I cannot wait for you to try one."

Before exiting the ballroom, Oliver caught Radclyffe's attention and made certain he understood to meet them outside when his dances with Miss Dorcas ended.

From the conservatory, they stepped out onto the highest level of the terraced garden. The formal garden behind the house, which had been recently refurbished, was well lit and populated with plenty of courting couples taking in the cool springtime air. Oliver and Doncroft found a place to perch on a low stone wall overlooking the fountain terrace.

He hated to admit it, because he hated to think anyone of lower rank than himself had anything nicer or better than he, but Wakesdown Manor far outstripped Chawley Abbey in grandeur. Too bad Edith Buchanan had two older brothers and was not heiress of the estate in addition to a large fortune.

He and Doncroft were halfway through the slim, fragrant cigars when Radclyffe joined them.

"I do believe our friend is about to break his own heart, pining after a woman he cannot have." Doncroft offered the open silver cigar case toward Radclyffe, but he waved it away.

"I have news on that front." Radclyffe straddled the wall on the opposite side of Oliver from Doncroft. "Negotiations between my father and Dr. Suggitt have ended with no engagement to his horse-faced daughter. For which I will live in gratitude my entire life. Once I hinted to Father that it might be possible for me to court Miss Dorcas Buchanan, he lost all regard for Miss Suggitt and her ten thousand pounds."

"Well, I hear there is to be a wedding in the family, so Miss Dorcas's mind will soon turn to matrimony." Oliver snuffed out the cigar, finding it too acerbic for his taste.

"A wedding?" Doncroft lit up a fresh cheroot. "Have you and Miss Buchanan come to terms, then?"

"I am not the one to be 'leg-shackled' just yet. No announcement has been made, but I believe Miss Dorcas's cousin Katharine will be exchanging vows soon . . . with Lord Thynne."

Oliver swung his legs over the wall the opposite direction from Doncroft so the acrid smoke did not blow directly into his face.

Radclyffe glanced toward the back of the house. "Now I understand why Sir Anthony withheld his permission for me to formally announce my intention to court Miss Dorcas. If the family is to be connected to a viscount, the value for each of the Buchanan girls on the marriage market will increase significantly, beyond the vast fortunes they bring with them."

Oliver sighed. "Yes, and you have the pick of the litter, I must say."

Doncroft guffawed. "Dear boy, are you having doubts about your arrangement with the oh-so-prickly Miss Edith Buchanan?"

"Not doubts, exactly. But I have no illusions as to what life with a woman like that will be like." He grunted. "Can either of you imagine my mother and Edith Buchanan living under the same roof?"

"Your hunting lodge in Middlesex will be much used, I wager." Doncroft stamped out the half-finished second cigar. "I am dry as a bone and in need of a beverage." He inclined his head and wavered a few steps before getting his footing and returning to the house.

"Are you certain Miss Dearing is to marry Lord Thynne?" Radclyffe sounded more like the hesitant, easily flustered boy of fourteen Oliver and Doncroft had taken on as a project at Eaton than the educated, wealthy man of eight-and-twenty he now was.

"Almost certain. Though, as you said, no announcement was made. Miss Buchanan has been expecting it for weeks." He did not add that his potential wife planned to try to stop the marriage from taking place.

"At least she will have her cousin's wedding plans to keep her busy and out of your . . . 'business' in North Parade." Radclyffe winked. "How goes it with the seamstress?"

Oliver shared Edith's demand that he never visit Miss Bainbridge again. "The first part of my plan goes into action tomorrow morning. I have something scheduled for each day of the coming week to make Miss Bainbridge think of me. It will culminate at our servants' ball, when I shall make my intentions known."

Radclyffe sat up straighter, surprise lengthening his face. "Surely you are not going to—"

"No. I will not tell her about the wager. She only needs to know I plan to make her fall madly in love with me. I care not about what happens after that." That strange foreign feeling tried to insinuate itself in his chest, but he once again ignored it.

"And if Miss Buchanan gets wind of it? What then?"

"She is not yet my fiancée or my wife. I am not formally courting her. She may do as she pleases; it makes no difference to me." Oliver rubbed his hands together. "However, it will make winning the wager that much more pleasurable to know I've done it under her express prohibition."

Yes, now more than ever, Oliver wanted to win that bet. Even if he did not have the challenge spurring him on, he would still want to woo Miss Bainbridge, just because Edith Buchanan had forbidden him from it.

This little scheme was turning out to be more fun than he could possibly have imagined.

$\mathcal{C}$addy tried to give the appearance of paying attention throughout the rector's homily; however, when Neal Stradbroke had entered the church just before service started, every pious and worshipful thought fled from her mind. He had been here every Sunday since his arrival in North Parade. But after watching him walk away with the two burly strangers yesterday, she had been prepared never to see him again—or not for a very long time at any rate.

The epistle to the Ephesians, from whence came the proscribed passage for the third Sunday of Lent, was one her father had studied and shared his thoughts about often. The rector of the St. Giles church had obviously not spent as much time developing his opinions of the text as Father had. And he was not so engaging a speaker as Father had been, which gave Caddy's mind yet more reason to wander.

When the congregation stood to sing the closing hymn, the sonorous bass voice coming from four rows behind wrapped around Caddy like an embrace. She found herself wishing it were more than his voice that embraced her. She remembered only too well what it had felt like to have him wrap his arm around her to help her up the stairs after her injury, and she had allowed herself to indulge too often in imagining what it would be like for him to wrap *both* arms around her. The idea of giving in to the strength and support he represented was too tempting.

Caddy stopped singing, closed her eyes, and prayed for God to renew her strength and resolve. After all, as Paul had written in the fifth chapter of Ephesians, *"Have no fellowship with the unfruitful works of darkness, but rather reprove them. . . . All things that are reproved are made manifest by the light: for whatsoever doth make manifest is light."* And what were secrets if not the "unfruitful works of darkness"? Although, since Dr. Stradbroke continued to cross her path, perhaps God was showing her that she needed to be the one to provide the reproof necessary for Neal to bring his secrets to light.

Just before the hymn ended, Caddy remembered Mr. Longrieve and sent up a quick prayer for his trial tomorrow. She then helped Mother with her cape before donning her own shawl.

Several ladies of their acquaintance surrounded Mother, remarking on her seeming recovery of late.

"I have the most wonderful new doctor. Oh, there he is. Dr. Stradbroke." Mother waved her handkerchief at him, and with a sheepish smile, Neal excused his way through the exiting parishioners in the central aisle to come to Mother's side.

"Good morning, Mrs. Bainbridge. You are looking well." Neal glanced over Mother's head and caught Caddy's gaze. "Miss Bainbridge."

"Doctor." Caddy glanced away, her cheeks burning with the frustrated longing in her heart to allow her attraction toward him to show.

Mother praised Neal's doctoring skills until his face was as red as Caddy's felt. Finally, he gently interrupted her. "If you will excuse me"—he inclined his head to the group—"I must speak with Miss Bainbridge."

At the glances exchanged among Mother's friends, even the tips of Caddy's ears burned. But she kept her expression as neutral as possible when she stepped around the far end of the pew to meet Neal in the side aisle.

He watched his hands as he turned his hat around and around in them. "Miss Bainbridge . . . I know I promised that I would attend the trial with you tomorrow. But urgent business calls me to London."

Caddy's stomach dropped as if she'd missed a couple of steps running down the stairs. "What manner of business could be more urgent than the trial?"

Pain—and a good measure of guilt—filled his blue eyes when he finally looked up from his hat. "I cannot tell you how abjectly I deplore the situation. However, I must be on a train bound for London this afternoon."

Caddy crossed her arms, wrapping her shawl tightly about her in the chilled air of the sanctuary. She had no right to ask, but betrayal knew no censorship. "Does this have anything to do with Mr. Birchip and Mr. Macquarie?"

Neal's normally ruddy complexion paled. He opened and closed his mouth several times, and he looked as if he waged an internal war regarding whether or not to reveal his secrets. "It is nothing untoward, I assure you. Simply a business matter that must be immediately attended to."

He hesitated, then reached for her hand and pressed it between his large, warm ones. "I will never be able to apologize enough that I must leave at such a time. But I can assure you that my thoughts and prayers will be with Mr. Longrieve the entire time."

She pulled her hand from his grasp. "And am I to inform Mrs. Longrieve of this for you?"

His obvious shock came from either the anger in her tone or her unspoken accusation of cowardice. "No. I am leaving here now to go see Mrs. Longrieve to tell her. I know I have not been as . . . forthcoming about myself as you would like, Miss Bainbridge, but I did hope that you would have a higher regard for me than that." He bowed, turned on his heel, and exited the church.

Caddy grabbed the back of the nearest pew to stop herself from running after him and apologizing. She did have higher regard for him than that—or she wanted to. But she could not give him the trust he seemed to desire as much as she desired his honesty.

After a moment to compose herself, Caddy sidled through the pew to join her mother—and stopped short at the end.

Oliver Carmichael stood, hands clasped behind his back, leaning in toward the small circle of women, speaking in a voice too low for his words to carry the few feet to Caddy.

Mother's friends wore expressions of awe that someone of Mr. Carmichael's rank would deign to come to St. Giles, and furthermore that he would make a point of coming over and speaking to a woman of their own social status.

He stepped back to allow room for Caddy to come out into the aisle. She hoped he hadn't noticed her hesitation. Though she did not care much for him, she could not afford to offend him.

She returned his greeting, then turned to Mother. "Are you ready to go?"

"Miss Bainbridge, it would be my pleasure to see you and your mother home." Oliver moved so he stood in the center of the circle of women, facing Caddy. "My carriage is just outside."

"Oh, no thank you, Mr. Carmichael. 'Tis only half a mile's walk. We would not imagine inconveniencing you for so short a distance." Caddy held her elbow toward mother, expecting her to immediately take the offer of support so they could leave. Mother pushed Caddy's arm away with a scowl before turning a beatific smile up at Mr. Carmichael again.

He returned Mother's smile and offered her his arm. "Then allow me to walk you home. I will not take no for an answer."

Most young women—and many older women, she observed from looking around at Mother's friends—probably found his playful grin and lowered chin charmingly handsome and irresistible. But with a mind still pondering what Neal Stradbroke's business in London could possibly be, she had no patience for Oliver Carmichael and his flirtations.

"Of course you may see us home." Mother wedged between Caddy and Oliver and hooked her hand into the crook of his elbow. "I would be ever so grateful for the support of your arm on the way. This is the first time in months I have felt well enough to walk to church. I am afraid I might tire out."

Caddy wanted to press her fingertips to her temples to try to alleviate the pounding caused by her mother's simpering expression as she gazed at Mr. Carmichael. But that would have meant drawing more attention than necessary to the bandage. Caddy had spent extra time this morning arranging her hair and morning cap to provide as much concealment as she could achieve.

As they left the church, to the shocked and delighted gasps of Mother's friends, Caddy could not keep her mind off Neal. Why did he need to go to London . . . and why so suddenly?

Her obsessive thoughts of the doctor made Carmichael's presence not quite so odious. She tightened the ribbon bow of her poke bonnet under her chin and stepped out into the uncertain blue-gray spring day behind her mother and Mr. Carmichael.

Mother kept Mr. Carmichael occupied with talk of her gardens from when she'd lived in the country as a girl and then at Father's parish houses. Caddy followed a few feet behind, allowing her mind to wander—creating scenarios of what Neal might do in London that he could not do in Oxford.

Perhaps Birchip and Macquarie were representatives of one of the lords of parliament who had heard of Neal's skill as a doctor—possibly a new treatment for gout or some other ailment of the aristocracy Neal had discovered—and had sent them to bring him to London to provide treatment. Unlikely. Maybe one of the royal children needed Neal's ministrations—or Prince Albert or Queen Victoria herself. There were always rumors floating about that one or more of them were in fragile health.

But as much as she respected his medical skills and knowledge, she doubted it was that which called him to London. Besides, he would not keep something like that secret. And he would not be living in rented rooms in North Parade or working in Jericho if he were providing medical services for aristocracy or royalty.

He could be performing some task for the government he could not talk about to anyone.

Caddy halted, gloved fingers pressed to her mouth. What if he were a spy? The secretiveness. The unwillingness to reveal much personal information. His reaction at seeing Birchip and Macquarie. It all fit.

What if Neal Stradbroke wasn't even his real name?

Mother glanced over her shoulder with a frown of reproach, and Caddy hurried to catch up with them. She fell into step beside Mother, on the opposite side from Mr. Carmichael.

A spy. It made sense. Only something like that would make him secretive and be of enough importance to draw him away from Thomas Longrieve's trial.

Or maybe—

"Miss Bainbridge, was that Neal Stradbroke I saw you speaking with at the church?" Oliver looked around Mother at her.

Caddy stopped herself from sighing. "Yes, it was."

"I heard that the two men who came into your shop looking for him last time I was there returned yesterday. I hope they did not inconvenience you in any way."

The discomfiture in Neal Stradbroke's expression upon seeing the two men had haunted Caddy since they'd parted company yesterday. She wanted—no, she *needed* to know what was going on. "They did not stay for long."

"I suppose Stradbroke told you this morning why those men came looking for him."

Caddy turned her head toward Oliver at the sound of knowledge in his tone. "No. Only that he must leave for London this afternoon and will be gone for several days."

Oliver pressed his lips into a frown, nodding. "That's understandable. I can imagine he would not want you to know who those men are and why they were here."

The tiny hairs along Caddy's arms raised, and her skin tingled. "But you have found out?"

"Yes. I have heard they are strongmen who work for a notorious gaming house in Manchester—or was it York?—and they were sent to collect what Dr. Stradbroke owes."

Caddy thought she might be ill. Not Neal. She would not believe it of him. Yet why would Oliver Carmichael tell her this unless it were so?

Mother put Caddy's roiling disbelief in words. "I cannot believe that is true. I am not impugning your honesty, Mr. Carmichael. But I believe you may have received false information."

He shook his head. "I have checked and rechecked my sources, Mrs. Bainbridge. I am sad to say it looks like the good doctor is an irresolute gambler. And a very unlucky one at that."

"No." Caddy's throat almost choked on the word. "That is not possible."

Oliver's brows arched up into the fall of curly hair over his forehead. "And you are able to rise to his defense because he has told you everything about himself? Are you certain he has held nothing back?"

Caddy tripped on an uneven cobblestone and pressed her hand to the wall of the tea shop for stability. No. Neal had not told her everything about himself. Just the opposite, in fact. She knew almost nothing about him. Not in specific terms. But he did not seem like the kind of man who gambled to excess. Or at all.

Of course, Alastair Hambleton hadn't seemed like the kind of man he turned out to be either.

Caddy fumbled with her reticule to fish out the key to her shop door. "Thank you for escorting us home, Mr. Carmichael. I wish you a good day." She all but pulled Mother through the door, which she closed almost before he'd said his farewell.

"Cadence Bainbridge, that was unconscionably rude. I would not blame Mr. Carmichael if he never calls on you again." Mother swept past, her full skirt pushing against Caddy's and throwing her off balance again. Caddy blamed her imbalance on the aisle's being too narrow for two wide skirts.

"Call on me? Is that what you think he's been doing?" Caddy pressed the heel of her hand to her side, wishing she could disrobe and spend the day in her dressing gown and slippers. She needed time to think, time to rest, time to clear her head.

"Why else would a gentleman of his rank come not just to North Parade, but to a dressmaker's shop?" Mother paused at the door to the stairwell and turned back to look at Caddy, her expression expectant of an answer.

"He . . . I do not know. But he has not made his intentions clear to me."

"He extended an invitation to you for the servants' ball at Chawley Abbey."

"Yes, Mother, the *servants'* ball. He did not invite me to tea with his mother or to a ball at which anyone of *his* station would be present. His invitation merely reminds me of my place in the world. I am welcome to socialize with servants, but not with those above stairs."

Caddy swallowed past tightness in her throat. "I have long since given up on the idea that a wealthy man of high social standing is going to swoop in and rescue me from my life of labor."

With a huff, Mother threw open the stairwell door and disappeared.

Mother had no one to blame but herself. She had been the one to indulge in reading fairy tales to Caddy about poor young girls being rescued by princes and dukes. Even as a child, Caddy suspected that Mother wished her life had turned out more like one of those stories. Not that Caddy doubted her parents' love for each other. But she knew how her mother hated the difficult life a clergyman brought to his family. And just when Father was about to move into a prime position in Oxford, which would have elevated not only his income but also the family's social status, he died. Caddy was fairly certain Mother still had not forgiven him for that. Her dream of living inside the city walls of Oxford, of participating in social calls and events among the elite of the academic and religious community there, was torn away from her. She had been relegated to living the remainder of her life on the outside, wishing to get in and knowing she never would.

Apparently, Mother believed Oliver Carmichael's sudden, inexplicable attention signaled the rebirth of her dream. But as affable as he'd always seemed, something inside Caddy warned her to keep her distance from him.

After a noon meal of bread, cheeses, and cold meat—and silence from Mother—Caddy changed into an old day dress and went down to the workroom. It needed a thorough cleaning and reorganizing, and she was in just the mood to do it, even if it did mean breaking the Sabbath with hard labor.

Hours later, with lamps burning and sweat rolling down her spine, Caddy stood with hands on hips and surveyed the room. Everything was back in its proper bin, container, drawer, or shelf. She'd found six silver needles, eight buttons, and too many pins to count amongst the dust, threads, and scraps caught under the armoires and chests of drawers. As much as she prided herself on keeping a clean workspace, the layer of dust and grime now covering her belied her efforts.

But now it was so clean Neal could perform surgery here.

Caddy closed her eyes and shook her head. She'd already expended too much mental energy on him today—after church and during the hours in which she'd been cleaning. She needed to move on, to think about something, about someone, else.

She doused the lamps and made her aching feet and legs carry her upstairs. Mother still sat in her armchair beside the fireplace embroidering a shawl, as she had done all afternoon. Caddy crossed the room to stoke the fire.

When Mother said nary a word and did not look up from her needlework, Caddy retreated to the kitchen, where she set the largest pot on the stove to heat water and pulled out the hip bath.

She'd once caught sight of an enormous porcelain bathing tub in a small room attached to Lady Carmichael's suite. Not only did it have its own permanent place, the maids did not have to pump water for it at the sink. A tap attached to the tub could be turned and hot water flowed freely to fill the bath.

Her own sigh caught her by surprise. She'd always been content with her life. Indeed, it was the only one she'd known. But her sojourns into the homes of her wealthy clients had given her a glimpse into what life could be like if one had the money to afford such luxuries as lady's maids and porcelain bathtubs.

She poured the boiling water into the small metal tub, refilled the pot, and heaved it back onto the stove. By the time she retrieved her toiletries and dressing gown from her room, the second pot of water was steaming.

The additional hot water filled the small tub halfway. Caddy filled the pot yet again and set it on the back of the stove to warm, to be ready to wash her hair in a little while.

Her bath did not take long, uncomfortable as the hip bath was. Oh, to have a tub like Lady Carmichael's, in which she could submerge fully—legs and feet included.

"Stop it. Be grateful you have this." Caddy spoke her reprimand aloud. "Think of those women at the castle with no tubs for bathing at all."

"Yes, those women do have a harder life than we do."

Caddy nearly jumped from the tub at her mother's soft voice. Even though only she and Mother were home on Sunday nights, she'd set up a screen for modesty's sake. Which was why she hadn't noticed Mother's entrance to the kitchen.

"Did you want to take a bath tonight, Mother?"

"No, I will wait for Mary's help tomorrow. I came in to see if you'd like some help washing your hair."

Frowning, Caddy reached for her towel. "You haven't had to help me with that since I was a young child."

"I know. I just thought . . . I thought it would be a way to apologize to you without actually needing to say I'm sorry."

Caddy finished drying and wrapped her dressing gown around her before moving the screen out of the way.

Mother sat at the table, hands folded, looking for all the world like a reprimanded child. "I never meant to push you toward Mr. Carmichael if you do not like him. I know what it is to have a mother whose idea of a good marriage is finding the wealthiest man whose attention could be captured."

"But Father—"

"Was not the man my mother wanted me to marry. She grew up a farmer's daughter and became a farmer's wife. When the son of the local magistrate—the man who owned the largest estate in the county—showed interest in me, my mother did everything she could to encourage the match. She cared not that he was boorish and rude, always making cutting remarks about people who were supposedly his good friends and wanting to pursue nothing more than sport and pleasure." Mother looked up. "I do not know if Mr. Carmichael is the same or not, but I will not do to you what my mother did to me."

Caddy sank into the chair across the corner of the table from Mother. She had never heard much about her grandparents. "What did she do?"

"When I refused to place myself in a compromising position so that he would be forced to marry me, Mama locked me in my room and withheld food, trying to get me to agree. She didn't know that I had already met and been secretly courted by your father and that I was already in love with him." A vague smile of reminiscence overtook Mother's face. "She also did not know that I was just as stubborn as she. And that Papa was sneaking food to me."

"How long did you stay locked in your room?" Caddy leaned forward, horrified at the story, but fascinated at the rare peek into her mother's past.

"Three days. Father finally convinced her that if I died of starvation, it would raise too many questions. And I realized I could use that against her. I refused to eat until she agreed that I could marry whomever I wished." Mother wiped at the moisture welling in her eyes. "If only Mama had lived to see you born, my darling daughter. She would have forgiven me for not marrying the magistrate's son."

Caddy gasped. "She never forgave you for marrying Father?"

Mother patted Caddy's hands. "She did. But whenever we had a row—which was quite often, given how stubborn we both were—she would accuse me of marrying your dear father just to spite her. She did grow to love him, though, in the end."

Shoulders slumped, Caddy sighed. "I shall never have that kind of love, I fear."

"I pray every day it will come to you. I had hoped . . . but, alas, I will not push my hopes and dreams onto you. You already try too hard to please me—you are so like your father in that. I am afraid that I might become my mother and you would give in rather than displease me."

"You make me sound so much better than I am." Caddy clasped Mother's hands in hers. "I do wish to please you, but I do not know that I would sacrifice a lifetime of happiness or love to do so." The corner of her mouth quirked up. "I can be just as stubborn as you if I want to."

Mother laughed and squeezed Caddy's hands. "Well, then, my stubborn child, before you devise a way to spite me just to prove me wrong, let us wash your hair and turn in for the night. And I will pray that love will sweep you off your feet."

Caddy stood and hugged her mother. "And I will pray that my feet stay solidly planted, even if I do, one day, fall in love."

Mother scrutinized her when she stepped back from the embrace. Caddy turned to pull the pot off the stove before kneeling at the tub and pulling the pins out of her hair. She feared she was well on her way to losing her footing when it came to a certain handsome doctor.

While Mother prayed her prayer, Caddy would pray that she did not come crashing back down to earth whenever Neal Stradbroke's secrets were revealed.

CHAPTER SEVENTEEN

_T_hese arrived for you a few minutes ago, Miss Bainbridge."

Caddy tossed her shawl around her shoulders and detoured from her path to the front door to stop instead at the counter where Phyllis stood gazing at an elegant nosegay of flowers in shades of pink and purple tied up with a purple velvet ribbon that lay on a square of brown wrapping paper.

"I wonder who they're from." She did not need to ask; she already knew. She'd sent a spool of that same velvet ribbon over to Chawley Abbey a few days ago.

"There was no note, miss, other than the one with your name on it."

"The messenger did not say who sent them?"

"They were on the front stoop when I arrived this morning." Phyllis leaned both elbows on the counter to bend over and smell the flowers.

If they were there when Phyllis arrived, they must have been delivered before dawn. Why would Oliver Carmichael go to such trouble to send her flowers?

The rattling of a carriage out on the street drew Caddy's attention from the blooms. "Have Nan take these upstairs. Mother will find a container for them."

"Yes, miss." Phyllis sounded disappointed that the flowers would not be hers to gaze at and smell all day. But Caddy did not want them drawing unnecessary questions.

"I am not certain what time I will be home. Let Mary know that Mother is not to wait for me for meals today."

"Yes, miss." Phyllis still did not look away from the pink rose she fingered longingly.

Caddy shook her head, hooked her reticule over her wrist, and tied her bonnet under her chin before stepping outside.

Johnny Longrieve hopped down from his seat. He looked as if he had not slept since the day of his father's arrest—and as if anything he'd eaten recently might be making a return appearance very soon.

"Miss Bainbridge—a moment, please." He took her hand and drew her away from the carriage.

Caddy gathered up words of encouragement and comfort, ready to assure the young man that his father would be treated fairly even if she had to fight for it with her last breath.

"Miss Bainbridge, before Dr. Stradbroke left, he asked me to take care of his chickens until he gets back from London. They're in a coop in the garden behind the apothecary. But . . . depending on what happens today, I might not be able to. Would you do it for me?"

Caddy hoped the lurch she felt in her middle at the mention of Neal's name—and at the idea of doing something nice for him—was not obvious to the boy. "Of course. But I do not believe it will be an issue. I fully believe your father will be coming home with us before the sun sets today."

She couldn't tell if Johnny's grimace was of pain or disbelief. She patted his arm. "Come, let us be on our way, and this sad situation will soon be behind us."

Johnny followed her back to the cab and helped her up into it. She greeted Mrs. Longrieve, whose stricken expression gave excuse for why the woman did not return Caddy's salutation. Caddy reached for the baby, and Mrs. Longrieve handed her over with no protest. Caddy sat on the seat opposite and cuddled the baby up to her chest. The infant had been bathed and powdered and dressed in a pristine white gown Caddy was fairly certain had been the child's christening gown. Ivy gurgled and cooed, the only happy creature in this sorry band of travelers.

At the castle, where Mr. Longrieve had been held since his arrest, Caddy handed the baby back to Mrs. Longrieve before expediting entry for the wife and son of the accused. She found out in which room the trial would be held and set off for it with confidence that was only partially an act. She knew her way around this prison, had been coming here since childhood. Although she had never been here for a trial that would determine the course of an entire family's future.

The courtroom was small and crowded, and the unwashed bodies of the prisoners awaiting adjudication created a wall of odor Caddy had to force herself to push through. She found two seats in the gallery for herself and Mrs. Longrieve. Johnny stood in the back of the room with several other young men.

"When do you think my Thomas will be here?" Mrs. Longrieve craned her neck trying to see down the line of men waiting in the wings for their turn to stand before the judge.

"I do not know. I was told only that he would stand trial today. Hopefully, we will not have to wait too long."

Caddy's hope proved true—but that did not make her feel any better. As each man came before the bench, it became more apparent that "trial" was a generous description of what was happening. No matter what any man—or any solicitor, for the few who could afford them—said in his defense, the judge reached the same verdict. Guilty. Which was followed by the same sentence: penal transportation, seven years of hard labor, and lifelong banishment from England.

After two hours of men being run through the courtroom, Caddy was making faces to entertain baby Ivy when Mrs. Longrieve gasped and grabbed her arm. Caddy looked up.

Thomas Longrieve, dressed in clean clothes and hair neatly combed, stood tall and proud just inside the door. He scanned the room until he saw his wife. He closed his eyes and heaved a deep breath, as if the mere sight of her were enough to bring him peace and contentment.

Tears glistening in her eyes, Mrs. Longrieve lifted Ivy from Caddy's arms and held her tightly, rocking back and forth on the hard, backless bench.

Envy twisted Caddy's heart. Even in such dire circumstances, the Longrieves shared such love for each other that an exchanged look was all it took to communicate support and caring. Unbidden, Caddy imagined Neal standing in Thomas Longrieve's position, and she knew that, in addition to being unable to hide her feelings for him, she would be unable to shield him from seeing her heart breaking.

She needed to face facts. She had fallen in love with Neal Stradbroke. Despite his secrets. Despite not knowing much about his family or his past. It did not matter. She knew his character, could see it in everything he did. She sensed his soul, for he put it in every word he spoke about his work and his desire to help people like those in Jericho. What difference did it make who his parents were or where he had grown up or what he had done before he came to North Parade?

None. All that mattered to her was knowing him and appreciating him for who he was now, for the kind of man he'd shown himself to be time and time again.

"Thomas Longrieve!"

Caddy straightened and put her arm around Mrs. Longrieve's waist as Thomas stepped up to the defendant's box.

The bailiff read the charges against Thomas. Several robberies in the North Parade and Jericho neighborhoods were mentioned. Caddy's optimism of a positive outcome faded.

"What say you to the charges?" The judge did not look up from the stack of papers in front of him.

"I am guilty as charged."

Mrs. Longrieve let out a low, keening moan and started rocking back and forth again.

"No!" Behind them, the crowd parted and Johnny pushed his way through to the front.

Caddy jumped to her feet and put herself in front of him. "Johnny, stop. It won't help."

But the seventeen-year-old, taller and heavier than Caddy, pushed her aside. He vaulted the balustrade that separated the onlookers from the court. Two burly bailiffs immediately grabbed him by the arms and started to drag him back to the gallery.

"My father is innocent!"

The judge called for order.

"My father did not do this, I say." Johnny pulled away from the bailiffs and rushed to stand between his father and the judge. "My father confessed to these crimes to protect me. I am the one who broke into the homes and shops and stole the money."

Mrs. Longrieve stood and shrieked. Caddy's shock delayed her reaction so that she almost didn't catch the woman before she fell to the floor in a swoon. She wrapped her arms around mother and baby and eased them back down to the bench with the help of a few nearby women.

An older woman produced a vial of salts, and within moments, Mrs. Longrieve began to regain her senses—in time to see the bailiffs lock her son in shackles.

The judge, from his lofty seat, watched the chaos unfolding as if he had a prime box at the theater. He looked as if at any moment he might rub his hands together in glee.

"What is your name, boy?" the judge boomed.

"John Longrieve, Your Honor."

"John Longrieve, because you have confessed to the same crimes your father has confessed to, you will share his sentence. Thomas and John Longrieve are both sentenced to penal transportation to Australia, seven years of hard labor each, and banishment from England." The judge pounded his gavel.

Mrs. Longrieve wailed and swooned again, this time leaning heavily into Caddy's side. Caddy quickly recruited two of the helpful women to hold up Mrs. Longrieve before standing and rushing to the balustrade.

"Your Honor, if I may speak on behalf of Thomas and John Longrieve." She had to yell to be heard above the cacophony in the courtroom.

"Request denied. Women are not allowed to speak in court!" The judge stood. "That is all for today." He swept out of the room, pulling off his periwig and wiping the sweat from his brow with it—and he did not bother to hide his smile.

Neal, oh, Neal. Her heart yearned for his presence. If he had been here, things would have gone differently. He would have stopped Johnny from throwing his life away. He could have spoken on Thomas and Johnny's behalf. If only he'd been here . . .

But he wasn't. He'd gone away, just when he'd been needed the most.

It took quite some time to get Mrs. Longrieve to leave the castle, and even longer for Caddy to unhitch the cab and start leading the horses out of the enclosed courtyard. She did not feel comfortable driving the large conveyance—much larger than her father's old curricle—through the crowd.

Outside the castle gates, she climbed up to the seat and snapped the lines, urging the mismatched but well-formed horses into a walk. Even over the noise of the street, she could hear both Mrs. Longrieve and the baby crying inside the coach.

Tears burned Caddy's eyes, and she swallowed hard a few times, trying to keep her emotions in check. She needed to be strong for Mrs. Longrieve until something could be done to get her husband and son released.

By the time the cab passed the city wall on the way north out of Oxford, Caddy could not hold in her tears any longer. She let them stream down her cheeks freely, since she could not take her hands from the reins. Her bodice grew tighter and tighter, and she struggled for breath.

How could this have happened? Why had God involved her in this situation if there were nothing she could do to change the outcome? And why would Neal have made her trust him and look toward him for strength and help and then leave when he knew he was needed?

Thankfully, the horses knew their way back home, since Caddy paid little attention. She pulled them to a stop outside the small stable behind the Longrieve house. Before dismounting the high seat, Caddy wiped the moisture from her cheeks and chin with her sleeves and pressed her cold, rein-sore hands to her face for a moment, hoping to eliminate any signs of sorrow.

The coach door swung open, and fresh cries from Ivy reminded Caddy of her responsibility. After setting the brake, Caddy climbed down as carefully as she could, though the closed coach rocked and swayed with the horses' stamping eagerness to return to their stalls. She reached the ground in time to take Ivy from Mrs. Longrieve as the pale, stricken-faced woman eased herself to the ground.

"Pack a bag for yourself and Ivy." Caddy shifted the baby up against her shoulder and patted her back. "You are going to come stay with me for a few days until we get this situation sorted out."

Caddy prepared herself for a fight, but Mrs. Longrieve shrugged and trudged into the house. Caddy packed clothes and other necessities for mother and child in the basket Ivy usually slept in during the day while Mrs. Longrieve sat on a kitchen chair, rocking back and forth, her eyes affixed on nothing.

It took some cajoling to get Mrs. Longrieve back into the cab, but with Ivy securely in her mother's arms, Caddy drove them back to North Parade and stopped at the livery, where she arranged for the horses and cab to be cared for. Hooking one arm through the handles of the basket and the other through Mrs. Longrieve's free arm, she led the grieving woman down the street to the shop.

"Once you are feeling better, we will see what we can do about you returning to your house. But until then, Mother and I will take care of you and Ivy."

Mrs. Longrieve made no sound in response, but fresh tears streamed down her cheeks.

"Perhaps there is something you can do to help out around the shop. I've found that industrious hands help one to think more clearly and . . . well, it's better to stay busy, isn't it?" After Father's death, Caddy had thrown herself into sewing, and she credited the activity of hands and mind with helping her through her grief. The same would be true for Mrs. Longrieve, she was certain.

Having her husband and son transported to Australia was the same as a death sentence, so Mrs. Longrieve had every reason to mourn.

Neal pounded on the door a third time, his anxiety increasing with each knock. He'd stopped at the castle on the way back from the train station. The visit with Thomas and Johnny Longrieve had been brief, but he'd learned everything he needed to know to move forward with his plan. But before putting it into action, he needed to talk to Mrs. Longrieve to make sure it would work.

Johnny—his protégé, the lad who'd made teaching someone to read too easy—had not been able to look Neal in the eye when he'd confessed his actions . . . and that he'd nearly let his father take the blame and the punishment.

Neal went around the row of narrow houses and let himself in through the back gate. The two-stall stable was empty and the cab was not parked on the patch of dirt where he'd seen it resting once or twice. He knocked on the back door. No answer.

Where could she be?

He went around to the front again.

The neighbor on the right stuck her head out the first-floor window of her house. "If you're looking for Winifred and the baby, the fancy lady took them away the day of the trial. Haven't seen them since." She shoved a seedling into the soil of her window box with a force that made the contraption groan.

The *fancy lady* could only be one person. "Thank you, Mrs. Hendricks. If anyone needs me, let them know I am back from London."

"Aye, that you are." Her spade flipped some of the dirt out of the box. "And if you find Mrs. Longrieve, you tell her that we're all praying for her man and boy."

"I will, and I'm sure she'll appreciate it." Neal picked up his valise and headed home, increasing his speed the closer he got to North Parade. When he'd first seen the recently developed street and buildings, he hadn't thought much of the town. How, after little more than a month, had he come to view it so fondly?

Or was it not the location but a certain person living in it that drew him like a honeybee to its favorite flower?

He grunted . . . and quickened his pace yet again. The entire four days in London, he'd been unable to get Miss Cadence Bainbridge out of his mind. At first, his thoughts had been filled with guilt from not being able to tell her the truth. Then guilt shifted to a longing to see her again, no matter what retribution might wait for him at her hand. He'd been almost at her doorstep when he realized he should call upon Mrs. Longrieve first.

Little had he known he could have saved time by giving in to the temptation to see Caddy first.

On North Parade, he stopped two doors down—where he knew he could not be seen through the shop's windows—and straightened his clothing and ran his fingers through his hair. Train ash fluttered down onto his gray traveling suit. He really should go home, wash, and change into fresh clothes before calling on Caddy—and before checking in on Mrs. Longrieve and the baby. But that would take time.

He brushed the flakes of ash from his coat and, straightening his shoulders, walked into Miss Bainbridge's shop.

To his utter surprise, Mrs. Longrieve looked up from the main counter. Her face was harder, more lined, than when he'd seen her on Sunday afternoon.

"Dr. Stradbroke!" She came around the counter and held her hand out toward him in greeting. He clasped it and returned the light pressure of her squeeze.

"How are you, Mrs. Longrieve?" He turned her so that the light from the windows shone on her face. Her cheeks were pale and she had dark circles under her eyes, but her gaze held a fraction of hope.

"As well as can be expected. I suppose you know about Johnny?" She pressed a fist to her lips and looked away from him.

Neal squeezed her hand again before releasing it. "I assure you, I intend to do whatever is in my power to mitigate the situation. 'Tis why I came straight to see you after visiting with Thomas and Johnny on my way from the station."

Winifred Longrieve lowered her fist and released a shaky breath. "It is so good to see you back safely. Miss Cadence has been worried about you. All of us were wondering when you might come back."

His gut twisted in anxiety and excitement. "Is she—is everyone well? Have my services been needed?"

Mrs. Longrieve shook her head. "No. Other than anything you might be able to do to help Thomas and Johnny."

She sounded so hopeful, Neal feared that his plan would be too much of a shock for her to bear. "Is Miss Bainbridge in? I need to speak with her."

"She is in the workroom. Shall I take you there?"

"I know my way. Thank you." He left his valise behind the counter, took a deep breath, and opened the door to the room where Caddy created the intricate fashions with which she supported so many people—her mother, Nurse Mary, the maid Agnes, the apprentices, Phyllis the shop girl, and now Mrs. Longrieve and baby Ivy. And she did it without complaint, as far as he could tell. He hoped that, perhaps, someday, he would be able to offer her the support she'd so long given to others.

CHAPTER EIGHTEEN

*C*addy looked up from the green wool gauze and her heart quickened. Her imagination was playing tricks on her—or else Neal Stradbroke had just stepped from her daydream into her workroom. She'd been about to chide herself for allowing her thoughts to linger on him. Instead she chided her heart for reacting at the sight of him.

She could not allow herself to be happy to see him—to rejoice at his return—when she needed an explanation for why he'd left at such a crucial time. The Longrieves had needed him. She'd needed him.

"Good day, Dr. Stradbroke."

"Good day, Miss Bainbridge. Miss Alice. Miss Leticia." He nodded at each of the apprentices in greeting.

Setting aside the wool, Caddy brushed stray threads from her apron to give her shaking hands something to do as she rose. "You've returned from London, then?"

She couldn't let him see that she knew how ridiculous the question was. He was standing here—of course he'd returned from London!

A twinkle sparkled in his blue eyes, though he kept his expression solemn. "Yes, I arrived not two hours ago. I stopped at the castle and saw Thomas and Johnny." He ran his fingers through his golden-brown hair; a few flakes of soot from the train snowed down and disappeared into the gray of his traveling suit.

Caddy dropped the pretense of disinterest in his presence. "Are they well? We have been unable to visit them since the trial. We heard they are being readied to be taken to Portsmouth, where they will be put on the ship bound for Australia." The very name of the place left a burning bitterness in the back of her throat.

"They will be on the train south tomorrow. That is why I came straight here—to find Mrs. Longrieve. I have a plan I believe will keep their family together, or at least allow them to be together after only a short separation; however, it must be acted upon quickly if it is to work."

To her left and right, Caddy could feel the curiosity of Alice and Letty, who looked as if they were diligently bent over their sewing, but their needles had stopped moving in and out of the fabric.

"I will ask Mrs. Longrieve to join you upstairs in the sitting room." Caddy moved to skirt around him, but he stopped her with a feather-light touch to her upper arm—though she'd never known the touch of a feather to burn so.

"Thank you for everything you have done for Mrs. Longrieve. Not for me, but on behalf of Thomas and Johnny."

Caddy's brows pulled together against her will, but she nodded as if he'd simply shared the London gossip. "We shall be up directly."

She had to intentionally keep her head from turning to watch him walk out of the room and around the corner to the stairwell. She waited until she heard the door at the top of the stairs close before heaving a sigh and allowing herself the briefest moment of joy at his presence in her home.

And on pain of torture, she'd never admit how long she'd spent each night he'd been away staring out her bedroom window at the darkened portals above the apothecary across the street.

When Caddy entered the shop, Mrs. Longrieve stood at the other end of the long room, helping a woman who appeared to be someone she knew pick out a cotton calico fabric. Caddy listened for a moment as Mrs. Longrieve explained the benefits of cotton over linen or muslin for work-wear. No matter what Neal's plan to get Thomas and Johnny released was, she intended to offer Winifred Longrieve a full-time position at the shop this very day.

"Phyllis, please take over for Mrs. Longrieve. Dr. Stradbroke needs to speak with her."

"Yes, miss." Phyllis scuttled around the main counter and down the long aisle of the store, and her counterpart came scurrying back with as much haste.

Caddy motioned for Mrs. Longrieve to follow her upstairs, and she did so without question.

When Caddy stepped into the sitting room, her breath caught in her throat, and she came close to swooning.

Dr. Stradbroke—tall, brawny, and devastatingly handsome—stood in the middle of the room with baby Ivy cradled in his arms, his cheek to her forehead, swaying to the rhythm of the old country tune he hummed to her.

Caddy pressed her hand to her chest and forced her lungs to fill with air again. He was just a man. Just a man holding a baby. Yet in that one instant, she'd caught a glimpse of the future she hoped to have. A future with him cradling and humming to *their* children.

Tears pricked her eyes at the unattainable happiness that came with the dream. For that's all it would ever be—a dream—unless the good doctor decided he could be honest with her about his past and allow her to know and trust him fully.

At the creak of the floorboards, Neal turned slowly toward the door. Unless he was very much mistaken, those were unshed tears glittering in Caddy's eyes. But why . . . ?

She wasn't looking at him—at least, not eye to eye. Her gaze was fixed on Ivy in his arms. His heart leapt and his innards twisted with the realization that he was seeing love, or something quite like it, in her expression.

"Here." Caddy's mother stepped forward and reached for Ivy. "I will take her into the bedroom with me and put her down for a nap to give you time to talk."

As soon as he handed the baby into Mrs. Bainbridge's arms, Caddy seemed to come back to herself as if shoved by an invisible hand. "I shall leave you to your talk." Caddy turned and softly latched the door behind her.

He waited until Winifred was seated before he perched on the front edge of the armchair with his back to the door.

"Have you discovered a way to free my man and boy, Doctor?" Mrs. Longrieve's expectation bordered on frantic.

He cleared his throat . . . twice. "No. Sadly, I do not believe there is any way to free them. While I was in London on other business, I spoke with a few men of the law. They said that once someone is sentenced to transportation, it is nearly impossible to get it overturned. The judges and magistrates are paid too well for each man they send to the ships bound for Australia."

Tears sprang to Mrs. Longrieve's eyes. "Then they're done for."

"Not exactly." Neal twisted the brim of his hat between his fingers. "You see, I have some money put aside. Quite a bit, actually. And when I was in London, I discovered it might be enough to convince a magistrate to commute the sentence of transportation."

Mrs. Longrieve gasped, pressing long, calloused fingers to her dry lips.

He held up his hand. "Unfortunately, I do not have enough money at my immediate disposal to get both Thomas and Johnny released. And I would not ask you to choose between them." Leaning forward, he pulled her hands away from her mouth and cradled them in his own, coming nearly off the edge of his chair to do so. "Instead of squandering the money on what could be a vain effort to try to get one of them released, I wish to propose a radical idea that will see your family reunited—in a way."

She nodded, tears streaming down thin cheeks. "I will do anything to bring my family back together."

Neal was glad Caddy had left the room. She would not only balk at his idea, she would decry it and do her best to convince Mrs. Longrieve not to go along with it.

"What is it, Doctor? What do I need to do?"

He cleared his throat one more time and tore his thoughts away from Caddy. "I have taken the liberty of booking passage for you on a ship leaving Portsmouth in four days' time. I will send letters of introduction with you so that once you arrive, you will be shown the highest hospitality by a good family."

Winifred stiffened and regarded him through narrow eyes, her head canted at an angle that screamed suspicion. "Arrive—where?"

His throat caught. He swallowed and looked her squarely in those questioning eyes. "Bathurst." At her continued expression of askance, he added, "It is a town in New South Wales, Australia."

Mrs. Longrieve gasped. "You're suggesting I go to Australia with them?"

"Not *with* them, exactly. But you would be in the same vicinity." He stood and paced to the fireplace, hands clasped behind his back. "Bathurst is a good place—much like the country villages here in England. And the people to whom I am sending you will care for you as if you are part of their own family."

"How can you know that?" The fear in Winifred's voice now had an edge of curiosity to it.

He regained his perch on the chair beside her. "Because the people I am sending you to are my family."

He took her hands in his. "I do not expect you to make a decision right now, but I will need to know soon. I booked the tickets while I was in London, because there was no time to waste. The ship leaves Portsmouth early Tuesday morning. We would need to catch the evening train on Monday to ensure you are there in time to board."

Mrs. Longrieve had gone chalky pale, but Neal knew it was from fear and indecision, not from any medical cause. "I shall call day after tomorrow to hear your decision. If you have any questions in the meanwhile, I am at your disposal. Oh, and I would appreciate it if you would not tell Miss Bainbridge of this arrangement."

Winifred frowned. "Why? She has been nothing but good to me."

"Miss Bainbridge can be . . . unreasonable when it comes to the subject of Australia."

A slight smile deepened the lines bracketing Winifred's mouth. "Aye. I've heard a few choice morsels about thieves and murderers from her over the past few days." Her eyes narrowed. "I know you're trying to protect yourself by not letting her know you have family there. But if my suspicions are correct and you've developed feelings for yon seamstress, best to tell her the truth as soon as you can. If she has the same feelings toward you, where your kin live won't matter to her."

"I hope you're correct, but I must wait until I feel the time is right. I shall see you on Saturday." He bowed to the woman, then let himself out of the room.

He was halfway across the street before he realized he'd left his valise behind the counter in the store. He paused, trying to decide if he should risk returning for it now or wait to get it when he returned in two days.

"Did you forget something?"

He closed his eyes against the waves of emotion Caddy's voice brought. Slowly, he turned. She stood on the walkway outside her shop, his valise hanging loosely at her side as if she were accustomed to carrying heavy loads. Given her line of work and the absence of a man in her shop, she most likely was.

A few strides closed the distance between them. He reached for the bag, but when his fingers wrapped around the handle, they wrapped around Caddy's fingers as well. Goose bumps raced up his arm at the contact, sending a frisson of electricity straight to his heart.

"May I know of your plan for Mrs. Longrieve?" She swallowed hard, but did not release the bag.

He wanted to tell her everything, but he did not believe she was ready to learn everything yet. "No. I am sorry. There are . . . delicate issues involved."

"Were these issues what took you away to London?"

"Not precisely."

She released a frustrated huff. "Then why did you go? The Longrieves needed you here for the trial. And some rather unsavory rumors have circulated ever since your sudden departure."

He decided to enjoy the chance to hold Caddy's hand, after a fashion, for as long as she wanted to keep possession of the handle of his valise. "What rumors?"

"That you are an inveterate gambler, and that Macquarie and Birchip work for a debt collector." She dropped her gaze to where their fingers entwined and pulled away as if she hadn't noticed his touch before.

He allowed the bag to swing down to his side. "I am no gambler, and I owe no debts."

She shook her head. He'd expected her to look relieved by his statement, but her dour mood persisted. "It doesn't matter if it is true or not—the rumors have permeated Oxford society. And I have . . ." She pressed her lips together and would not meet his gaze.

"You have . . . ?" he prompted.

She squared her shoulders and raised her chin, her stormy blue eyes meeting his. "I have had three customers cancel orders for gowns because, they told me, they do not want to patronize a seamstress who associates with a known reprobate."

His heart sank. Never before had the secret of his past affected anyone but him. He'd managed to keep it hidden so well that no one in Hampshire had learned the truth until after Grandmamma's death. And he'd been keeping his secret from Caddy—from everyone in North Parade and Jericho—to protect her. To keep this very thing from happening.

"Can you not tell me why you went to London? Can you not share with me what terrible thing happened in your past that you're afraid others might find out?" Caddy took a step forward, her throat exposed as she lifted her chin high to maintain eye contact with him.

The words formed in the back of his throat. "I was—" The expectation in Caddy's eyes, and the slight part of her lips, made his heart race. He could not bear to see her once again dissolve into anger and disgust. "I cannot. It is . . . If it became generally known, my medical practice would crumble."

He backed away from her, ready for her to tell him to leave and never return.

She matched his steps, staying mere inches from him, even though she had to cant her head back fully to look up into his face. "I do not know what could be so bad that you cannot tell me, even knowing that I would keep any confidence you share. I will not try to force it from you. I hope, someday, you might come to trust me enough to tell me. However, there is something I must know."

He steeled himself for the question he was certain she would ask, trying to decide if he was willing to lie to her about his place of birth.

"Can you promise me that you are not doing anything nefarious or criminal? I believe you are a man of integrity, but I may be risking my business by continuing to associate with you if your secret involves anything illegal."

He set his valise on the street and clasped Caddy's right hand in both of his, bringing it to his lips. The contrast of the soft skin on the back of her hand to the calluses on her fingertips and palms reminded him of everything he admired and respected about her. He pressed her hand to his chest over where his heart pounded. "I promise, I am involved in nothing criminal, nefarious, or illegal. And I swear that one day I will tell you all. But now . . . The time is not right."

Her eyes flickered as they danced back and forth, searching his. Finally, she nodded. "Very well, then. Tea is in one hour. I hope you will join us."

Neal opened then closed his mouth. After everything that had passed between them . . . after he'd told her he did not trust her enough to share his secret with her . . . she invited him to tea? "I would be honored." He kissed the back of her hand again, released it, and picked up his valise.

She backed away from him until she bumped into a protruding window box with a slight grunt, her aim for the door having been slightly off.

He grinned at her, tipped his hat, and backed away a few steps until she disappeared inside the shop. She waved at him through the window in the door. He waved back. Then, whistling an old country tune, he returned to his flat to bathe and change clothes to be presentable for tea with Caddy Bainbridge.

She might not be ready now to hear of his origin, but he was certain—at least, he prayed he could be certain—that once she fell in love with him, she would not care that he'd been born in the place she seemed to hate the most.

He had a feeling that would not be too long from now.

CHAPTER NINETEEN

*E*dith climbed gingerly from the carriage, stiff after the hour-long ride from Wakesdown to Chawley Abbey. She had no desire to spend time with Lady Carmichael, but if she planned to marry the woman's son, she might as well start learning how best to endure her company.

The butler ushered her straight into the house and up the wide, worn stone staircase in the medieval building. If Edith had her way, a new, modern mansion would be built on the next rise over—higher, with a more commanding view of the surroundings. She'd be more than happy to allow Lady Carmichael to have this monstrosity as her dower house. Even with the carpet runners, wallpapers, and tapestries, a chill hung in the air that could never be chased away in an ancient heap like this.

She waited to be announced before sweeping into the sitting room, then dropping into a curtsy in greeting.

"Miss Buchanan, please, do come in and sit." Lady Carmichael waved a bejeweled hand toward the two armchairs opposite the settee where she sat. "You have had a long drive. May I offer you tea or some other refreshment?"

Though parched, she did not want her future mother-in-law to believe her gauche by taking tea before teatime. "No, thank you, my lady." She folded her gloved hands demurely on her lap and did her best to appear shy and retiring.

"I hear your house party was a *grande réussite*. Every young woman who has called in the past weeks has had nothing but Wakesdown Manor and the Buchanans on her lips." A slight smile played about the corner of her thin mouth. "And the Americans. I have heard no end of your cousins, the tall, good-looking Americans. Though the praise is more flattering toward the young man than his sister. Am I to understand correctly that your *cousine* has landed Lord Thynne? How on earth did she manage to steal him away from you, my dear?"

Anger, hot and sticky like melted candle wax, oozed through Edith, but she did her best not to let it show. She cocked her head and pursed her mouth in a coy smile. "Now, Lady Carmichael, how could I even think of Lord Thynne when there has been no one for me but Oliver—Mr. Carmichael—since we were children?"

Actually, the first time she'd met him, and for at least ten years afterward, Edith had done her best to avoid being in his company. It was only after seeing how many young women flocked to him in the drawing rooms and ballrooms of London during her debut season when she'd forced herself to reevaluate her feelings toward him.

Lady Carmichael simpered, her expression looking no more genuine than Edith's felt. Her brows—as pale as Edith's were dark—raised a bit more, adding even more ridges to her fore-head. "Yes, well, childhood fancies rarely lead to lasting attachments as adults. But *c'est la vie*." The baroness's rings sparkled in the sunlight beaming in through the old leaded-glass mullioned windows as she waved her hand.

Annoyance dripped down Edith's spine at the woman's affectation of throwing in French words and phrases. It was her way of reminding others that she had spent part of her girlhood in Paris when her father relocated the family there after the war and then returned to England a very wealthy man.

Edith thought it only served to remind people that Lady Carmichael came not from the aristocracy or the gentry but from the merchant class. According to Edith's father, it had been quite the scandal when the heir to Chawley Abbey and the Carmichael barony had married a woman well below his social station, no matter how wealthy her family.

Which gave Edith the perfect argument against Lady Carmichael's insisting the daughter of a baronet was not of high enough birth to marry her son.

"When do you leave for London, my lady?"

Lady Carmichael picked an invisible speck of something from one green silk sleeve before answering. "Monday. Tonight we will bid *adieu* to our household with the servants' ball. So naturally, we cannot travel tomorrow. Lord Carmichael is very traditional and believes it would blacken our souls to board a train on Sunday. So we wait until Monday. Do I remember correctly that your younger sister is being presented this season?"

"Yes. The fifteenth of April. We also plan to leave for London next week so she has time for her final fitting before we go to court."

"You went to a modiste in London rather than depending on our local talent?" The baroness twisted a long gold chain around her finger.

"Yes. And after what has happened with my local seamstress, I am very happy we did."

Lady Carmichael stilled, eyes widening. "Oh? Has your seamstress been involved in a scandal?"

"Not a true scandal, no. But some unsavory rumors have been connected with a man she has been known to keep company with."

"Do tell." Lady Carmichael leaned forward, her face more animated than Edith had ever seen it.

Like a coconspirator, Edith also leaned forward, lowering her voice. "Apparently, my seamstress started keeping company with a young doctor who was new to her area. One day, two strangers appeared and started asking after the doctor. No one knew anything about any of the three men. Then last week, the doctor suddenly disappeared and has been gone ever since. Mr. Carmichael says the two men were debt collectors and the doctor is an unrepentant gambler." Edith gave a delicate shudder and shook her head. "I always thought Miss Bainbridge of better character, but now that her true nature has revealed itself, I can breathe easier knowing I did not put my sister's presentation gown in such low hands."

Lady Carmichael stiffened and her eyes narrowed. "Surely you are not speaking of Miss Bainbridge?"

Edith widened her eyes in feigned shock and remorse. "Oh, dear, I had forgotten Oliver said you occasionally patronize her. But did he not tell you of the woman's . . . indiscretion? 'Twas he who told me, after all."

Oliver's mother looked down at the green silk gown she wore as if she wanted to tear it from her person. "Yes, I do occasionally use Miss Bainbridge's services. But if she has been keeping company with a reprobate, I am glad I do not currently have any gowns commissioned with her." She pressed the back of her left hand to her mouth. "Oh, dear."

"What is it, my lady?" Edith hoped she looked concerned instead of gleeful at her coup in eliciting such a reaction from the woman who seemed to know everything about everyone in Oxford long before anyone else.

"Oliver has invited Miss Bainbridge to the servants' ball. Now that I know she is a loose woman, I am worried . . ." She let her voice fade out.

"About what?" A trickle of concern seeped into Edith's consciousness.

"Worried that he might be planning to make her his mistress—if he has not done so already. The last time he did something like that, we were out a tremendous amount of money, after sending the girl off to the country to have the babe in secret before giving it up to a barren marquess and his wife to pass off as their own."

Edith imagined that the fee they took from the marquess for securing the child in secret more than compensated them for whatever expenditure they'd laid out for the mother of Oliver's illegitimate child.

Her stomach knotted at the idea that Oliver had a child—a son most likely—out in the world somewhere. Not that she looked forward to carrying or bearing children herself. But if it had happened once before, what was to keep it from happening again? And while little scandal would be attached to an unmarried *Mister* Carmichael getting a working-class girl pregnant, it would be different for a married *Lord* Carmichael. This proclivity must be ended now, before they married.

A glance at the enormous clock in the corner of the room told Edith her fifteen minutes had expired. "Lady Carmichael, it was lovely to see you. I hope we might meet again in London." Edith stood.

"I imagine that with your sister's presentation, you and she will be invited to all of the best gatherings, so I am certain we will see each other again within the fortnight." Lady Carmichael inclined her head by way of farewell.

Edith dipped her curtsy, then turned and left the room.

It wasn't until the carriage was almost twenty minutes down the road from Chawley Abbey that it struck her. Lady Carmichael's revelation of the birth and subsequent hiding away of Oliver's offspring—the baroness would not have told just anyone about that. Since Edith had never heard of it, and the Buchanans and Carmichaels had known one another for as long as she could remember, the Carmichaels had been successful in keeping the issue quiet. No scandal had ever come about from it.

Lady Carmichael was testing her. If the secret leaked, Lady Carmichael would hear about it, and then she would know that Edith could not keep confidences. And that would give Lady Carmichael more ammunition to use in her war against Edith's marrying Oliver.

But if Edith could not find anyone else this season who would marry her—and who would elevate her at least as high as marrying Oliver would—she needed to still have the option of marrying him.

No matter how tempting sharing this information—at the right time, of course—with her friends might be, she must keep it to herself.

For now. If Oliver did anything to welsh on their arrangement, Edith now had the perfect ammunition to get him back in line. Perhaps, instead of testing Edith, Lady Carmichael's purpose behind sharing the family's deep, dark secret was the baroness's way of telling Edith she wanted her to marry Oliver.

⁂

Caddy watched as Letty pulled the hot rod from the lock of hair and it bounced over her shoulder in a perfect ringlet. She'd noticed the apprentice's skill with dressing her own hair long ago,

so she'd offered Letty an afternoon off next week in exchange
for helping her prepare for the ball at Chawley Abbey.

The mother-of-pearl comb sparkled at her crown, assisting
the hairpins in holding up the high knot from which the cascade
of curls fell to tickle her neck and exposed shoulders.

The ivory taffeta gown with its overlay of veil-thin silk embroidered with blue flowers had been made for Edith Buchanan . . .
who canceled her order after the gown was mostly finished. The
style had come from the spring *Godey's* magazine, so she knew
it was the height of fashion. She needed to be cautious with it
tonight; she'd keep it and sell it ready-made from the shop later.

"All finished, miss. And a fine head of hair you have too. It's
hard to tell with it always in a chignon or a snood." Letty eased a
couple more long curls over Caddy's right shoulder, where they
rested on her collarbone. "You look so much younger this way."

Letty's face went pink when she looked up and caught
Caddy's gaze in the mirror. "I'm sorry, miss, I didn't mean—"

Caddy laughed—but the sound ended as a choking cough at a
knock on her bedroom door.

Mother stuck her head in. "He's here. I have seen him into the
sitting room."

The tight-laced corset that allowed Caddy to wear the dress
would not allow her to breathe deeply, so instead she held her
breath and counted to ten. To twenty. To thirty. Finally, her heart
rate moderated. She took up the pair of fingerless lace mitts from
her small dressing table. With them securely in her left hand, she
lifted the overly full skirts and petticoats to make sure the fragile
silk tissue overskirt did not catch on anything and rip on her way
out of her room.

Outside the sitting room, she paused, squared her shoulders,
took a few shallow breaths, then opened the door. She measured
her steps to make the bell-shaped skirt sway just so.

Neal Stradbroke stood facing the fireplace, hands clasped behind his back. He turned languidly. Then he stiffened, his eyes widened, and his lips parted, and a low breath huffed out between them.

Pleasure heated Caddy's cheeks to what she hoped was a becoming color. "Dr. Stradbroke." She practiced the deep curtsy she would make when presented to the Baron and Baroness Carmichael in about an hour.

To her delight, Neal flourished a bow that wouldn't have been out of place in the court of Queen Victoria. "Miss Bainbridge." He straightened and re-clasped his hands behind his back, rocking from heel to toe. "If I may say so, you look lovely tonight."

"Thank you, kind sir." Caddy tried to simper, then laughed at herself for even attempting it.

"I see you have removed the bandage." He came forward and reached for her, brushing an artfully arranged wing of hair from her forehead to reveal the scar underneath.

"I could not have my hair washed and coiffed with it in place, could I?" She swallowed hard as she leaned her head back to continue looking into his impossibly blue eyes. Robin's egg blue. She had a bolt of brocaded silk just that color—it would make a beautiful waistcoat. Not that she had seen Neal wear any waistcoats that weren't dark enough to hide the signs of his trade—black, brown, navy. Tonight, he wore one of a dark purplish-indigo that made his hair look blonder, his eyes bluer.

She sighed.

"Did I hurt you?" He jerked his hand back from where his fingers had been gently probing the scar.

"No. You did not."

"Last night at tea, you mentioned you wanted me to come by tonight before you leave for your . . . event." His voice turned strained and his mouth settled into a firm line.

Caddy's heart gave a little thrill at the hint of jealousy. When she'd told him last night of Oliver's inviting her to the Chawley servants' ball, he'd almost choked on his tea. "Yes. I hoped I might be healed enough that you could remove the stitches."

The stoniness in his mouth extended up to his eyes. "No. You are not healed enough. Besides, you will have to wear a bandage for several more days after I remove the stitches, as it might bleed a little afterward."

Caddy knew she should be disappointed, but the continued need for medical attention meant more excuses for seeing Neal—and for being in close proximity to him.

"How much longer do you think it will be?" Her voice came out raspy and breathy due to the strain on her throat from leaning her head back so far to look up into his face. When had she moved so much closer to him?

"Hmmm?" Neal's finger traced her hairline down her cheek to untangle her earbob from a wispy ringlet. "When?"

Caddy's breath hitched. "The stitches . . ."

"A few days."

"Oh."

His finger trailed down the cording of her throat, pausing over the pulse pounding there. His face eased into a dreamy smile. "Your heart is pounding."

"I know."

"Why?" A bit of slyness entered his expression.

Caddy didn't care. "Because you're here."

Neal bent and pressed his lips to hers, his hand stealing around to cup the back of her neck. Caddy raised up on her toes to get a better angle and slid her hand up his arm to encircle his neck.

When she'd told Alastair she would marry him, he'd kissed her. His dry, slightly rough lips had pressed to hers for the briefest moment. Until now, she had not known a kiss could be more—oh, so much more. Neal's soft, warm lips moved over hers, and she knew she had never truly been kissed before. She arched her neck back and to the right, and Neal wrapped his other arm around her waist, pulling her closer.

Caddy's limbs went numb, and the only things she could feel anymore were her lips and the heat building in her chest. She never wanted this moment to end.

Almost as suddenly as he'd started the kiss, Neal ended it. He released her and stepped back, breathing hard.

Caddy grabbed the back of the settee before she collapsed onto the floor in a melted heap.

"I beg your pardon, Miss Bainbridge. I should never have taken such liberty or forced myself upon your person."

Strength fueled by incredulity flowed back into Caddy's limbs, and she closed the gap between them, grabbing the lapels of his coat. "I do believe you may now call me by my Christian name, Neal. And you have nothing for which to apologize." She released his lapels and pressed her palms to his cheeks, forcing him to look down at her. "You did exactly what I have been hoping you would do for some time now."

Neal gently extricated himself from her grasp, capturing and holding both of her hands in his. "You say that now. But once you know the truth—"

A soft knock interrupted his thought. Mother entered the room, clearing her throat. "The carriage from Chawley Abbey is here for you, Cadence."

Neal kissed her clenched fists, squeezing his eyes tightly closed in the moment he lingered over the gesture. "I will see you . . . another time." He edged around her, took up his hat and kit, and with a nod to Mother, left the room.

Disappointment stung Caddy's eyes.

"Caddy, the carriage," Mother prompted.

"Tell them I am not coming. I cannot go to Chawley Abbey."

Mother entered the room, arms akimbo, expression stern. "You must. You do not tell me much, but I hear the girls talking. I know you have lost the business of many of your regular customers recently. You cannot afford to alienate Lady Carmichael at this of all times. I do not know what passed between you and Dr. Stradbroke just now—though by the looks on both of your faces, I imagine he stole a kiss. But no matter your feelings for him, you have a responsibility to your business to make an appearance in society and to assure the baroness there is no reason for her to take her patronage elsewhere."

Caddy's jaw hung slack. Mother had not lectured her like that in years. Not since before Father died. Obviously Neal's presence and attention had been good for her as well.

With a sigh—or as much of one as she could heave—Caddy accepted her shawl from Mother and swung it around her shoulders before stomping down the stairs . . . while still being cautious with the gown. Her kid dancing slippers did not make much noise, even on wooden stairs, more's the pity.

When she stepped outside, she gave the footman who assisted her into the coach no reason to think she was anything but happy and excited to be going to the ball.

She would go. She would be pleasant to all. She would toady to Lady Carmichael. But no one could stop her from dwelling on Neal Stradbroke and the fire—now banked to glowing embers— caused by his kiss.

CHAPTER TWENTY

*O*liver paced the vestibule just off the great hall, where all was prepared for the servants' ball. The coach bearing Cadence Bainbridge should have been here by now. Even though he could not lead off the dancing with her—no, that . . . *privilege* was reserved by tradition for his mother's lady's maid—he wanted to be certain to greet her and let her know, by deed if not by word, that she should consider herself the honored guest tonight.

That should soften her toward him.

He didn't have much time left in which to woo and win her before the Great Exhibition started. Especially since M'lady expected him to travel with her and Father to London on Monday and, once there, to stay for the duration of the season. If he were there and Caddy were here, he would not be able to work on breeching her defenses.

"There you are, Son." M'lady swept into the hall, her cloth-of-gold gown—or close approximation, anyway—glimmering in the dim candlelight. "I'd hoped to speak with you before the ball."

"About what?"

"About your connection with the unfortunate Miss Bainbridge."

"Unfortunate?" He crossed his arms and glared at M'lady. Though he'd made disparaging remarks about the seamstress to Doncroft and Radclyffe, hearing someone else speak of her less than kindly gave rise to something inside him he couldn't—or didn't want to—identify.

"Yes. Miss Buchanan called this afternoon and shared some interesting news with me."

Oliver listened with growing anger as his mother shared the gossip—nay, slander—Edith had poisoned her mind with about Cadence Bainbridge.

Taking a deep breath and dropping his arms to his sides, Oliver waited until she'd finished speaking. "I assure you, madam, there is nothing untoward between Miss Bainbridge and the doctor. Her moral fortitude is too high to countenance such a thing. Besides, she is not more than acquaintances with him, despite what Miss Buchanan might have told you. So his sins should not be visited upon Miss Bainbridge."

Though he'd started the speech out of habit of taking the opposite side of anything his mother supported or believed, by the end of his speech, he found himself growing heated in his defense of the seamstress.

Could it be? Could he have genuinely come to care for her?

No. Surely not.

M'lady arched her brows imperiously. "Believe what you will, Son, but those kind of people do not live by the same morals as we do."

He snorted. "No. Those kind of people almost always have higher morals than we."

With a snap of fabric, M'lady spun and stomped through the door to the great hall.

A bit off balance by his reaction to his mother's denigration of Miss Bainbridge, Oliver paced the entry hall.

He must win Miss Bainbridge over tonight. He could close the deal by getting her to agree to meet up with him at the Exhibition. Once she was put off her guard by the sights and sounds and inducements of London and the looser morals of town life, he would finish his seduction.

"My lord, my lady, Mr. Carmichael . . . Miss Cadence Bainbridge." The butler stepped aside and Caddy passed into the vestibule from the entry hall. Oliver had ordered the carriage driver to bring her to the main entrance, not the servants' door in the back.

Oliver found himself taken aback at her appearance. He'd never considered her a beautiful woman—she was too old for that appellation. She was handsome in her own way. Tonight, however, she came as close to beautiful as she might ever manage. And the gown she wore, with wispy gossamer over rustling taffeta, made her look like a princess straight from a Grimm fairy tale.

"Miss Bainbridge, you are a vision." He lifted her hand to kiss it, careful to touch his lips to the fingers left bare by the mitts she wore.

Her cheeks pinked at the compliment. "Thank you, Mr. Carmichael."

He offered her his arm and escorted her into the great hall. Her skirts billowed out like summer clouds when she dropped into a deep curtsy before his parents.

"Welcome, Miss Bainbridge." M'lady looked none too happy that the seamstress had entered through the front of the house.

"My lady, my lord. I cannot express my gratitude for the invitation to your home."

Oliver choked on a laugh. Caddy had been in this house more times than he could count, between fittings and deliveries of his mother's gowns. But he supposed she meant being a guest for the first time. He would remind her later that *he* had extended her the invitation, not either of them.

In high dudgeon, M'lady preceded them into the hall. Oliver's father stood beside her, looking at Caddy a few times, winking at her twice.

Oliver's stomach soured at his father's obvious attempt at flirting with Caddy. To this day, no one was certain if the servant girl's babe had been Oliver's or the baron's. Not that it mattered. The marquess had been happy to replace his wife's fourth stillborn child with a living boy with half an aristocratic pedigree.

Dressed in the closest thing they had to finery, the servants of Chawley Abbey lined the perimeter of the great hall, their anxiety and excitement almost tangible.

Oliver lay his free hand over Caddy's, where it rested lightly in the crook of his elbow. "I must begin the evening by apologizing for not dancing with you first. You see, there is a tradition to this kind of thing, which unfortunately dictates that I must dance with M'lady's maid first. And then the housekeeper, and then the head housemaid. But I trust you will not be too bored waiting for me to do my duty before I can get on to the pleasurable part of the evening." He tucked his chin and gave her his most charming look.

Caddy nodded. "Oh, do not concern yourself with me, Mr. Carmichael. I am certain I can make my own way tonight."

She sounded too cheerful when she said it. Oliver fought against a frown and a rebuke. Like a horse not quite broken, he must let her have her head for now. Soon enough, he would be reining her in and teaching her exactly how she was supposed to respond to him.

He walked her to an unoccupied corner of the large room, kissed her hand, and promised her he would be with her as soon as possible.

He'd just stepped out onto the floor with M'lady's French maid when he saw Caddy dancing with the footman he'd sent to fetch her. She laughed at something the gangly youth said and shuffled her feet to cover for the young man's misstep in the schottische.

The souring that had started with his father's obvious attempt at flirting with her turned into a full-blown stomachache as jealousy filled his craw. And it wasn't because he might lose the bet; he'd lost plenty to Doncroft and Radclyffe in the past, and he was certain he would lose more in the future. No. He could not fail in this because he did not want to think there was a woman alive who would fail to fall for his charms. Never before had a woman turned him down. Even when she initially said no, he'd managed to wheedle and flirt his way into changing her answer into a yes.

He would not allow Caddy Bainbridge to be the one woman who turned him down. Especially not now that he realized *he* had fallen under *her* spell.

The first three dances seemed interminable, but finally he pulled away from the tall, lean head housemaid and shot like a well-thrown dart to where Caddy was about to take the dance floor with Father's valet. The servant stepped aside as soon as Oliver held his hand toward Caddy.

"Oh, but I already told Mister—"

"No, miss, no." The valet wisely shook his head and backed away farther. "'Tis better you dance with Mr. Carmichael." He bowed and walked away.

Caddy frowned, then quickly changed her expression to one more neutral as she let Oliver lead her to the floor for a waltz.

"I must say, you look absolutely ravishing tonight, Miss Bainbridge." Oliver took the lead of the dance with a firm hand, but a few steps into it realized Caddy needed no tutelage on how to dance.

"Thank you, Mr. Carmichael."

"And you are a lovely dancer. Where did you learn?" He added an extra turn to see just how well she could follow him.

She did not miss a beat. "I learned in finishing school."

"Truly?" He frowned. Only wealthy families sent their daughters to finishing school. From everything he'd learned about the Bainbridges, they most definitely did not fit into that class, even before her father died. "Then how did you end up becoming a seamstress rather than entering society and becoming the wife of a rich merchant or squire?"

Color rose high in Caddy's cheeks, and her lips curled up in a half smile, but her eyes gave away her shock at such an indelicate question.

Not the way to win her affection, Carmichael, he chided himself.

"My father was friends with the headmaster of the school and saw to my admittance and continued enrollment. But even with the cost of tuition waived, I still needed money for books, clothing, and other sundries. So I used a skill learned at my mother's knee and from a family friend to repair and create gowns for my schoolfellows. When I completed school, I apprenticed with the same family friend in her shop in London before returning here to use what I had saved to start my shop. My former classmates were among my first customers and are still the most valued ones."

"I am certain your father would have been proud of your accomplishments." Oliver bowed as the waltz ended, then extended his hands to her for the polka the quartet in the corner started next.

Caddy looked over her shoulder at the valet and other male servants standing to the side for lack of female partners. But Oliver took hold of her hand and waist and led her into the rollicking steps of the dance.

"My father would have been more pleased to see me as the wife of some wealthy merchant or squire. That was why he arranged for me to attend school." She pressed her lips together as if to indicate there might be other reasons her father would not have been proud of the person she'd become, but Oliver knew better than to push the point. Aside from the fact that he really did not care for the details of the seamstress's background and relationship with her vicar father, he'd never had romantic success with a woman who had been pushed to delve too deeply into the emotional turmoil of her past.

Oliver would have been content to dance with her all night—telling himself it was because she was by far a better dancer than any of the servants. But as soon as the polka ended, his father cut in and whisked Caddy away for the next dance. Oliver excused himself to have a cup of punch with M'lady, who sat in her throne-like armchair overseeing the festivities with a slight frown. She kept a hawk-like watch on her lady's maid—the French puff who thought too highly of herself and was an accomplished flirt—so she did not notice when Father managed to maneuver Caddy to the edge of the room and then disappear with her down the darkened service corridor.

Knowing his father's intentions and worried for Caddy's virtue, Oliver hurried around the perimeter of the room and lifted a candelabra from a side table.

As he suspected, at the other end of the hall, Father had trapped Caddy against the wall and was doing his best against her struggles to try to kiss her and lift her skirts at the same time.

"I say, my lord!" Oliver put as much outrage into his voice as he could, but his heart had quickened at the glimpse of plain white stocking under the edge of Caddy's froth of petticoats. "Unhand her this moment."

The baron cursed and continued trying to maul Caddy. Oliver set down the candelabra and grabbed his father by the shoulder. Tomorrow, once his father was sober, he would most likely not remember his son's manhandling of him.

"Lord Carmichael, please, pay Miss Bainbridge the respect she deserves as a *guest* in our home." He took Caddy's hand and pulled her behind him. "I believe it is time for you to say your good-night, sir."

Oliver waited until the baron staggered the rest of the way down the hall to the stairs, then he turned to face Caddy. "I offer my most abject apologies, Miss Bainbridge. If I had known my father would behave so abominably toward you, I would never have let you dance with him."

He reached out and adjusted the lace fall on the short sleeve that rested just below the tip of her shoulder. When his fingertips inadvertently brushed her skin, she jerked back. Here was no wanton who pretended outrage with one man only to fall into the arms of her rescuer. He'd guessed she'd be more prudish than that.

"Come, let us get you back to the society and security of the ball."

"If you please, Mr. Carmichael, I know it would be a great imposition, but I would very much like to go home." She smoothed the wing of hair over her forehead with trembling fingertips.

"Yes, of course. I will drive you myself."

Her eyes widened, and she gasped. "Oh no. I could not ask that of you."

"But I cannot ask the driver and footman to leave the ball. It is their one night of frivolity before going back to the daily drudgery of work. Besides, I feel responsible for what happened here tonight. Driving you home is the least I can do." He offered his arm to escort her back to the great hall, taking up the candelabra with his free hand.

"Then I accept." She lightly rested her hand in the crook of his arm and allowed him to escort her back to the main part of the house.

Rather than the closed coach that had brought her, Oliver had arranged for his two-seater high-flyer to be made ready before the ball in preparation for driving her home. While he had not expected to be taking her home so early, he was pleased with how well his plans had turned out.

He tucked her in against the chill spring air, then climbed up and took the reins. "When do you think you will go to London to visit the Exhibition, Miss Bainbridge?"

"I had hoped to be there for the opening, but I was unable to secure tickets for that day. I shall go, instead, the week after. I understand that many of the items to be exhibited have not arrived yet, so there will likely be much more put out on display after the opening."

"I am looking forward to seeing all that the world has to offer. It has been a few years since my grand tour of the continent, and I am certain much has changed since then."

"Where did you go on your grand tour?"

If he were not mistaken, he heard genuine interest in her voice. He smiled into the darkness. "France, naturally, Spain, Italy, Greece, a summer in the Carpathian mountains, several other little countries in the eastern part of Europe, then Bavaria and France again."

"And which was your favorite?"

"Paris. No other place can compare. Not even London."

"I see." She sounded less enthusiastic now.

"If you could travel anywhere in the world, where would it be?" He needed to engage her, to make her want to see him and spend time with him.

"As a seamstress, I suppose I should say Paris, where the great designers are, or Italy, where they make such fine fabrics. But I am a country girl at heart. The wilds of America have always sounded fascinating to me. Or even farther away like . . . like Australia."

"Australia?" Oliver barked a laugh. "A land filled with brigands, thieves, and cutthroats? Why on earth would you want to go there?"

He felt her shrug against his shoulder. "I have heard that Australia is not as horrible a place as we may have been led to believe. I have been reading about it recently, and I learned of several expeditions of settlers—good Christian people—who chose to go to Australia to build new lives. And now that gold has been discovered, I am certain even more people will choose to make their lives there."

Considering she was the only "good Christian" person he knew, Oliver did not feel adequate to comment on her statement. "I suppose we should wait and see what happens in the next few years, then."

"Yes, I suppose." Her soft voice drifted away on the breeze, and Oliver had a feeling he'd lost her in a world of her own imagining.

They neared North Parade, so he needed to hasten the conversation along. "Miss Bainbridge, I wonder, if it is not too much of an imposition, whether I might ask you to wire me, or write to me, to let me know when you will be at the Exhibition so I can meet up with you and take you around to show you what I've discovered there."

"I . . . I do not know. I am certain you would much rather spend your time showing Miss Buchanan or some others of your own . . . circle of acquaintance around. I would not wish to be the cause of your being subjected to gossip and rumors."

He pulled the gig to a stop in front of her shop. Before he could get out and help her down, she climbed out.

"Thank you for a lovely evening, Mr. Carmichael."

He caught up with her at the door when she paused to fumble in her reticule for the key. "Miss Bainbridge, please say you'll meet me at the Exhibition." He could not let her go without a promise—he might not see her again otherwise.

"I cannot agree to meet you there." She looked up at him, her eyes gray in the waning moonlight.

He recognized the moment she softened toward him—she lowered her gaze and her square shoulders rounded.

"However, should I run into you, I would be happy to accompany you on a tour of the Great Exhibition."

Oliver grinned and raised her free hand to kiss the backs of her exposed fingers. "Thank you, Miss Bainbridge. I shall count the days until I see you again in London."

"But—"

"Nay—while you may not be able to promise to meet me, I do promise that I will try my best to see you there." He bowed and leapt back into the gig, waiting until she'd gone inside and locked the door behind her before driving off.

Now the only thing he needed to do was ensure she did run into him there. And though he'd begun learning his tactics from his father, he'd perfected them beyond his tutelage. Caddy would never try to push Oliver away when he cornered her and stole the kisses that would win his bet. And the Exhibition was by far the perfect place for it to happen. He'd scout out a corner where he could do it and make sure Doncroft and Radclyffe were there to see it.

Once that conquest was complete, he could resign himself to courting and marrying Edith Buchanan.

CHAPTER TWENTY-ONE

After completing his rounds in Jericho on Saturday, Neal bypassed the apothecary shop and headed across the street. Both Phyllis and Mrs. Longrieve were assisting customers when he entered Caddy's shop, and several others waited for their turns to have fabric or notions cut to their specifications.

He angled his head toward the door to the workroom, and Phyllis nodded with a shy smile and a blush that brought the illusion of contours to her thin cheeks. The woman whose fabric the shop girl measured gave him an appraising, almost knowing, look.

His breath caught in his throat. Unlike calling on a woman in her home, which might be kept somewhat private, Caddy Bainbridge's situation—with so many eyes observing her every move—ensured that everyone in North Parade knew he was courting her.

He stopped short of the door, his hand reaching out for the knob. Courting? Were they truly at that point? Nothing had been said to define their relationship, but yesterday's kiss made it impossible to think they were anywhere but on the road to the altar. And while he used to balk at the idea of marriage, he'd thought of little else since meeting Cadence Bainbridge. He could only hope—pray—she felt the same. Especially once she knew the truth.

And because of her he was praying again. The realization made him smile. She'd been a good influence on him, most likely without even realizing it. After all, he'd only returned to church because she was guaranteed to be there.

With a deep, calming breath, he opened the workroom door. His heart, however, was anything but calm when Caddy looked up at him. She knelt on the floor in front of a dress form, pinning the hem of a dress the rusty-orange color of a sunset.

He offered her his assistance in rising and did not want to release her once she was on her feet. But with Letty, Alice, and Nan looking on, he had no choice but to relinquish her hand.

Without a word, she led him from the workroom and up the stairs to the family quarters. But instead of the sitting room, she led him to the back of the apartment and opened the door to one of the bedrooms.

"Mother, Dr. Stradbroke is here."

Once Neal saw Mrs. Bainbridge, he was glad he had not stopped at home and left his kit there. He wrapped his free arm around Caddy's waist, both to give her a squeeze of reassurance and to move her out of the narrow passage between wardrobe and bed.

Mrs. Bainbridge's breath came in short gasps and the gray hue of her skin bore witness that this was no feigned illness. One touch to her forehead established that she had no fever, but his stethoscope confirmed the congestion in her lungs.

"It's pneumonia, isn't it?" Caddy hovered behind him, and her warmth seeped through his frock coat.

"I do not believe so. Lung infections are common among those with weak hearts. Has she been complaining of pain in her side?

Did she have a chronic cough?" He moved the stethoscope to listen to her lungs through her right side.

"She's had a chronic cough ever since I can remember, though it has sounded a little worse the last few days. But she has not complained of pain in her side, not to me. Mary?"

Neal glanced over his shoulder to see Caddy chewing on the tip of her thumb, her face drawn in anxiety. Mary rose from the straight-backed wooden chair in the corner of the room, her face almost as gray and wan as Mrs. Bainbridge's.

"She complained of pain only after her cough worsened and became more frequent."

Neal listened to his patient's left side—first her lung, then her heart.

"Nan and Letty were both ill earlier this week." Caddy pressed forward, her skirts now pressed up against his leg. "Nothing more than mild fevers and running noses and sneezing, but I tried to keep Mother away from them."

He straightened, set the stethoscope aside, and laid his hands on Caddy's shoulders, waiting until she turned her worried eyes upon him. "I am certain you did everything you could to minimize the risk to your mother." He looked over the top of her head to Mary. "I do not mean to sound indelicate, but I must ask. When she coughs is there any . . . discharge?"

Mary nodded. "Aye. Started off as a whitish yellow, but then became darker."

He blanched. "Any traces of blood?"

"Oh, no sir." She glanced at Caddy with a grimace. "Darker . . . yellow."

Neal drew a relieved breath, then returned his gaze to Caddy. Her face still turned up toward his, her eyes wide and searching. He lifted his left hand and ran his thumb along her cheekbone. "It sounds like bronchitis. I shall go to the apothecary and have him mix an expectorant elixir. She will need to cough out the congestion. It will take a few weeks for her to recover fully." He squeezed her shoulders. "But she will recover."

Her throat worked hard as she swallowed, and she blinked a few times. "Thank you."

Leaving his bag for the moment, he gently escorted her into the hallway, closing the door behind them. "Why did you not send for me?"

Caddy frowned. "Did you not receive my note?"

"No. If you sent someone with a note, he never found me."

"I left it at your flat. I thought you had seen it and that's why you came."

He chuckled and almost unconsciously brushed aside the wing of hair hiding her stitches. "I didn't stop at my flat. I came straight here . . . because I wanted to see you."

Even her forehead turned pink and warm with the force of her blush. "People are starting to gossip about the amount of time you spend here."

He cupped her cheek with his hand and leaned forward to kiss her forehead just at the hairline where the scar disappeared. "Let them. I have nothing to be ashamed of in people knowing that I fancy you."

A delicate shudder passed through her, and he smiled, placing another kiss at the soft V between her fine, dark eyebrows. Like hers, his breathing quickened. He raised his right hand and settled it on her waist, his fingertips pressing into the small of her back, drawing her closer.

"There is still so much we do not know about each other."

Neal kissed the bridge of her nose. "Yet that has not stopped us from falling—from forming an attachment." He wasn't certain what kept him from admitting he'd fallen in love with her, but he needed to be certain of her feelings before he proclaimed it.

Her eyes fluttered closed, and he dusted each eyelid with light kisses. Her hands came up between them to rest flat against his chest. He wished he did not have a coat and waistcoat to muffle the warmth of her touch.

To his astonishment, she pushed herself away from him. "No, Neal. It has not stopped us from forming an attachment. But I cannot—I will not—put myself into a situation in which I will likely be hurt again."

"Again?" He let his arms fall to his sides. "What do you mean?"

She turned and paced to the window at the end of the narrow hall. "When I was twenty years old, I was engaged to be married."

Neal's knees almost buckled. Caddy had loved another man? And loved him so much as to want to marry him? He swallowed hard. "Will you tell me of it?"

Caddy wrapped her arms around her middle as if trying to ward off a chill, even though the sunlight coming through the west-facing window heated the hallway quite efficiently.

When she did not speak, he resigned himself to the knowledge that she did not trust him. And why should she? He had shown time and again that he did not trust her with his deepest secret. He did not deserve to know hers.

With a sigh, he moved toward the bedroom door. Mrs. Bainbridge needed her cough medicine, and helping her get well was all he could do right now to continue working to gain Caddy's trust.

"His name was Alastair Hambleton."

Behind her, Neal's footsteps halted. Caddy could not turn to look at him. Once she told him this, once he knew how simple and gullible she'd been, he'd lose all respect for her.

"I met him in my last year of apprenticeship with Mrs. Gregson in London after my father's death. He was also an apprentice, to a solicitor whose office was in the same street. It started innocently enough. I would see him at the farmers' market or at church. He finally asked if he could walk me home one Sunday. I told him I wasn't allowed followers, but he said to think of him as a friend who wanted to ensure I arrived home safely."

The flow of air from the window turned chill, and Caddy pulled the sash closed. Her breath fogged the glass when she leaned her forehead against it.

Behind her, Neal made no sound, but she could sense his presence.

"After several weeks, instead of walking straight home, we took a turn around the park. He expressed such an interest in my work, and it had been long since I had anyone in whom to confide, that I shared more with him than I should have. He was so charming, so amiable. No man had ever paid such attention to me. I was flattered and beguiled into believing him in love with me, and I in love with him."

Warmth stole across her back, and she turned, breath catching in her throat at Neal's sudden nearness. She'd been so wrapped up in her memories that she had not heard him traverse the creaking wooden floor toward her.

"What did he do to you?" His blue eyes held an anger she had never thought to see there.

"Nothing to me, not exactly." She leaned against the windowsill, her head resting on the glass, cushioned by the thick coil of braid covering her back. "Through me, he learned which of Mrs. Gregson's clients were the wealthiest and which had the most to lose if they became involved in a public scandal." She dropped her gaze to his deep indigo waistcoat. "He . . . became close to the women, then compromised them. He threatened to tell their

husbands—or to provide proof of the affair to the newspapers—
and made them pay him to stay silent."

Neal clasped his hands tightly together and pressed his
thumbs to his forehead, drawing Caddy's gaze up once more. His
eyes were squeezed shut and his mouth formed a thin line.

Her throat closed. She knew he'd not take it well that she'd
allowed herself to become embroiled in such a scheme, even
unwittingly. "I became suspicious of his activities because he had
much more money than he should have as a lowly apprentice to
a little-known solicitor on the fringe of London society. I began
to pay closer attention to his activities. And I saw him flirting
with our customers. Then not just flirting, but climbing into their
carriages and being driven away by them, to return hours or even
days later. And we rarely saw those same women in the shop
again."

She turned to look out the window, unwilling to see the
certain censure in his eyes. "I did not confront him, though. I
believed myself in love with him, and I thought my love would
be enough to make him see the error of his ways and change.
So when he proposed marriage to me, I accepted. Three days
later, as we walked together in the park, several constables surrounded us and arrested him." She trembled at the memories
overwhelming her. "I was taken in for questioning and held for
three days."

Warm, strong arms wrapped around her from behind. Tears
pricked Caddy's eyes as Neal enveloped her with his strength,
but she could not accept the support he offered. She did not
deserve it.

"I told them what I suspected, and once they determined I had
not taken part in the scheme, they released me. But despite how
much Mrs. Gregson defended me, no one believed I was as innocent as I claimed. And I knew I was not completely blameless.

I should have reported him to the police as soon as I suspected him of wrongdoing."

Neal's chin rested on her shoulder, and he pressed his cheek to hers. "You are not responsible for what he did. You are as much his victim as any of those other women."

"Mrs. Gregson had to move her shop and change her name— she goes by Madame Renard now. Since she moved closer to the West End, her business has improved."

"I would count that a blessing that came from a terrible circumstance. I imagine she would as well." The vibration of his deep voice tickled her back, and his breath made her cheek tingle.

She tentatively rested her arms atop his, which encircled her waist, and she released some of the tension from her spine, absorbing the strength his embrace offered. "Madame Renard helped me return to Oxford and set up shop. Originally, I was in a tiny storefront several streets off of High Street in Oxford proper. When I learned of the development of North Parade, I was one of the first to purchase a lot and have my shop built."

"You have not been here long, then?"

"Only a little more than a year."

Neal huffed a low grunt. "Yet you are already well known and highly regarded throughout the area. The way people talk about you, it sounded as if you had always been here." He disentangled himself from her and turned her to face him. "Now I understand why you go to the castle each week, and why you give so much of yourself to take care of others and expect nothing in return."

She cocked her head, frowning. Gazing into his sapphire eyes, she almost forgot the subject of their conversation. "Why?"

"Because you feel like you owe the world for your sin of falling in love with the wrong man." He tucked a stray strand of hair behind her ear, his eyes searching hers. "Which is why you are afraid of falling in love again."

Caddy bit her lips, pulled away from him, and took a few beleaguered steps down the hall. "I am afraid of falling in love . . . with you." She rubbed her upper arms, suddenly cold now that she was away from his overwhelming nearness. "Do you not now see why honesty is so important to me? Why I refuse to give my heart to someone who cannot tell me all there is to know about himself? Someone who is obviously keeping a secret from me?"

She watched him carefully as he considered her words. The openness and, dare she think, love in his eyes vanished behind a wall of protection.

Holding back tears of disappointment, Caddy nodded and took in a shaky breath. "I see. Obviously you do not care enough about me to share your secret with me." She crossed her arms and took a few steps farther back. "I thank you for tending to my mother, Dr. Stradbroke, but once she is recovered from this illness, I believe we will once again depend on the services of her former physician."

No longer able to face him, she turned. Instead of entering her mother's room, she went into her own, closing the door firmly against him just as tears began sliding down her cheeks.

She pressed her back to the door and slid down to sit on the floor, burying her face in her apron and allowing herself the indulgence of silent tears. Why couldn't he love her enough to tell her the truth about himself? Surely it could not be as bad as what she had just shared with him.

The need to swear him to secrecy hadn't occurred to her until now. Of course, he was good—excellent—at secret keeping, so she had little concern that he would spread word of her checkered past. And she doubted that most of her customers who hailed from Jericho, those who had become the mainstay of the shop, would have cared.

But she had already seen how even a hint of scandal could affect her dressmaking business among the women from the upper echelon of Oxford society—and that based on rumors that had proven to be untrue. If her current customers learned she had once been held by the London police for three days . . .

A sob tore from her throat. She trusted Neal not to reveal her past to anyone. So why couldn't he trust her to do the same?

CHAPTER TWENTY-TWO

$\mathcal{N}$eal held baby Ivy in one arm and offered the other to assist Mrs. Longrieve down from the cab. He paid the fare and dismissed the driver. He could walk the distance to the inn where they had stayed last night to gather his bag before heading to the train station.

On the quay, he spotted a stout older woman in a dark blue dress who seemed to be scanning the crowd. He waited until she looked their direction, then waved. She nodded and bustled toward them.

"Dr. Stradbroke?" The wind gusted, and she raised a large hand to hold her bonnet securely to her head.

"Thank you for meeting us here." He motioned for Mrs. Longrieve to come forward. "Mrs. Longrieve, this is Mrs. Allison, the nurse I have hired to travel with you."

Mrs. Longrieve's finely boned jaw dropped open. "No, Doctor, I cannot—it is too much to ask of anyone else to suffer my fate."

"Pshaw." Mrs. Allison waved her hands in protest. "I do not know what fate you think you face, but let me assure you that you will find Australia a beautiful land with hospitable people ready to welcome you and your little mite."

"Are you . . ." Mrs. Longrieve looked between Neal and the nurse. "Are you from there?"

"Right you are, my dear." Mrs. Allison took the baby from Neal. "I came to England to bring my last dear charge to be finished off and presented, and had I not seen the doctor's posting in the paper, I might have gone mad with grief on the voyage home." She cooed and cuddled the baby. "But now I shall have days full of the joy of a bairn in my arms again."

"But I cannot afford—"

Neal stopped her with a hand to her arm. "Mrs. Longrieve, you do not need to worry about it. Mrs. Allison has been paid in full to see to you until you arrive safely at my family's estate in Bathurst."

Winifred's pale brows shot up. "Estate?" Her voice came out a weak rasp.

He chuckled. "It is a rather grand word for a place where cattle and sheep are raised, is it not? But do trust that you will be well looked after, as will Ivy, and that your husband and son will be welcomed as soon as their time of service has passed."

"I will be allowed to work to earn my keep, yes?"

"Naturally. I knew you would have it no other way. But you will be cared for and looked after until your family can be reunited." He handed her single large valise to the sailor loading luggage onto the small ferry that would see them out to their ship. "Please write when you arrive and are settled. So long as nothing happens to the ship on which I sent the letter to my family, they should be expecting your arrival. And they should already be at work to discover exactly where Thomas and Johnny have been sent to serve their time."

He handed her an envelope. "Here is a letter of introduction, just in case my previous letter has not arrived by the time you do."

She tucked the letter into her reticule. "I do not know how we will ever be able to repay your kindness, Dr. Stradbroke. Truly you have been too, too kind to us."

"Your family was among the first to welcome me to Jericho. Consider this repayment for your hospitality and friendship."

"True friendship never needs to be repaid." She gave him a watery smile, then gave him a quick kiss on the cheek. "Thank you, Doctor. For everything."

He waited until the ferry reached the large steamer out in the harbor before leaving the port and walking up Portsmouth's High Street to the inn. The walk from there to the train station was short, and he arrived in plenty of time to catch the train to London.

No matter how much he wanted to return to Oxford and set everything right with Caddy, he'd given his word that he would return to London to assist Macquarie and Birchip for the remainder of the week. He'd let his regular patients know, and had arranged for the apothecary's assistant to check on them while he was away. But he had not had a chance to inform Caddy of his planned absence.

What would she think of him disappearing for almost a week after their last encounter?

A few hours later, he climbed out of another cab and entered the gate of Hyde Park after showing his committee credentials to the soldiers guarding it. Before him, the Crystal Palace sprawled like a giant glass-and-iron mountain range, so long that the opposite end disappeared into the misting rain and fog. He entered through the eastern end of the building and made his way down the enormous structure, cringing at the noises of hammering, sawing, yelling, and banging that naturally came with the activity of building display spaces and breaking open shipping crates and setting up for the Exhibition.

Just past the south entrance, in the center of the third mile-long expanse, Neal caught sight of several familiar faces. Macquarie waved him over to join the group as they stood looking toward the south.

"We're behind the Canadian exhibit?" Neal stopped behind Macquarie and three other committee members who stood with arms crossed.

"Aye. And a display from the West Indies is between Canada and us." Macquarie shrugged. "No sense in complaining. At least New South Wales has its own designated display space. None of the other colonies do. They are displaying in an area they're calling the British Possessions of Australasia."

"I received the wire that the shipment from my father's estate arrived two days ago." Neal followed Macquarie beyond Canada and the West Indies to the smaller-by-half space allotted for New South Wales.

"I went to the docks myself to receive it." Macquarie waved toward a towering stack of crates. "Your father's goods arrived with a shipment of goods from several other estates."

Neal divested himself of coat and waistcoat and untied his cravat. "Shall we start unpacking, then?"

Macquarie gave him a crooked smile. "In a hurry to be back on your way to Oxford? No sense in denying it. Do not forget, I had the honor of meeting the charming seamstress who caught your eye."

Neal grimaced and turned to lift down a small crate from atop the pile.

"What? Am I wrong in believing I saw signs of affection there?"

With no one else he could talk to, words tumbled out of Neal's mouth before he could stop them. "No, you did not imagine it. However, I have made a total blunder of it all, and I do not know how to rectify the situation before I lose her completely." He explained Caddy's disparagement of Australia and everyone from there, along with her displeasure at his inability to trust her. He did not, however, share Caddy's secret. He would take that to his grave.

"Just tell her, mate. If she loves you, where you were born won't matter."

Neal pried the top off of a second crate and handed the hammer and pry bar to another man before unpacking the fur pelts—skins from animals he should be able to identify, but which he had not seen in twenty years. He'd been but a boy last time he'd seen a kangaroo or a wombat, and trying to tell the pelts apart was impossible, for him at least. Would Caddy understand why that made him sad? Why he wanted to go back for a long visit? Or would she balk at the idea of visiting his father and stepmother, aunt and uncle, based on her fear of a land of which she'd only heard bad things?

He wanted to believe Macquarie. And perhaps, once his role in the Royal Society for the Industry of New South Wales was complete, he would tell her.

Neal threw himself into the physical labor of unpacking and then breaking down the crates. Day after day, he worked himself to exhaustion unloading, creating and checking inventory lists, and moving items around the display space as directed by the more senior members of the committee.

He ensured everything his father had consigned for display had arrived and was properly labeled—wool, grain, caskets of the fattest salted beef, copper ore and tools, and lithographs depicting the rich farm and grazing land around Bathurst, as well as the town and its citizens.

He nearly devoured the lithographs—recognizing his aunt's precise hand in the fine ink lines. He had a stack of pictures at home that she'd drawn for him and sent him over the years; images that kept him connected to his true homeland, the place of his birth.

If he showed those to Caddy, maybe she would begin to understand why Australia—or New South Wales, at any rate—was not as bad as she believed.

Somehow he had to get past her prejudice to show her the good of the place so that, even if she never came to love it, she could at least appreciate it. Because now more than ever, after seeing all these reminders of the place, he wanted to take her there. And to introduce her to his family as his wife.

⟡

Edith's chest burned at the sight of her cousin Kate entering the sitting room on the arm of Stephen Brightwell, Viscount Thynne. But she reminded herself of the announcement that would be made at dinner, and she found a true smile.

"Cousin Katharine. Lord Thynne. Do come meet the baron and baroness." Edith beamed at them. Kate seemed taken aback by Edith's friendly demeanor and lagged behind Lord Thynne until he appeared to be pulling her by the arm. She recovered herself and regained his side.

Edith introduced them to Baron and Baroness Carmichael, and after the pleasantries, Oliver gave his greetings to them. Once all of the guests arrived, Edith graciously positioned Kate and Stephen at the door to lead everyone in to dinner.

Between his escorting Kate into the dining room and his assisting her with her chair, Lord Thynne's connection to Kate was obvious and every head in the group of guests nodded in understanding. Tonight Sir Anthony would announce the engagement of his niece to the viscount.

And then Edith would make her announcement. She glanced down the table and smiled sweetly at Oliver as her father assisted her with her chair.

Lord Thynne came around and took his place at Edith's left hand. She smiled across the table at Kate as if there had never been any enmity between them.

Edith relished the soup course, knowing what would come at the end of it, sending an empty bowl back with the footman to the kitchen. She dabbed at the corners of her mouth with her napkin, then beamed at Papa when he stood and raised his glass.

"Friends, thank you for coming. Three days ago, we celebrated my daughter Dorcas's presentation at court, and many of you joined us here for the reception afterward. Ladies and gentlemen, Miss Dorcas Buchanan."

Wishes for health and happiness followed the raising of glasses. Dorcas blushed prettily. Edith stopped herself from a sardonic lift of her eyes heavenward and raised her glass in honor of her sister.

Several people put their glasses down, but picked them up when Sir Anthony raised his again. "Tonight, we have more good news to celebrate. Please join me in congratulating Lord Thynne, whose proposal of marriage to my niece, Miss Katharine Dearing, has been accepted."

The guests tittered and wished Kate happiness and congratulated Lord Thynne. Edith kept a smile plastered on her face as Kate blushed and feigned embarrassment. Edith knew better. The scheming fortune hunter had been after this since she arrived in England. But that was all about to end.

Papa had just regained his seat when Edith stood, heart racing with anticipation. "Father, may I say something?" She beamed such a smile across the table at her cousin that Kate's face drained of color. Ah, so she was worried. As well she should be.

"Yes, Edith, of course. I am certain your cousin and Lord Thynne would be happy to hear your best wishes." From his tone and expression, he obviously had no idea what his niece had been up to mere hours ago right in his own back garden.

Edith raised her glass. "To my cousin Katharine. You came as a poor relation to snare a rich husband, and you performed beyond everyone's expectations."

Gasps and whispers followed this statement. Papa stood. "Edith, that is quite—"

"And to Lord Thynne. May you find happiness in your choice of a wife. And may you be ever ignorant of her true nature—or at least possess the ability to turn a blind eye when you find her sneaking out of the house to carry on an affair with the landscape architect you have hired to redesign your gardens."

Lord Thynne's chair crashed to the floor. A phalanx of voices swelled around Edith, but she had no attention except for the woman seated across the table from her. Within minutes, the dining room was cleared of everyone save Edith, Kate, Lord Thynne, and Papa.

Lord Thynne paced the length of the room behind Edith, but she could not pull her gaze away from Kate long enough to gauge his reaction. Finally, he stopped to stare into the fireplace behind the chair in which Sir Anthony sat slumped, hand over his eyes.

"I must speak with Katharine alone."

Kate flinched at the viscount's soft voice. Papa lowered his hand from his eyes and pushed himself unsteadily to his feet. He wrapped his hand around Edith's, squeezed painfully, and dragged her from the room.

"What was the meaning of that?" He grabbed her by the shoulders and shook her. Edith's sense of triumph vanished. Never before had her father laid a hand to her in anger. In fact, she had never seen him so angry in her life.

"I am telling the truth, Papa. Kate kissed the garden designer this very morning. And it is not the first time. They sneaked off for an assignation in the garden folly several weeks ago too."

"How do you know of this?" Sir Anthony shook her again, then snatched his hands back as if only now realizing what he was doing.

If she told her father she'd had one of the maids follow Kate to see if she would do anything that Edith could use to break up the engagement with the viscount, Papa would not be happy with her. "My maid told me. She was . . . out for a walk and saw them go into the folly together, then close the door. She was curious, so she peeked through the window and they were kissing."

Papa rubbed his hands over his eyes and then through his silver hair. "Why did you not bring this to my attention—privately?"

"I thought nothing of it, then. At the time, Kate and Lord Thynne were not engaged." And that was true. She'd wanted better ammunition to use against her cousin than one stolen kiss on a rainy afternoon.

The dining room door opened, and Lord Thynne came out into the hallway. Edith's heart leapt. Surely he would thank her for saving him from marrying a faithless woman and show his gratitude by asking for Edith's hand in return.

"Sir Anthony, would you please come in for a moment? There is something I need to discuss with Miss Dearing, and I believe you should be present."

Papa nodded, then turned back to Edith. "Go up to your bedroom. We are not finished with this conversation."

Edith almost laughed at her father's severity. Once he witnessed the dissolution of Kate's engagement, he would be thrilled to come to betrothal terms for Edith to marry the viscount.

In her room, Edith sat at her dressing table and examined herself in the mirror. She imagined herself at a state dinner at Buckingham Palace, answering to the name Lady Thynne. She had never seen the Thynne viscountess's coronet, but she was certain it would look magnificent in her raven hair. And the gowns she would have . . .

She sighed. No more lowering herself to visiting a dressmaker's shop. No, the finest modistes patronized by the other ladies of the high aristocracy would clamor for her business. She would finally be able to tell Lady Carmichael exactly what she thought of her. And she would laugh behind her fan at, if not give the cut direct to, whatever woman Oliver ultimately convinced to marry him.

Once she had given Lord Thynne an heir, she might even take Oliver as a lover. If she could find no one better with whom to tryst.

Her bedroom door banged open and Papa marched in, her lady's maid following demurely behind. The young woman did not look up at Edith even after executing her curtsy.

"Pack up all of your mistress's belongings," Sir Anthony directed the maid in a chillingly calm voice.

Edith bounced from her stool, tripping over her petticoats, but quickly regaining her balance. "Papa, what—?"

"You are returning to Wakesdown on the first train to Oxford tomorrow morning." He turned to leave the room.

She ran across the rug and caught his sleeve. "What? Why?"

He once again took her by the shoulders, though this time he did not shake her. "I have grown tired of your antics, Edith. I overindulged you after your mother's death, so it is my fault your character is lacking. I spoke with your maid. She informed me—I believe honestly for fear of being turned out with no reference—that she followed your cousin Katharine at your behest and reported back to you on her activities."

"But if Kate had acted with propriety, there would have been nothing for her to report, would there?"

"That is not the point. Ever since your cousin arrived, you have been nothing but a contentious woman, inhospitable at best, downright vicious at worst. I know you are disappointed that Lord Thynne did not offer for you. I was as well. I invited him here with that very hope. But with the way you have been behaving the last few months, had he asked for your hand, I would have pointed out all the reasons he would not want it."

Papa leaned his head back, eyes closed as if in great pain. "You will leave for Wakesdown in the morning, where you will have time and solitude to think about what you have done and to pray for forgiveness."

Tears sprang to Edith's eyes—tears of rage rather than repentance. "But . . . the season. How will I find a husband if I am not here?"

"God save any man who would wish to court you when you behave thusly toward a member of your own family. You will return to London only at my invitation, once I determine you have had enough time away to change your ways."

He pulled away from her and left the room, softly closing the door behind him.

Edith threw herself across her bed and pounded her fist into her pillow. How dare her father speak to her so!

She would show him; she would show all of them. Edith Buchanan was not to be crossed.

CHAPTER TWENTY-THREE

$\mathcal{O}$liver escaped his mother's ranting by slipping up to his room as soon as the carriage arrived at their townhouse. All the way to the Buchanans' city home, she'd indulged in a tirade about how degrading it was that they'd accepted the invitation from the baronet—it would look as if she could not garner better invitations from those of higher rank in London. But then, to have been present when Edith Buchanan caused what might be the biggest scandal of the season—unthinkable! He wasn't certain she'd paused to breathe the entire drive home.

No doubt, when she recovered from the shock, she would be certain to tell all her friends exactly what happened because she had witnessed *everything*.

After freshening up, Oliver went back out, having the driver drop him at the club he and his friends frequented when in London. Not as posh as the more prestigious London establishments, Boodle's attracted politicians as well as aristocrats from the more rural shires. While Oliver didn't go in for politics, he found himself much more comfortable around the country set than the London snobbery he'd experienced at other clubs.

In a back room on the second floor, he found Radclyffe looking on as Doncroft finished a rousing round of cards.

Radclyffe looked at Oliver in surprise, then checked his pocket watch. "You are two hours earlier than you estimated."

Oliver nodded. "I shall tell you why when Doncroft can join us. This is a story that must be savored. But first—I'm half starved. Dinner was called off on account of . . ." He grinned at Radclyffe. "But I shall tell you of that shortly."

He motioned for a footman, and fifteen minutes later sat down to a steaming bowl of stew and a fresh loaf of bread. No ostentatious French food here. Just hearty country fare—the kind he got at home only when he went down to the kitchen and ate the food meant for the house staff before dinner. Though all he'd had at the Buchanans' tonight had been soup, he imagined Edith had set out a menu fit to please the most snobbish of society matrons, a few of whom had been present.

He chuckled, remembering the scene after the soup course. He could not have orchestrated his escape from his agreement with Edith any more perfectly. Given his mother's reaction, the recoil from the shot Edith had taken at her cousin would knock her off every invitation list for the remainder of the season. He could not marry a woman who had been given the cut direct by London society and make her the future Baroness Carmichael.

The last bit of gravy had been soaked into the heel of the loaf of bread when Doncroft joined them, jangling his coin purse before tucking it into his pocket.

"Either I am drunker than I realize, or you got here early." Doncroft slouched down into the chair opposite the small table from Oliver.

Oliver wasted no time in telling his two closest friends what had happened at the Buchanan townhouse tonight.

Doncroft crowed with laughter; Radclyffe frowned with what looked like genuine concern.

"Do not tell me you are sorry for the Dearing woman. If she was indeed sneaking kisses with the gardener, she deserves any censure that comes upon her." Oliver waved over a footman to clear his bowl and plate and refill his glass. He motioned his friends to three comfortable club chairs away from the roaring fireplace. Though outside, the evening had brought cold rain, inside, the club was more than warm enough without sidling up to a fire.

"It is not the Dearing woman I worry about. It is Miss Dorcas Buchanan—and how this will affect her season."

Doncroft leaned over and punched Radclyffe's arm. "All the better for you if it does affect her season. You knew the young bucks would swarm around her once they realized that a dowry the size of hers comes with such a pretty face. But if she is cut from the invitation lists, you have much less competition to court her and win her hand."

"You are right about that." Radclyffe's face transformed into a smile as he pondered Doncroft's words. "Though I would hate for anything to mar her debut season, I do actually hope that her sister's actions will mean she gets struck from the invitation lists."

Doncroft gave Oliver an exasperated look, and both shook their heads. Sometimes Radclyffe could be so simpleminded.

"What will you do about Edith Buchanan?" Doncroft asked.

Oliver shrugged as if he did not care. "She has broken our agreement and engaged herself in scandal. I am a free man now."

"I visited my mother today." Doncroft drained his glass and waved for a footman to refill it. "Apparently the dowager Baroness Cranston has returned to London now that her period of mourning is ended. While my mother told me this in hopes I would snag the young widow of a wealthy baron, I have my eyes set elsewhere."

Oliver leaned back in his chair, fingertips pressed together in a steeple. Baroness Cranston. If he recalled correctly from her debut around five years ago, she had been a pliable, buxom redhead with a pleasant laugh and a sweet smile. "She has no children?"

"None. But Baron Cranston was quite old."

Oliver tapped his fingers together. "Yes, quite old." He nodded and sat up straight, lifting his glass high. "Gentlemen, to a season of conquests."

They joined the toast.

"Speaking of conquests, how goes it with the seamstress?" Doncroft waved the footman over again and took the bottle of brandy from him before shooing him away.

Oliver tried to hide a grimace at Doncroft's question.

"Do not tell me you are losing the stomach for the seduction of the woman. Or has she turned you down outright?"

More than he hated hearing Caddy Bainbridge disparaged, he despised being teased, especially by Doncroft. "No, of course not. With Edith now out of the picture, I intend to escalate my plans for Miss Bainbridge."

Two hours later, Oliver climbed the stairs to his room in his parents' London home. His friends had been quite helpful in rounding out his ideas to close the deal with Caddy. Especially Radclyffe. The man had been a secret romantic all along. Dorcas Buchanan was bringing out the best in him.

Begging and pleading had not helped. Nor had tears. Edith dropped with more force than necessary on the plush seat of the private first-class compartment on the train. Not only was she being banished from London. But after all the trouble Edith had gone through to show Lord Thynne the kind of person her cousin was, he was going to marry her anyway.

At least Kate had to go stay at a home for wayward women until he returned from his holdings in Argentina to prove she could be faithful to him. Edith could take a modicum of pleasure that she wasn't the only one being punished for Kate's perfidy.

When her maid opened her mouth to speak, Edith quelled her with a quick glare, and the girl left the compartment to go ride in third class.

The trip home seemed to stretch out forever, but they arrived in Oxford before noon. True to his word, Papa had wired ahead to alert the Wakesdown staff to send a carriage for her. The trunks full of Edith's gowns, the ones she'd had made in London as well as those made in North Parade, weighed down the back of the carriage and made the ride bumpier than usual.

Halfway to Wakesdown, Edith banged on the roof of the coach with her parasol. It rolled to a stop and one of the footmen opened the door. "Yes, Miss Buchanan?"

"Take me to Miss Bainbridge's shop."

He looked down, uncertain. "That is on the other side of Oxford, miss. Are you certain?"

Edith leaned forward, shaking the tip of her parasol in his face. "I am certain that if this carriage does not turn around in five seconds, there will be a driver and a footman without jobs once we return to Wakesdown."

"Yes, miss." He closed the door, and about ten seconds later, the carriage made a wide, cumbersome turn and headed the opposite direction.

Edith did not look in her maid's direction, as she did not want to see the confusion written on the young woman's face.

If she could not keep her cousin from marrying the viscount, the least she could do was ensure that Oliver did not engage in an affair with her seamstress.

The trip from the west side of Oxford, back through town, and then up to North Parade took almost an hour. By the time the carriage rolled to a stop, Edith found herself wishing she'd gone home and seen to this task tomorrow.

She straightened her skirts as soon as she stepped down to the walkway, feeling a momentary despair at the wrinkled state of the wool organza. But that was only until she saw the handsome giant of a man with light hair standing outside the shop door, staring at it as if trying to will himself to enter.

Edith's mouth went dry at the sight of him. She'd seen tall men, and she'd seen handsome men—some of the handsomest England had to offer. But she had never seen one built like this one: broad shouldered, lean waisted, and long legged.

Mayhap she would allow Oliver his little dalliance with the seamstress if she could strike one up with this man.

Before she could speak, he entered the shop, a determined set to his square jaw. Edith followed him, her curiosity making her forget why she'd come here in the first place. Why would a man like him be entering a women's dress shop alone?

Edith's eyes were still adjusting to the dimmer interior of the store when Cadence Bainbridge emerged from a door behind the counter that ran across the end of the narrow room.

"Dr. Stradbroke, how may I be of—" The seamstress broke off when she saw Edith behind him. "Miss Buchanan. What a pleasure to see you. How may I be of assistance?"

The doctor turned and stepped aside, allowing Edith to sweep past him. She swung him a sultry glance before stepping forward to accept Miss Bainbridge's greeting.

The bell on the front door jangled again.

"Special delivery for Miss C. Bainbridge." The messenger, in the train company's livery, held a letter-size packet aloft.

Caddy stepped forward and extended her hand for the delivery. "I am Miss Bainbridge."

After she signed his delivery schedule, he handed her the parcel.

She slid it into the pocket of her apron, then started to turn back toward Edith.

"If you please, miss, I'm to wait for a reply."

Edith swallowed her groan of frustration and shot the handsome doctor another inviting glance. But he wasn't looking at her. His eyes were fixed on Cadence, watching her long fingers untie the twine that held the packet together.

When she unfolded the exterior parchment, four smaller pieces fell onto the floor.

The shop girl who stood nearby bent to pick them up, then squealed in excitement. "Oh, Miss Bainbridge. Passes to the opening day of the Great Exhibition—and train tickets to London! Whoever is it from?"

"Never you mind—"

But the girl, who could not be any older than Dorcas, sneaked a glance at the letter over Caddy's arm before the seamstress could hide it.

"Mr. Oliver Carmichael." The shop girl danced around with the passes and tickets. "Opening day of the Exhibition." She stopped. "You will get to see the queen in person!"

The other women in the store crowded around the shop girl.

Edith thought she might be ill. Oliver had sent passes—which were not easy to come by—and train tickets to Cadence Bainbridge of all people? Why hadn't he sent them to the woman he was planning to marry?

She stormed out of the shop and flung herself into the carriage. "Take me home!"

Oliver had thrown the gauntlet now. She would return to London and arrive in time to thwart anything he might be planning to do with Miss Bainbridge. She did not know how yet—for Father surely would not be happy to see her show up on the doorstep of his house before he decided to lift his banishment. But she would do it. Somehow.

Neal closed his eyes, waiting for a shattering sound when Miss Buchanan slammed the front door. But instead of the windows breaking, he felt as if shards of glass had pierced his heart.

Why would Caddy even consider him as a suitor when she had the only son of a baron courting her? He forced his eyes open, ready to leave, but the messenger blocked his exit.

"Phyllis, that is quite enough, thank you." Caddy held out her hand, palm up, her expression stern.

The shop girl stopped dancing around and placed the passes and tickets in Caddy's hand.

Finally, Caddy turned to face Neal. "I—"

But whatever it was, she could not bring herself to say it. She stalked from the shop back into the workroom.

He should leave, and he should do it now while she was gone. But the messenger still stood in front of the door, and Neal's riding boots seemed to have grown roots into the floor.

Several long minutes later, after Phyllis had returned to cutting fabric and the other customers to picking out ribbons and buttons, Caddy returned, drawing everyone's gazes. Behind the counter, she pulled out sealing wax and folded a new note around Mr. Carmichael's and the passes and tickets. She made sure everything was held within the parchment before sealing it and then tying it up with twine.

She handed the packet back to the messenger along with a coin. "Please see this is delivered to Mr. Carmichael in London by the next train. No response is necessary."

An ember of hope flickered to life in Neal's chest. He could not have mistaken that for anything other than Caddy turning down Mr. Carmichael's generous gift. And she wouldn't have done that unless . . .

She gave him a tight-lipped nod, then spun on her heel and returned to the workroom, closing the door between them.

Well. That hadn't been quite the response he'd hoped for. But she had acknowledged his presence. That was better than yesterday and the day before, when she'd seen him in the street and looked right past him.

He sighed, then looked down at a feather-light touch on his sleeve. Small, precocious Nan stood there looking up at him. With a crook of her finger, she motioned for him to lean over. He crouched, balancing himself with one knee on the floor. "Yes, Nan?"

She leaned forward until she was almost cross-eyed keeping eye contact with him. "Do not give up, Dr. Stradbroke. Miss Caddy might be angry at you right now, but I know she misses you. I've seen her staring out the windows at the apothecary shop or whenever she thinks you might go by on the street."

The ember of hope ignited into a flame at the girl's words. "Thank you, Nan."

"She really does want to go to the opening of the Exhibition. She just doesn't like that Carmichael fellow, and I don't either." Nan nodded, grinned, then skipped away to continue sweeping the floors.

Caddy wanted to go to the opening of the Great Exhibition. Neal was in a position to get her a pass—several, in fact—if he acted quickly. But would Caddy accept the peace offering, or would she turn him down as unceremoniously as she had Mr. Carmichael?

Only one way to find out.

CHAPTER TWENTY-FOUR

*N*eal had been in London for a week after taking Mrs. Longrieve and Ivy to Portsmouth. He'd come back for three days and then left again. And now, more than a week after that awful scene he'd witnessed when she'd received the delivery from Oliver Carmichael, he was still gone.

Caddy punched her pillow and tried to get comfortable. But ever since she'd told him about Alastair, she'd been unable to sleep, not knowing if there was any chance that they could find happiness together.

She climbed out of bed and sat in the chair beside her window. Across the street, the windows of Neal's apartment were dark, as they'd been the past several evenings. Of course, if he'd been home, a lighted window this late at night would have meant something bad had happened somewhere for the doctor to be awake.

Caddy turned her eyes up to the star-strewn sky. As a child, when she couldn't sleep, the advice her father had given her was to pray. For letting anxiety or worry needle her until she could not sleep kept God from being able to do His work. Or so Father had said.

"Gracious God in heaven," Caddy whispered, her breath fogging the window, "I miss him." Now who wasn't being completely honest? "I love him. I want to be with him. But how can I when he can't trust me? The only thing I can think is that his secret is something that will hurt me deeply. Therefore, I need Your help. Whatever it is, whatever secret he is keeping, change my heart, Lord, to be able to accept the truth, no matter what it is." She went on to pray for her mother and her continued recovery from bronchitis, for Mary, Phyllis, and the apprentices. "And please watch over Neal, dear Lord. No matter where he is, let him be safe and know that he is loved. Amen."

Shivering, Caddy climbed back into the bed and drifted almost immediately to sleep.

The next several days were busy, finishing orders for women who hadn't canceled their requests for gowns to wear to the opening of the Great Exhibition. With each stitch, Caddy tried to convince herself she was not jealous. She'd held two passes in her hands. It would have been so easy to accept them and go, to tell herself that it meant nothing.

But she could not have abided that lie. It would have meant something to accept such a gift from a man like Oliver Carmichael. The latest bit of gossip about Oxfordshire's most sought-after bachelor was that he was courting a young dowager baroness just come out of mourning and seemed very likely to marry her.

Caddy snorted. That must not sit well with Edith Buchanan.

She set her hands down in her lap and closed her eyes, praying for forgiveness for such an uncharitable thought. Edith Buchanan was obviously a very unhappy woman, and the only way she had found to cope with her misery was to take it out on others.

Out in the shop, the bell on the front door clanged—a sound that had become more and more common as the time for the opening of the Exhibition drew nigh. The sound filled Caddy's heart with both gladness and dread. She was thankful for the extra business to make up for that which she'd lost due to the rumors about Neal. But she dreaded the idea that she might get to the point where she could no longer accept any more orders and would have to turn potential customers away.

A light tap preceded the workroom door opening. "Miss Bainbridge, there's another special delivery for you." Nan's brown eyes sparkled.

Caddy groaned and set her sewing aside. Letty and Alice, who'd been told the story of Oliver's delivery, exchanged significant looks, and their giggles followed her out into the shop.

Instead of a messenger, however, *he* stood there. Neal Stradbroke, his golden-brown hair gleaming in the sunlight streaking in through the windows behind him, stood just inside the front door, hands clasped behind his back.

He gave her a smile when he saw her, but it was tenuous at best. He extended a thin packet toward her with a slight bow. "Special delivery for Miss C. Bainbridge."

Once she took it from him, he reached behind him for the doorknob. "No reply is necessary." He disappeared into the mid-morning glare.

Caddy carried the letter upstairs to her room and closed the door, ensuring privacy.

She slid her thumb under the seal and popped it open. As had happened with Oliver's delivery, other slips of paper slid out when she unfolded the outer parchment.

In Neal's no-nonsense handwriting, she read:

Monday, 28 April 1851
North Parade, Oxfordshire

My dear Miss Bainbridge,

Please accept the enclosed as tokens of my regret for having hurt you by what I have done and said. Or, to be more precise, what I have not said. I have been selfish in not telling you the truth about myself, meaning only to guard against personal pain and sorrow, not thinking of what it was doing to you.

There is so much I need to tell you, so much of my heart I want to share with you. But before I can, I need to know if you can forgive me for hurting you so.

You need not reply to let me know whether you accept my peace offering or not. If you do, please meet me near the south entrance of the Crystal Palace behind the Canadian timber display on the first of May at eleven thirty in the morning. If you do not come, I will have my answer.

Yours affectionately,

N. Stradbroke

Caddy lifted the smaller of the two scraps of paper that had fallen to the coverlet. A pass for the opening day of the Great Exhibition. Unlike the one Oliver had sent, which would have allowed her to sit in the stands near the stage to listen to Queen Victoria's opening address, Neal's ticket was general admission, granting the bearer admittance but no special privileges once inside. The other, larger piece was a train ticket. Not first class, as Oliver's had been, but still the comfort of second class.

She pressed the pass and ticket to her lips to muffle her cry of happiness, then looked up toward the ceiling. "Thank You, Lord."

To keep the letter, ticket, and pass safe, she tucked them into the front of her father's Bible, which she kept beside her bed. Back downstairs, she took her sewing up again with a joy she had not felt in many years—since long before Father died.

At dinner, with Mother, the apprentices Mary, Agnes, and Phyllis present, Caddy knew she had to tell them.

"I will be taking my trip to London earlier than expected."

Everyone looked up from her dessert, eyes wide.

"How much earlier?" Mother asked.

Caddy cleared her throat. "I am leaving day after tomorrow."

"But that means . . ." Nan counted on her fingers. "That means you are going for the opening."

"I thought you sent the tickets back to Mr. Carmichael." Phyllis licked her spoon before setting it down.

"I did. I received an invitation from someone else to attend on opening day, and I am accepting it."

Mother's pale blue eyes lit up. "Does this have anything to do with the special delivery that Dr. Stradbroke brought today?"

Caddy's cheeks burned. "Yes. Tomorrow, I will wire Madame Renard and let her know to expect me a week early. I leave on the eleven o'clock train Wednesday morning.

The rest of the evening was spent with everyone crowded into Caddy's small room, advice flowing freely as to which gowns she should take to consign in Madame Renard's shop and which one she should wear to the opening of the Exhibition.

After sending the girls upstairs to bed and getting Mother and Mary off to do the same, Caddy collapsed onto her bed among a froth of gowns and petticoats.

If her suspicions were correct, Wednesday, the day before the opening, the train would be so crowded that a large trunk full of clothing would not make her a favorite among other travelers in the second-class car. So she put everything away and packed only what she would need for a few days in town. She considered taking the gown she had worn to the servants' ball at Chawley Abbey, but the memory of what happened that night made her shudder and shove it to the back of her wardrobe. When she went back to London later this summer to take the girls and Mother to the Exhibition, she would be sure to take that gown to sell. Until then, she wanted it out of sight.

Besides, that was a ball gown. And even though many women would wear dresses fit for a dinner or ball due to the grandeur of the event and the presence of the queen and royal family, Caddy wanted to make sure she dressed in something that better suited her station in life. She was not a member of the gentry or aristocracy, nor would she become one through marriage, so she had no reason to dress as such.

She wondered what the wife of a doctor in a suburb of Oxford would wear. She smiled as her hand fell to the perfect dress. She had not worn it in a long time, which meant Neal had never seen her in it. And the bright color would ensure he would be able to find her. The last thing she wanted was for them to miss each other in the crowd and for him to decide she had chosen not to forgive him.

Edith arrived at the train station early Thursday morning. She yelled at the driver for stopping too far from the building, but when she climbed down from the carriage, she understood why. The station was mobbed with people obviously wanting to catch the first train to London to be sure not to miss the queen's opening speech.

As a holder of a first-class ticket, which she'd had the foresight to send a servant for last week, Edith was ushered through the crowd and to the front car of the train. But even first-class passage did not guarantee her privacy. She found herself sharing the compartment with a couple and their three boisterous children.

By the time the train reached London, Edith had mentally prepared a strongly worded letter that she planned to write to the railway company demanding that they ban children from first-class cars in the future.

Since she could not go to the house, as Papa still had not given her permission to come back, Edith followed the crowd from the station the half mile to Hyde Park. She had not yet managed to secure a ticket, but she was certain she would be able to get in.

Just her luck, several people outside the high fence surrounding the park were selling tickets. Edith balked at the price quoted her by the man she approached, but she pulled out the coins and paid him, taking the pass in exchange.

She ventured into the park in the slow-moving queue, but broke away from the teeming mass as soon as she could find room to walk. She found herself in a large garden, which would have been pleasant except for all the other people walking in it.

How would she ever find Oliver among these thousands of people?

And then, as if by a miracle, the crowd parted ahead of her and she saw him. Dressed in brown worsted, his light hair roguishly tossed by the spring breeze that threatened rain at any moment, Oliver seemed to be following someone through the crowd.

Edith lifted her skirts and hastened after him, slowing when she drew near enough to be certain it was him.

A light drizzle began, and almost everyone in the garden dashed for the doors at this end of the Crystal Palace.

Oliver, however, had caught up with whoever he'd been chasing down. With his hand clamped around her elbow, he turned the woman in the rusty-orange dress toward him.

Edith gasped and lifted her skirts to run toward them, but suddenly, an arm snared her around the waist and pulled her behind a large oak tree.

Reginald Doncroft pressed his fingertips to her lips to shush her, then leaned around the tree to observe Oliver.

Edith struggled to free herself from Doncroft's grasp, but he did not loosen his hold.

"Be still," he hissed, "and watch."

Oliver pressed Cadence Bainbridge against the base of a large statue and kissed her.

"I never thought he'd be able to do—"

The sharp crack of a slap cut off Doncroft's words. Cadence ran toward the building, rubbing the back of her hand across her mouth.

Doncroft laughed. "As I suspected. She'll never want anything do to with him. I warned him he should not put money on the chance of seducing a woman like that. Too prudish." Doncroft looked down at Edith, his pale eyes narrowed, head cocked as if seeing her for the first time.

"Are you saying he wagered that he could seduce my seamstress?" She clenched her hands into fists, ready to go after him and tell him exactly what she thought of that.

Doncroft caught her around the waist again. "As you can see, he did not win the wager, so there is nothing to worry about, is there?"

Edith struggled against him, but the heat coming from him made her want to draw closer as the drizzle turned to a genuine rain. "Release me this instant. I wish to go inside now."

"Do you?" He pressed her back against the tree. "Why are you so determined to marry Oliver Carmichael? You know he would never make you happy."

Edith snorted. "And you would?"

"You and I are of a kind, Miss Buchanan." He ran a finger down her neck, chasing a raindrop. "We understand each other."

"I do not know how you can say that when we have hardly ever spoken."

"We do not need words."

Edith barely had time to draw a breath before Doncroft lowered his head and kissed her, his lips ravaging hers, drawing from her a hunger she'd never experienced. She returned his kiss with equal measure, half passion and half loathing for the man who drew such a reaction from her. She knew all about Reginald Doncroft and his exploits. And she knew he would make any woman he married miserable with his penchant for seducing maids in back stairwells. But she could not deny her physical reaction to him, no matter how wrong it was.

A sharp gasp and a man's shout drew them back to the world of reality.

"Edith!" Dorcas stood under a large black umbrella held by Oliver's other friend, Radclyffe. He must have been the man who shouted. "What are you doing here? Are you intent on completely ruining our family's reputation? It is bad enough what you did to Kate, but now you allow yourself to be compromised too?"

Edith pushed away from Doncroft. "You are one to speak, out here alone with a man."

Dorcas gazed soppily up at Mr. Radclyffe. "Sebastian and I are engaged to be married. He was supposed to meet his friends in the garden, and I begged to come with him so we could tell them together." Dorcas folded her hands, prim as a schoolmarm, and frowned at Edith. "Were you so desperate to marry that you had to force a man to compromise you?"

When had her sister turned from a milquetoast into the tigress who now stood before her? Had falling in love given her so much confidence she could now stand up to Edith?

Beside her, Doncroft laughed. He yanked Edith back into his arms and kissed her again. Then he returned his attention to Dorcas. "I assure you, your sister has not been thoroughly dishonored. If a few stolen kisses necessitated a wedding, there would be many more forced marriages than there are." He touched the dripping brim of his hat, then jogged off toward the building, laughing.

Dorcas slid her hand into the crook of her fiancé's arm. "Father will be so angry if he learns you came back to London without his permission. You should probably go home—back to Wakesdown."

Edith wanted to scream at the unfairness of it all. Not even a month after her presentation, and Dorcas was engaged.

"Also, you should know that Oliver Carmichael has asked Lady Cranston to marry him and she accepted." Dorcas looked up at Radclyffe, then down at the gravel path. "I thought you had feelings for him, though now I am not so certain."

Edith was not so certain herself anymore.

"Miss Buchanan, you are getting soaked." Radclyffe shrugged out of his overcoat and placed it around Edith's shoulders, drawing her under the umbrella and stepping out into the rain himself. "We should see you to your father's townhouse. I am certain you have a good reason for being here against your father's wishes. If you explain to him why you returned to London, perhaps he will understand and forgive you." Radclyffe gave Dorcas a sickeningly sweet smile. "I believe he is in a forgiving mood of late."

Edith looked between the two. Oliver was lost to her. Lord Thynne was too. All she had left to her was the comfort and support of her family. And with Dorcas now the golden child, maybe Edith could use her sister's favor with their father to reenter his good graces.

"I do want to go see Papa. But . . . do you think we can stay, just to watch the opening ceremony?" She raised her brows in an innocent expression. She might yet see Oliver and change his mind.

Dorcas's pious face finally broke into a smile. "Yes, let's. I would not want to miss it for the world."

$\mathcal{C}$addy kept wiping the back of her hand against her mouth, unable to get the feeling of Oliver Carmichael's lips to go away. At least his father had the excuse of drunkenness when he'd attacked her at the servants' ball. Oliver hadn't smelled or tasted like he had been drinking when he accosted her in the garden.

He'd approached her as if he'd known she would be here. Upon questioning how he had found her amongst the throngs of people crowding into Hyde Park, he confessed that he'd had someone watching Madame Renard's shop and home. Oliver had followed her from the shop to Hyde Park, then pretended he'd happened upon her.

And to think that she had started to like the man.

With thousands of others, Caddy pressed toward the center of the enormous hall. Not only did she need to get to the middle, she had to get past it. According to the map in the commemorative booklet she'd purchased while standing in line to get through the doors, the Canadian exhibit was on the far side of the central transept. With the queen scheduled to give her speech to open the Exhibition at noon, it seemed everyone in London, and half the rest of the world's population, crowded into the Crystal Palace to partake of the momentous occasion.

She never should have worn a dress with such a full skirt. She pardoned and excused herself numerous times as she squeezed through the tightest spaces in the crowd. Though no one was rude to her, the closer she got to the transept, the less amiable people were about moving so she could pass.

Her heart raced. It had to be near eleven thirty already, and she was only halfway to the transept.

She paused and lifted the broach watch pinned to her bodice. Ten more minutes until she was supposed to meet Neal—and it must have taken near half an hour to get this far.

Panic began to build in her chest. While trying to be as polite as possible, Caddy pushed her way through the crowd in earnest.

"Excuse me, please. I beg your pardon. I need to get through. It is urgent, I promise. I apologize. I have no desire to take your spot. I must get through to the other side. Someone is waiting for me." On and on through the seemingly endless sea of people.

She finally caught sight of the crystal fountain, the centerpiece of the transept. She looked at her watch again. Eleven thirty-five.

She had to keep going. Neal could see the crowd. He should know how hard it would be for her to get through.

Please, Lord, let him wait for me. Don't let him lose hope.

Near the stage, under the giant canopy hanging from the transept roof, a band started playing. The crowd around Caddy pressed forward, nearly sweeping her from her feet. She struggled for balance, then kept pushing against the tide of onlookers, not caring what was happening near the stage, only wanting to find the Canadian timber display.

Ten minutes later, Caddy looked up at the CANADA sign and took a trembling breath. *Please let him still be here.*

She pushed out of the crowd and into the display of wood, both rough and prepared lumber, from Britain's North American colony. Here, out of the main avenue of the Crystal Palace, the crowd thinned.

Behind the Canadian space, another sign indicated she'd entered a display from the West Indies. Surely this was not where he'd meant for her to meet him.

She kept walking, her hope draining and trickling away just like the beads of sweat down her spine.

Beyond the West Indies, she saw a sign that brought her up short. NEW SOUTH WALES.

Against the exterior wall of the building, below the windows letting in the uncertain gray light from outside, the display from the Australian territory was small and rustic. Wool and grains, copper ore and tools, and fur pelts along with drawings of the animals they'd come from. Caddy reached out to touch the red fur that had come from a kangaroo.

"Beautiful."

Her heart leapt into her throat, but she didn't turn at the familiar voice. "How big do they get?"

"The largest I've seen was almost five feet tall, fully extended."

"You—you've seen one for yourself?"

"More than one. When I was a boy, I helped the drovers keep them out of the sheep and cattle paddocks, or else there wouldn't be enough grass for the livestock."

"You visited Australia when you were young?" Caddy continued to run her hand along the grain of the short, smooth red fur.

"No. I lived there."

Warm hands settled on Caddy's shoulders, and she allowed him to turn her to face him. Her heart pounded violently at the sight of him, and it took all her strength of will to keep from wrapping her arms around his neck and kissing him. But other people wandered around in the nearby displays, and she did not want to embarrass him.

"Caddy, I was born in Australia. My father went there as a surveyor with the Royal Society for Industry in 1820. My mother's family were also going—her father was the head of the expedition—and they fell in love and married on the ship on the way there." He let one of the ringlets draped over her shoulder curl around his finger. "I was born two years later, after they settled in Bathurst. When I was four years old, my father discovered gold in the process of sinking a copper mine. The government made him keep quiet about it. So he extracted as much of it as he could and told no one. When I was eleven, my mother died. She had wanted a different life for me than the hardscrabble one she'd seen in New South Wales. So my father sent me back to England to live with my grandmother and attend school."

Caddy waited for the rest of his confession. "And?"

"And what?"

"That's your big secret? That you were born in Australia and lived there until you were twelve?"

He squinted and cocked his head. "And my family is now among the wealthiest in the land?"

Laughter, full of joy and relief, bubbled up through Caddy's chest, and she let it out, finally allowing herself to throw her arms around him in a hug. "You're certain that is all? You aren't keeping any other secrets from me?"

Neal took hold of her upper arms and pulled her away from him. Consternated, she frowned at him.

"Do you not understand what I'm telling you? I am one of those people you cannot abide. One of those criminals, one of those wild Australians who are nothing more than thieves and cutthroats."

She reached up and caressed his cheek, reveling in the rough stubble she could feel just below the smooth surface. "I do not know what you are talking about. Australia may have some convict settlements, and convicts are used to augment the labor force. But so many good, hardworking people have settled there that it has become a lovely, hospitable place."

⁂

Neal stared at her in awe and wonder. To hear his own flattering description of his homeland coming from Caddy . . . if he could have measured his heart, he was certain it would have been twice its normal size.

"So it does not bother you that I hail from a land best known as a penal colony?"

"Was not North America filled with penal colonies at one time?" She waved toward the Canadian display several yards away. "Look at how respectable they are now." She settled her hands on his lapels. "Besides. After being corrected on my assumptions about Australia, I have educated myself and read about it. I have never before relied solely on rumor and innuendo as fact, and I knew I could not do so in this case either. The circulating library in Oxford had several volumes of essays from visitors and emigrants alike. And they all described it much the same way you did."

"I cannot believe I put you—put both of us—through unnecessary anxiety over so simple a matter as my birthplace. But after my grandmother's death, when her will was read and it became common knowledge, I lost all of my patients and I was shunned from taking part in any of the village's social events. They assumed—wrongly—that my mother had been a convict.

They made up all kinds of stories, one worse than the next. I had to leave before I hurt someone in anger."

Caddy smoothed her hands down his lapels, and his skin tingled. "I cannot believe you would ever do anyone physical harm on purpose."

"I wouldn't . . . except when it came to the possibility of needing to defend my mother's honor." He waggled his brows at her.

A gong drew their attention, and everyone around them moved toward the main avenue.

"It is time for the queen's speech." Neal traced the scar on Caddy's forehead, disappointed that she'd gotten someone else to remove her stitches.

"We should go listen."

She did not move.

He didn't want to either. "We seem to have been left quite alone for the moment." He leaned down just as she raised up on her toes to meet him. An electric charge bolted through him at the touch of her lips. No matter how much he wanted to do otherwise, he kept the kiss short and sweet, then wrapped his arm around her waist and led her into the fringe of the crowd.

Even with as quiet as so many thousands of people could be, he could not hear the queen's words clearly. Neal kept Caddy with the crowd until the ceremony ended with a rousing rendition of Handel's "Hallelujah Chorus." He then pulled her back toward the New South Wales exhibit.

Shortly, Macquarie, Birchip, and the remainder of the committee joined them, ready to greet visitors and answer questions.

Macquarie and Birchip greeted Caddy warmly, apologizing for not revealing the reason they'd sought Neal when they met her at the shop. "The states did not have time to get up a committee to send from Australia, so they left it up to those of us who live here in England already. I'd heard of a doctor in Hampshire

who was Australian by birth and thought we should recruit him."
Macquarie cuffed Neal's shoulder. "But by the time we caught
up with him, he had already been run out of his home and practice. Is it any wonder he did not want anyone else to know where
he was born?"

"And were you born there, too, Mr. Macquarie?" Caddy
dragged her eyes away from the bolt of tweed wool fabric Birchip
had just pulled to show a group of women.

"Yes, and proudly so. My great-grandfather was sent there
nigh on a hundred years ago, after being convicted of stealing
bread to feed his family. His wife managed to arrange passage for
herself and their seven children. My great-grandfather escaped
the convict colony—Van Diemen's Land—and they made their
way inland from Sydney and homesteaded. When my great-
grandfather discovered both copper and coal on his land, he
became a very wealthy man. Of course, his name wasn't originally Macquarie, and he never told anyone what it was so that he
couldn't be caught and sent back to serve the remainder of his
sentence."

Neal almost laughed at the shocked expression on Caddy's
face.

Macquarie leaned close. "Of course, he could have made the
whole story up."

Caddy laughed, and Neal's chest almost burst with his love
for her.

Once Caddy had a chance to see everything on display,
Macquarie told Neal to take her around the rest of the Exhibition
or he'd do it himself. Happy to oblige, Neal offered Caddy his
arm, and they moved out into the wide, main avenue. They con-
sulted Caddy's guidebook, and Neal insisted they start upstairs,
where the largest displays of silks, woolens, lace, and other fabrics
were.

Caddy pointed out several plaids and brocades she thought would make beautiful waistcoats for Neal. He, in turn, draped a silk as light as angel feathers—and just as white—across Caddy's shoulders and a lace shawl over her bonnet.

"You will make a beautiful bride," he whispered, leaning close.

"Only if someone asks me to be his wife." She pinned him with a challenging look.

"I thought I should wait until we were in the garden, for a more romantic setting."

Caddy fingered the lace hanging beside her soft cheeks and her eyes changed from challenging to inviting. She held her hands out as if to encompass the entire display. "This is my garden, Neal."

"Then, Miss Cadence Bainbridge, will you do me the honor of becoming my wife?"

"Before I answer that, I need a promise from you."

His heart throbbed with unexpected anxiety. "Yes?"

"Promise you will always be honest with me, even when you think it might hurt me."

"I promise. But only if you do the same."

Her smile was beatific, but he could see the pulse pounding in her throat. "I promise."

"Then I will repeat my question. Will you marry me?"

"Yes, Dr. Neal Stradbroke. Nothing in the world would make me happier."

Because of the crowds around them, Neal dared not kiss her properly. Instead, he raised both of her hands in his and kissed them, then held them to his chest.

A cleared throat hinted they had blocked this part of the display too long. Caddy set the lace and silk back on the table, then wrapped her hand through Neal's elbow and allowed him to lead her away.

"Neal, do you want to return to Australia—to live, I mean? I can tell you miss it, and you must still love it because it's your home." Caddy's bonnet blocked her face, so he wasn't certain exactly what she was thinking.

He pulled her to the railing that overlooked the main floor below, then tilted her head up with a crooked finger under her chin. "Yes, I would like to go back to Australia. I want to see my father, and meet my stepmother and half-brothers and -sisters. But I have not thought of it as home in a while now. Ever since I met you, in fact." He traced her chin with the tip of his finger. "My home is North Parade in Oxfordshire—because that's where you are. For the rest of my life, you will be my home, no matter where in the world that may be."

Ignoring the crowds and decorum, he leaned down and kissed her, as he had been wanting to do for the past . . . forever, if he were honest with himself.

And he would be, too—with himself and with her. Honest now and forever.

Follow the Heart
KAYE DACUS

Available Now